A Man for The Summer

Allys Reid

Chapter One

It could turn out to be a lovely morning, thought Calista, as she looked out at the sky from her kitchen window.

To the East, the clouds rolled over the Cascade Mountains, tumbling like fluffy white balls of cotton, down the treed hills, toward the town of Ocean Dunes.

To the South, she could see that the rain had already started, moving in from the Suislaw National Forest. In a few minutes, it would drench the yard and the long dirt road from the highway to the handful of guest cottages that fanned out in an arc around the main guest house.

Calista Blake elbowed the screen door open, shimmied sideways onto the wide porch, and struggled with her tray of muffins and coffee, keeping them level as she hurried to the door of one of the five cottages.

She knocked on the door and waited politely. The door opened and a man, middle aged and impatient-looking, glared out at her. He looked her up and down, ogling her, then shook his head.

"Hi. I brought your breakfast, Mister Jameson." Calista said. "Where would you like it?"

He shrugged. "Oh, yeah, right. Look, miss, we're not very hungry. Matter of fact, we have to head straight back to San Diego, right, hon?"

He looked over his shoulder at a woman, also around his age, who was combing her hair and frowning at the dresser mirror.

"Right. San Diego." She repeated. "I want to get going, Ted."

The man turned back to Calista. "Anyway, sorry about this, but we really have to leave- very important business."

The woman put the comb into her purse and snapped the latch closed, firmly. She marched past Calista, out the door to a parked car.

The man watched her go then reached into his pocket. "It's fifty for the room, right?"

He pulled out money and placed it on Calista's tray. "Sorry again for the short notice. Bye."

He picked up a suitcase and stopped at the door, waiting for Calista to move out of his way.

Calista shrugged sadly. "It's too bad you have to leave. I do hope you come back soon."

He looked her up and down, deciding what to say. "Yeah, sure." He said, simply.

The woman in the car waved at him. "Come *on*, they're holding the room for us." She called.

He joined her, tossed the suitcase into the back seat and they drove north, away from San Diego.

Calista was still standing in the doorway of the cottage, still holding the tray in her hands, as the car bounced down the rutted road. She sighed and walked slowly back to the main house.

She went through to the kitchen, placed the tray on the dining table and removed the tea towel covering the muffins. A creaking sound behind her made her look back at an old woman, in a thick bathrobe and fuzzy slippers, who sat across from her at the dining table.

"Morning, mother." Calista said. "We just had a runaway. At least he paid for the night's stay first."

Calista's mother picked out one of the muffins and broke off a piece. She took a bite and grunted.

"Well, at least they left us the food." She joked. "We've got breakfast."

Calista looked out the window. Streaks of rain now struck the glass at an angle, moist diagonal marks, gently at first, then heavier, getting louder and louder, until it sounded like a long ocean wave, a sustained roar of water on the roof and the road.

The rain would probably last all day, Calista thought. She wouldn't be able to mow the lawn or hang laundry out to dry, and she'd have to wait until it evaporated before she could even think of painting the fence by the road.

Calista's mother poured herself a coffee from the carafe on the tray and sat back.

"These aren't half bad." She muttered. "I like this flavor, Cali."

"Yeah, I like them too." Calista agreed. She poured coffee for herself, and the two women sat quietly for a moment.

"You know, mom, I really think we need to get someone in, a handyman to help get the place spruced up before the summer season."

Her mother shook her head. "We can't afford that, Cali. We're barely hanging on as it is. Paying for help would sink us."

Calista stared into her coffee cup. The guest house had been her father's, and the land it was built on was his father's before him. Back then, when central Oregon was just a blank space between San Francisco and Portland, the land had already been in her family for years.

Now, the hotel, which had never been very successful, might have to be sold. Calista would have to find a job in town, and get an apartment away from here, away from her beloved beach, away from the place where she'd lived all her life.

She shrugged. "I don't know, mom. I've said it before; I think we need to fix the place up. If we're going to lose everything anyway, I figure we should risk it- go out with a bang, if nothing else."

She looked out the kitchen window. The rain, heavy now, bounced off the ruddy clay of the driveway, forming puddles here and there, little pools of red mud that slowly flowed downhill toward the beach.

"All right then, Cali, let's do it. If we're going to go out, let's go out in style." Her mother smiled.

She reached under the table to a shelf and pulled out a telephone book. She opened the book to the middle and flipped through pages, looking for a name.

"Here we are, The Penny Pincher newspaper." She announced.

"Going for the big spend, mom?" Calista Joked. "The Lincoln City Gazette isn't good enough?"

Her mother shook her head. "I don't want to attract any vultures. If people think we're really desperate, lord knows how many shady carpenters and plumbers and whatnot will knock on the door. Not to mention more of those real estate folks- if they smell blood they'll never leave us alone."

After breakfast, the rain fell just as hard, the air just as cold, and the red clay still oozed its way down the road, through the wild grass to the beach. Calista wrapped a trench coat around her, pulled the collar over her hair, ran to the old station wagon they kept out back and took the highway into town.

She drove along the Coastal Highway, through the forest, following the road as it veered away from the water, then breaking from the cover of the trees into a grey overcast, and it turned west toward the water again.

A few minutes later, the occasional barn on the roadside gave way to houses, then more and more houses, closer together, then all at once the road widened, and side streets branched out, with a Dairy Queen and a gas station on opposite corners of one intersection. This was downtown Lincoln City.

Lincoln City did not look like the typical small town most people think of, when you say 'small town'. There was no town square, no quaint city hall opposite a school, no founder's statue. It was a scattering of houses and businesses up and down the highway, getting denser for a while then thinning out at the south end of town, away from Calista's hotel.

Calista decided she'd drop off her ad after she caught up with the local gossip, so she passed the Dairy Queen and turned right at a parking lot by a high sign that read 'Whale View Diner'.

She walked into the diner and sat at one of the counter stools.

A waitress, in a thick sweater and slacks, waved at her from the far side of the diner and walked over.

"Hey Cali, how're you doin'?" She smiled.

"OK, Jan. Fine, I guess." Calista shrugged. "Waiting for the tourist season to start."

"Figure you'll have a good year?" The waitress asked, a little too curiously. Her husband sold real estate part time, besides working in the local John Deere dealership. He was eager to buy her hotel, she knew.

"Yeah, I think it's going to be a great summer. We've already got a bunch of pre-books." Calista lied.

The waitress slid a glass of water and a coffee in front of Calista. Calista nodded, accepting them, then took a sip of water.

"How's work going?" The waitress continued. "You're still doing the books for some of the farmers out your way, right?"

Calista nodded. The few dollars she made as a bookkeeper helped keep the hotel going, but it was nowhere near enough to have them survive if the guests stayed away.

"How's Maisie doing?" The waitress asked.

"Mom's doing well, thanks. How are you doing? Business picking up for the summer yet?"

The waitress shrugged. "This place ticks along. I got regular hours. Glen's doing his bit, too. His main job's fine, he says. People gotta buy tractors. Still, he's hoping the real estate end takes off. He figures that's a way better way to make a living. Anyhow, take your time. Let me know what you want, hon."

The waitress poured a fresh coffee for the only other patron, a small man in a windbreaker, chatted with him for a minute then came back to Calista.

"So, what can I get ya?"

Calista didn't bother looking at the menu, chalked on the wall behind the waitress. She knew it by heart.

"Just a tuna salad on white, Jan. thanks."

The waitress wandered off to the kitchen, and Calista opened out her purse, looking for a piece of paper, the ad she would place after she ate.

The diner's front door opened, ringing the small bell over the entry, and Calista casually glanced over to see who had come in. As the door opened, a low roaring sound, rain falling on the front mat, rumbled through the diner.

The waitress, also hearing the bell, came back from the kitchen to greet the new patron. She stopped and grinned.

The new patron was a man, somewhere in his thirties or possibly his early forties, wearing jeans and a leather bomber jacket over a navy blue tee shirt.

He was tall, slim, with a mop of wavy blonde hair and a slight stubble of beard, carrying a motorcycle helmet under one arm.

"Hello." He said, simply. "Can I sit anywhere?"

The waitress smiled broadly at him and patted the counter. "Sure, hon. Why don't ya sit right here? You want coffee?"

He smiled back and nodded. "Yes, thanks."

The waitress poured him a cup of coffee and leaned in close as she slid it toward him.

"Here you go, hon." She said.

He sat two stools away from Calista and placed his helmet between them. He nodded politely at her.

"Ma'am. Good morning." He said.

Calista nodded back. "Hello. It's kind of a wet day to ride a motorcycle."

"Yeah, it sure is. That's why I decided to stop here- I figured it might let up, so I waited for a while."

Calista turned slightly on her stool, facing the man. "Where are you going?" She asked.

He smiled- a warm, inviting smile. "Nowhere special, just heading north for now."

Calista grinned. "If you don't know where you're going, how will you know when you get there?"

He laughed out loud. "You sound like a bumper sticker. Actually, I'm taking the summer off- clearing out some mental cobwebs."

"Taking the summer off? Are you a teacher, or what?"

He shrugged. "No, just taking time from my regular job. I had the opportunity to get away, so I'm taking the summer off."

She swiveled to face him head on and rested her elbow on the counter. "Should I be looking for your picture on the wall of the post office, or what?"

He laughed out loud again. "No, I'm not wanted. At least, not in that way."

"What is it you do?" Calista asked.

He thought for a moment. "My job is in in construction."

Calista sat up. "Construction? Like, carpentry, woodwork, things like that?"

"Yeah, I suppose you could say so."

"Are you looking for work? We're looking for a handyman." She asked, hopefully.

He shook his head. "No, I'm not, and I don't think you could afford me. Besides, as I said, I'm taking the summer off."

The small man in the windbreaker said goodbye to the waitress, left a dollar on the counter and walked out, making the doorbell ring again.

The waitress disappeared into the back of the diner, and Calista leaned forward, speaking softly.

"It's just that, you see, I'm about to put an ad in the paper: we need a handyman, someone to help us out at our guest hotel. I'd rather it wasn't someone from around here, you know."

"Why is that?" He asked.

 "People can get very nosy, and after they come into your home, they gossip. That's why."

He looked at her for a long minute. "Can I see your ad?"

She took a folded-up piece of paper from her purse and carefully passed it to him, like showing him a secret message.

He unfolded the paper and read it aloud. "Wanted- a man for the summer. Rate of pay negotiable."

He read out the phone number. "Sounds like you're advertising for a boyfriend." He grinned.

She scowled and took the paper back from him. "They charge by the word. I was trying to be brief."

He smirked. "Define 'negotiable'."

She frowned and folded the paper back up. "So, are you interested in the job after all, or just curious?"

He took a sip of his coffee and shook his head. "Sorry, I plan to be in Portland this afternoon, then hopefully stop in Seattle by nightfall. As I said, I'm taking the summer off."

Calista looked out the window. The rain had eased, and was now just a light mist, covering the road with damp fog.

"What are you doing in Seattle?" She asked.

He took another sip of coffee. "Actually, a buddy of mine lives in Anchorage. I figure after I hit Seattle I'll ride up the Alaska Highway to see him."

Calista shrugged. "Well, I figured I'd ask, anyway." She stuck out her hand. "I'm Calista, Calista Blake."

He took her hand. His hand was warm, slightly rough. He placed his other hand over hers.

"Brandon Cooper. Calista, that's a lovely name. Your family's Greek?"

"My father taught history at Tillamook High. He had a thing for the classics- my name was an occupational hazard, I guess."

The man nodded. "Good thing he didn't teach shop. You could have been called 'Bandsaw'."

Calista laughed and covered her mouth. "I've never heard that one. Good one." She took a sip of water.

The waitress brought out Calista's sandwich and leaned in close to Brandon.

"So, hon, what would you like?" She asked, purring.

"Just a slice of apple pie, thanks." He said.

The waitress was still leaning close. "You want to have some ice cream with that, hon?"

He shook his head, and the waitress walked slowly away.

Calista watched her go. "I think she likes you."

"I guessed. Is she like that with many people?"

"Only with men who don't live here."

The man sipped his coffee again. "Calista- she was the mother of Arcas, the lover of Zeus?"

Calista raised her eyebrows. "That's very impressive. Most people think it's just a name."

"It means 'most beautiful' in Greek. I see it's appropriate, too."

Calista blushed. "My, you're a smooth one, aren't you?"

The waitress brought out a slice of apple pie, far bigger than it should have been, and placed it ceremoniously in front of the man. "Here you go, hon. Take your time. More coffee?"

He looked up at the waitress and smiled warmly. "Thanks so much. You're very sweet."

She straightened up and fanned her face, then went back to the kitchen.

Calista chuckled. "She'll be talking about you for weeks, you know. She'll embellish the story with all these things you supposedly told her."

They ate, talked about Lincoln City, the weather, and nothing in particular, and glanced over at each other when the other wasn't watching, then the man picked up his motorcycle helmet and stood up.

"Thanks, I enjoyed the conversation, and good luck finding someone. It was nice talking to you." He said.

The waitress pulled his bill out of her apron and handed it to him.

"Can I get Miss Blake's bill as well, please?" He asked casually.

Calista stood up and shook her head. "No, no, really. That's not necessary." She argued.

"Nonsense. It's my pleasure." He smiled. He looked at the two bills, pulled some cash out of his pocket and placed it on the counter. "That's good, thanks. Keep the change." He said.

He stretched his hand out again. "Miss Blake, best of luck with your search. Goodbye."

Calista took his hand, automatically, and the man left. The door closed. The waitress watched him go.

"Hey Cali, ya think he likes women? I mean, a guy looks like that, he HAS to like women, right? I mean, if there's a god in heaven then he has to..."

"I get it." Calista interrupted. "Yeah, I think he likes women."

The waitress rested her elbows on the counter and stared out as the man put on his helmet and started up his motorcycle. He leaned across to the sidecar and snugged down a canvas backpack wedged into the passenger seat. He threw a lean leg over the seat and rode off, headed north.

"OO-EE. Another reason to love Levi's." The waitress joked. Calista rolled her eyes and said nothing.

The rain stopped; the sun came out, weak at first through the thin clouds, then the street began to dry off. Calista left her coat in her car and climbed the steps to the newspaper office, on the second floor of a small commercial building. There was a pet groomer and small engine repair shop on the ground floor, and a tiny loading bay out back where young men in old vans loaded up the free newspaper twice a week and delivered it all over Lincoln City and the surrounding area.

Calista walked to the single counter on the second floor and waited. A minute later, a man in black slacks and a rumpled white shirt greeted her.

"Hi. Yes?" He asked, hurriedly.

"I'd like to place an ad." Calista said. She carefully took the paper out of her purse and handed it to him.

He unfolded it and read it over. "That's it? OK, um, four dollars and twenty cents."

She handed him a five-dollar bill and he rummaged through a drawer for change. He finally found three quarters and a nickel, then he slid them across the counter to her.

"It'll be in Friday's paper. Thanks. Bye." He said simply, and walked away.

Calista walked slowly back down the stairs to her car. It felt like she had just cast the last desperate lifeline to save her family business, the last chance to fix up the place before the summer season, just in time to entreat travelers to stay there, even though it was a little out of the way and far from the tourist spots further up the coast.

She was already in town- should she go to the bank while she was here? She could take a few dollars out of her account, buy groceries, and pay some of the bills that had been collecting dust on her side table.

Then she would head back to the house and decide what to do first. Yes, that would be it. She'd do that.

By two in the afternoon, the red clay driveway was dry, but the heavy morning rain had made the ruts in the road even deeper, and her car bucked and bounced along as she drove back home.

Calista's mother was on the front porch, wearing Capri pants and a sweater, sweeping dust off the porch and onto the grass.

"Hey, Cali. How'd it go in town?" Her mother asked.

"I put the ad in, paid the phone bill, and dodged Jan's questions. I still think her husband wants to buy this place if we're willing to sell up. She seemed way too interested in how we were doing. Anyway, the ad will be in the paper Friday, so let's see how it goes. We'll have to weed out the losers and the scam artists, I suppose, but hopefully we get someone who'll work out."

Her mother chuckled. "You always were the practical one. All right, Cali, let's see what the cat drags in."

"Ah." Said Calista, "And a passing motorcyclist bought me lunch."

"Really?" Her mother raised her eyebrow. "Was he cute?"

"Honestly, mom."

They had dinner together sitting huddled at the small table in the kitchen, then her mother went through to the back room to watch TV and sew, while Calista sat in a corner of the room with a favorite book, and listened to music on the radio. By ten thirty, Maisie was asleep in her armchair. Calista woke her up and both women went upstairs to bed.

Chapter Two

The next morning, bright sunlight pierced the gap between the window frame and the roller blind in Calista's room. Calista woke up early and went out to the cottage that the couple had abandoned yesterday. She pulled the sheets off the bed, fluffed up the comforter and vacuumed the carpets, then she cleaned the bathroom sink and shower.

She carried the sheets back to the main house to go into the laundry. The dryer was still not working- an expensive repair, she'd been told, but now that the sun was out, she could hang them up to dry.

Her mother was in the kitchen, flipping eggs in a frypan. She saw Calista walk past on her way to the laundry and called out to her.

"Hey, Cali. Breakfast will be ready in two minutes."

"Thanks, mom." She called back.

They had toast and eggs, sitting at the same kitchen table, then Calista looked at her watch.

"Nine o clock. I'm going to go get the mail." She announced.

She walked out the side door and sauntered down the long driveway to the highway, thinking about the ad.

The house had been her home all her life. Her mother hoped they would keep the place afloat, but Calista knew that there was not much chance they could turn it around. There were fancy hotels to the north, up in Seaside and Astoria, and there were new casinos further south at the California border.

This stretch of Oregon coastline, however, was mostly overlooked- the poorer cousin. The very thing that she loved about her home, the seclusion and privacy, was the thing that made it hard to find people who wanted to stay there.

Calista reached her mailbox, a wooden model of the main house, and flipped open the back. No mail. At least there were no bills today, either.

She headed back toward the house, deciding what to do next. There was grass to mow, windows to wash, and a host of other chores to do.
She also had to do the accounts books for her neighbor, Freda Parsoner. Freda and her husband owned the land beside the hotel, and they kept dairy cows, but Freda was not very good with numbers, and Calista's math abilities were much appreciated by the Parsoners.

Maybe if the paper came out early on Friday, Calista thought, she'd get a response that morning, and she could have the man start the following Monday. Maybe even work for part of Friday. Maybe. There were too many maybes. Maybe her husband could have had more life insurance.

The steady sound of a thump-thump-thump in the distance brought her thoughts back to the present.

The crop-dusters and aerobatic pilots sometimes flew along the beach; they would skim low over the wide sands and wave at her if they passed close to the house.

This sound was different, though. It was slower, closer. Calista looked back to the road. Coming toward her, improbably, was a motorcycle with a sidecar- the man from the diner, the one who was headed for Alaska.

Calista froze, wondering what he wanted, curious about why he was here, whether she only imagined seeing him.

He stood up on the foot pegs of the motorcycle and nodded at her as he approached.

"Hi there." He said. "Where should I park?"

Calista waved silently at a gravel area beside the main house, and the man revved the engine on the big bike and rolled smoothly to a stop beside the porch. Calista walked briskly, not quite running, to meet him as he got off and shut the engine down.

He tugged his helmet off and casually smoothed his hair back. He placed the helmet on the seat of the motorcycle and smiled at Calista.

"Hi, I figured I'd drop by and take a look at this place of yours." He said. His voice sounded like a warm blanket, inviting and cozy.

Calista felt a rush just listening to him. "What about that trip up the Alaska Highway?" She was afraid of what his answer might be, that this was just a quick visit by him, but she still had to ask the question.

"I stayed over in Portland last night. I was hoping I'd get to Seattle, but the rain yesterday made me stop in that little diner of yours, and it threw my timetable off." He smirked. "Anyway, I called my buddy, and it turns out he isn't even in Anchorage right now."

"Where is he, then?" Calista asked, curious.

"He flew to Bali. He's doing some geological surveys in Indonesia. Somehow, you know, it didn't seem like a good idea to fly all the way to Indonesia just to say hello."

Calista stared at him, looking up at this man who had just fallen into her life. He seemed so at ease with himself, so comfortable with who he was and what he was doing.

"Anyway, so, what work did you need done?" He asked.

Calista wasn't listening. "Sorry, what?" She asked.

"Did you want to show me around? You said you needed some work done around the place."

Calista's mother wandered out onto the porch and stared at the stranger. She stepped down onto the grass and walked slowly toward him. He strode over to meet her and held out his hand.

"Hi, you must be this young lady's sister." He smiled. Calista's mother blushed.

"I'm Cali's mother, Margaret. Everyone calls me Maisie." She said. She took his hand, gingerly.

He wrapped both his hands around hers and nodded. "I'm Brandon. It's a pleasure, Maisie." He said.

Maisie turned to Calista. "He *is* cute. You should keep this one around, Cali."

Calista frowned, embarrassed. "Mom, please."

Maisie turned to face the man. "I'm sorry, it's Brandon, you said?"

"Brandon Cooper, yes. So, did you want me to look over this place of yours, and see what it needs?"

Calista looked at her mother for direction. Maisie smiled and shooed them both away.

Calista sighed and said "All right, come with me. I'll give you the grand tour."

Calista stuck her hands in the back pockets of her jeans and stretched, loosening up for the day.

She noticed the man furtively looking at her curves, his eyes racing from her knees to her neck and back. She stood straight and glared at him. "None of that." She snapped. "If that's why you're here, forget it."

He shrugged. "Sorry- it's an automatic reaction to being around a beautiful woman."

Calista smirked at the compliment then frowned and shook her head. "I advertised for a handyman, nothing more. Do you still want to look it over- I mean, the property, look over the property?"

He stopped smiling and got serious, businesslike. "Sure thing. Let's see what work you want done."

She led him out to the far cottage, the one that the couple had left the day before. She pointed to a crack in the porch wood, splinters in the paint here and there, and a host of other small things. He took it all in and said nothing. She showed him the other four cottages; the same general work needed to be done, the same sorts of things were wrong, and still he said nothing.

"So, what do you think?" Calista asked him, finally.

"I think you should sell the property and buy a house in town." He said. "You have a beautiful location here, but the cottages need a ton of work, and right now this looks like a sinkhole for cash."

Calista glared at him. "Yes, well, thanks for taking the time to come by and look at our place, but obviously you have other, more important, things to do."

He shook his head. "Look, you asked me what I think, and I'm just saying that from my professional point of view, fixing up this place would be expensive, and you probably couldn't afford it. That's all."

Calista glared at him. "This land has been in our family since the First World War. We've kept it in good times and bad, and I intend to make sure we have it a century from now, if I can."

She walked away from him, toward the house, and waved over her shoulder. "You can find your own way out, Mister Cooper?" She called.

He got on his motorcycle, started the engine and wordlessly drove back out to the road. Calista went into the kitchen and sat at the table with her mother. She was shivering, she realized, trembling with anger at this man and his cavalier attitude to her home, her life in this place.

Her mother looked at her. "Cali, what's wrong? Isn't he interested in the work?"

Calista shook her head. "He said to tear the place down. No, actually he said sell the property and move into town. He called the hotel a 'sinkhole for cash'."

Maisie shrugged. "Well, he may be right at that, hon. We haven't had a really good year for over a decade. Ever since that new highway got built, nobody much comes this way anymore."

Calista stared at her. "You too, mom? You're giving up on the hotel, too?"

Maisie shook her head. "Hon, I'm an old woman. You're barely thirty. You've still got time to find someone else, maybe have kids, live somewhere nice. This is all I know, the hotel's all I got. But you, you've got a life in front of you, hon."

Calista sighed. "Ed was not the kind of man dad thought I'd marry, but he was a good man, mom. He loved you and he loved me, and he loved this place as much as we do."

"You can't wish for what isn't. Nature has its own agenda, Cali. You can't let the past hold you back. Ed was a good man. But he's gone, and you're here. It's time to move on with your life."

Calista leaned her elbows on the table and rubbed her face with her hands. She was angry now, determined. She had to find some way to save the place. There had to be a way. Out the window, the thump-thump-thump sound came back. Calista told herself she was imagining it- this time it really must be a crop-duster. No, it wasn't.

She got up and walked out onto the porch. The man was just getting off his motorcycle and putting his helmet on the seat. He shook his hair back and smiled at Calista.

"So, miss, what does that job pay, if I were to take it?" He asked.

Calista's heart raced, but she frowned. "It pays minimum wage. Forty hours a week at minimum wage."

She said it defiantly. If he was just playing with her, she wanted him to get it over with so she could go back to work. He shook his head.

"Uh-huh. No good." He said. "I'd like room and board."

"Room and board plus minimum wage?" Calista asked. Now her heart was thumping through her chest.

He shook his head. "I don't need the money. I'll take the job for just the room and board."

Calista walked down two steps from the porch and sat down. "Why?" She asked, firmly.

"Are you looking a gift horse in the mouth?" He grinned. "No, I see your point. Why would I do that?"

He pointed to one of the cottages. "I'll tell you a secret. I've worked hard all my life, and the thought of just sitting around in a hotel room all summer watching TV holds no appeal. This is a challenge, and you had the guts to tell me to get lost when I gave you the bad news. I like that. So, forty hours for just room and board, is it a deal?"

He stuck his hand out. Calista took it, cautiously. "Deal." She said. "Come inside."

She went ahead of him into the kitchen. "You've met my mother, and we have a lady who comes in to clean once or twice a month, if we're busy. That's us, all of us. Mom, Brandon says he would like to take the handyman job."

She sat at the table, beside her mother, and Brandon sat across from the women.

"Missus Blake. Calista says you have some work you need done."

Maisie smiled at him and patted his hand. "Anything you can do to help is appreciated, son. Cali told you what the job pays?"

He smiled. "Yes. I counteroffered."

Maisie frowned. "I don't know as we can pay much more than that, son."

Calista leaned forward. "He doesn't want money, mom, just room and board. That's all."

Maisie looked at Brandon, surprised. "You don't want to get paid for working here?"

He shook his head. "As I told your daughter, I don't really need the money, ma'am."

Maisie leaned back in her seat. "You're not on the run from the police, are you?"

Brandon leaned back and laughed loud, a hearty laugh. "That's a good question. No, I'm not. Calista can take my driver's license into town and check me out, if you like. In fact, I insist on it. You both need to know that I am who I say I am."

Maisie waved her hand. "Time enough later for nitpicking. Why don't you get settled? We have a great spare room upstairs, down the hall from the bathroom. There's another one downstairs, too."

Brandon shook his head. "Actually, seeing as it's just me and you ladies here, I think it would be more appropriate of I was to sleep in one of the cottages, don't you think?"

Calista hadn't thought of that. If he slept in the main house, people would talk. "Oh, right. I showed you number four earlier- it's probably our best cottage."

"Great. Let me unpack my stuff, then I'll get going." He said. "Just so we're on the same page, this is only for the summer, right? We're in late May now. I'll be gone by mid-August. Is that still all right?"

Maisie smiled at him. "I'm sure any help you can give us will be greatly appreciated, Mister Cooper."

"Brandon, please."

"Brandon it is." Maisie said.

Calista walked with Brandon out to his motorcycle and watched as he carefully pulled a backpack out of the foot well, then he reached in and pulled out a folding suitcase. It was new, expensive looking, a brand Calista recognized from a fancy magazine someone had left behind once. She said nothing.

She showed Brandon to his cottage, with its faded beige paint and a creaky wooden porch, and opened the door for him. She waved at the room as he walked around inside it.

"This is the main room. Here is the small kitchenette and writing table." She said, almost mechanically.

"The bathroom is around the corner, and the bed is right there." She said this almost with embarrassment, as though he might infer something from the statement.

He looked around, admiring the cottage. "This is nice." He muttered. "It has possibilities."

Calista sighed, deciding to ask him the question she had been curious about. "So, where exactly are you from?"

"San Francisco." He said, simply.

"Is there a Mrs. Cooper?" She asked. She immediately regretted asking it.

"You're wondering about me- because I'm from San Francisco?" He asked. He seemed amused.

"Look, it's none of my business what you do, I mean like, I mean, you know."

He was grinning broadly now. "So, would you like me to hold your mouth open while you change feet?"

Calista blushed a deep red. "Listen, it's not my business. I hired you to fix up the place, that's all."

Brandon nodded. "Fair enough. The place it is. As a start, though, I have a couple of days' grungy laundry. Can I do a load or two before I get going?"

Calista walked him to the main house and its laundry room. "The washer works well, but you may have to wait until we get a dry spell to hang the clothes up. Our dryer is on the fritz."

"Really?" He asked. "What's wrong with it?"

"The man said something costly was broken. He told me what it was, but I didn't understand what he meant."

Brandon turned the dryer on. It sounded like a jet engine. "Your drive belt is slipping, I think."

He looked around. "Where do you keep your tools?" He asked.

Calista led him to the basement. "We have all sorts of tools here. My husband was fairly good with his hands- he liked working around the place, and he had everything we needed down here."

Brandon nodded. "It's a nice basic shop. Where is your husband now?"

Calista shook her head. "Gone. He had an aneurism, and he died about six years ago."

He winced. "I'm sorry to hear that. It must have been hard for you to keep going here."

Calista nodded. "Yeah, they say it gets easier with time. I'm still waiting."

Brandon gathered tools and parts as they spoke, looking up and down at the pegboard with its pliers, screwdrivers and wrenches as he listened to her.

He went upstairs, unplugged the dryer, and started disassembling it.

"So you haven't remarried, then." He said.

"No."

"Are you dating anyone?" He popped the back cover off and crawled down onto his shoulder, reaching into the mechanism.

She thought it was none of his business. "No. I'm busy enough just taking care of this place." She said.

"You don't have children either, I gather."

She frowned. "Why would you assume that?"

He glanced up at her and smiled. "You're saying 'I' and not 'we'. Your mom didn't mention grandchildren, either. Most of the older ladies I know, if they get stopped for speeding they show the cop their ID and school photos of little Tommy or Wendy."

Calista chuckled. She was on her knees behind him now, looking over him at the dryer.

"What are you doing, exactly?" She asked.

"I'm greasing up the idler pulley." He said.

He got up and reassembled the dryer, smoothly and quickly. It had all taken under ten minutes. He started the dryer up. It was almost completely silent.

"That's terrific. How long will it stay this quiet?" Calista asked.

"A couple of years, I guess. The shaft was rusty, that's all." Brandon said.

Calista fumed. "He wanted a fortune to fix it. That bastard- it just needed some grease?"

Brandon smirked at the outburst. "Maybe he was going to use some really expensive grease?"

Calista sat on the floor with her knees up to her chest, hugging her legs. She sighed and looked Brandon over, carefully.

"Listen, we're just two women, all alone here, and some people seem to think they can just take advantage of us, you know?"

"Your mom said that, yes. Are you asking me if I'm setting you up to take advantage of you?"

Calista hadn't thought of that. "I don't know. Are you?"

Brandon shook his head. "Listen, if you ever do think that I am taking advantage of you, let me know. If you decide that you're uncomfortable with me here, I'll leave. No hard feelings, no questions asked."

Calista nodded. "Fair enough. Thanks for fixing the dryer, too. That'll help us out a lot."

Brandon reached his hand out and Calista took it. He pulled her up, but she leaned forward at the same time and propelled herself forward, bumping into him.

They both stood there for a brief moment, not moving, then she backed up a half step.

"Sorry, that was an accident." She muttered.

"My fault, purely." He said softly.

For days afterward, her mind came back to Brandon, pressing himself against her for those few seconds. How he felt, how he smelled, how his eyes looked as he gazed down at her. For days afterward, his own thoughts went to the same thing, too.

Chapter Three

The next morning, Calista woke up early. It was six fifteen, and the sky out her window looked like it couldn't decide what to do. There was a thick, solid overcast that seemed to go from Portland down to California, and small, fluffy Cumulus clouds here and there under the overcast, speeding along at their own pace. Out over the ocean there was a sliver of dark blue sky, tantalizingly close, but not quite close enough. She rolled over, thinking about the man in her guest cottage, and about pressing herself against him in the basement.

Calista sniffed the air. Coffee- she smelled coffee. She pulled her robe over her pajamas and headed downstairs. Maisie wasn't up just yet, apparently. Calista was halfway down the stairs when she saw a large pair of boots walk past the kitchen doorway. Calista froze. Who was inside her house?

The boots walked slowly out of the kitchen and toward the base of the stairs. As they got closer, she realized it was Brandon. He poked his face up the stairs and smiled at her.

"Good morning. I made coffee for you. Can I assume you like coffee?" He spoke softly.

Calista nodded. She crept gingerly down the rest of the stairs, holding onto the banister for stability, and followed him into the kitchen. He poured a mug of coffee and placed it in front of her.

Calista nodded and pulled it close. "What are you doing up so early?" She asked.

He looked at his watch. "It's almost six thirty. I should be out working already- let's chalk up this late start to the first day on the job."

Calista smiled and took a sip of coffee. It was exceptionally good. "Where did this coffee come from?" She asked.

Brandon smiled. "Your cupboard. It's your coffee."

"No way." Calista said. She shook her head. "Our coffee does not taste like this."

"Your coffeemaker was running cold- the coffee wasn't perking properly. I adjusted the thermostat." He explained.

"I didn't know we had a 'coffee thermostat' tool." Calista challenged.

He pointed at the cupboard drawers. "A meat thermometer works really well in a pinch."

Calista thought of something- the front door was locked at night. "How did you get in?" She asked.

"Through the door." He answered.

"We lock up at night."

He shrugged. "It wasn't locked."

Calista didn't quite believe this. She decided to put that aside for now. She took another sip of coffee.

Brandon looked at his watch. "OK, time for me to get going." He said.

"Have you eaten already?" Calista asked, quickly.

"Um, no. Just coffee." He answered.

"Didn't you want toast or eggs or something?" She asked.

"I don't know how to make eggs." He confided. "Just coffee."

Calista grinned. It somehow made her feel better that she could do something he couldn't.

"Sit." She ordered. "How do you like your eggs?"

"Over easy. With whole wheat toast, if you have it."

Calista lit the gas on the stove and plunked bread in the toaster. Within three minutes, Brandon was wolfing down breakfast, hunched over his plate, scooping egg white onto his toast.

Calista watched him, amused, and slurped her coffee. She took a bite of her own toast and put her cup down.

"So, Brandon, what part of San Francisco are you from?"

"How do you mean?" He seemed to stiffen a little at that.

"It's a big town, not like Lincoln City. I hear there are lots of different neighborhoods, all with their own personality. Where were you in San Francisco?"

He sipped his coffee and placed it slowly on the table, considering his answer.

"I grew up in a house on Jackson Street. It's in an area of town right outside Russian Hill, beside Chinatown. Have you heard of it?"

Calista shook her head.

"Ever see the movie, 'Bullitt'? Part of the chase scene was filmed right in front of our house, I'm told. That was a long time ago, though." He seemed quite proud of that.

"Do you like living in a big city?" She asked.

"It's what I know. If I'd grown up here, it might seem completely strange to be in the city all the time."

A sound behind them made them both turn around. Calista's mother stepped gingerly down the stairs to the main floor, and padded her way into the kitchen.

She smiled warmly at Brandon. "Good morning. You found your way in, then."

Calista looked at her. "Did you unlock the door this morning, mom?"

"Yes, hon. Is that fresh coffee I smell?"

Maisie poured herself a coffee and put bread in the toaster. "It's part and parcel of getting old, I suppose. I woke up before six, and I saw Brandon clearing some wood from around number three. I figured he might want to come in and help himself to breakfast, so I unlocked the door for him. You made coffee, did you?"

Brandon nodded. "Yes, thanks."

Calista relaxed. "Try the coffee, mom."

Maisie poured herself a mug and took a sip. "Oh, my. This will certainly wake me up."

After breakfast, Brandon asked Calista to walk around the property with him. She made notes of things to be done, he suggested the easiest, least expensive ways of doing things, and they agreed which jobs should be done first.

He looked at his watch. "All right. Let's stop for a break, shall we?" he pointed toward the west.

"How far is the ocean from here?" He asked.

Calista smiled. "Come, I'll show you."

She walked him through a gap in the scraggly pine trees, along a sandy pathway in the grasses, and over a slight rise in the land. As they crested the rise, Brandon could see the low, flat beach open out before him. It stretched on forever; in the light fog of the morning, the ocean disappeared into the mist at the horizon.

Calista continued on for a few yards, and the pathway widened to a flat area, about ten feet square, with a checkerboard of flagstones laid down, and a cut down oil drum in the middle of it, set up as a fire pit.

"We used to come here all the time when I was growing up." Calista said. "My dad made this for us, and we'd come here on summer nights to cook hot dogs. In the winter, we'd bundle up and come here to watch the waves pounding in all the way from Japan."

She pointed along the beach, remembering. "Sometimes we'd find beach glass. There were these huge blue and green glass floats that broke free from fishing nets, and they'd wash up here. I had a collection of them, I don't know, forty or fifty of them at one point. For a while I was selling them to the local gift store- tourists love them. Now I do bookkeeping for our neighbors."

"What happened to your dad?"

She shrugged. "He was a lot older than mom. She was in high school when he was teaching there, but they only met ten years later. By then he was a forty-five-year-old bachelor and she was twenty-six."

She stopped. "Why am I telling you all this? I never tell people this much about myself."

Brandon smiled softly. "People like talking to me. I'm just that kind of guy."

He looked back at the house. "I should get to work. Come on, let's go back."

He hiked up to the top of the rise, and Calista tried to follow, but she stumbled back slightly and flailed her arms.

Brandon reached out and grabbed her outstretched hand. "Here. Hold on." He said.

He pulled her up gently, firmly, and Calista moved toward him. She picked up speed, and realized with a start that she was about to slam into him again, chest to chest. She dug her heels in and stopped just short. 'That was close'. She told herself. She didn't realize she'd said it out loud.

"Could have been interesting, though." He smirked.

She smiled and looked up at him, wondering what was going through his mind. He seemed amused by her, and he seemed to like talking to her, but had she misread what he expected out of the summer?

Was she more hopeful for what could happen, rather than afraid of what might happen? Enough of that kind of talk, she told herself. Stop it- think about what he's supposed to be doing here.

They walked back to the house, along the same path. Brandon looked over his shoulder at the beach.

"You know, I could make that path wider, clean it up so guests will want to go out there." He said.

"That would be good." Calista said. She kicked at the red clay of the road, dodging wet potholes.

"I'd be a lot happier if we could fix this, though." She muttered.

Her toe dug up a clump of red muck, and her foot flicked it off into the grass. "Everybody hates this road. It's our biggest eyesore."

Brandon looked down at the mucky path. "Maybe I can help you with that, too." He said. "First, though, I need to go into town for an hour or so. Can you spare me?"

Calista nodded. "Sure, see you later, then." She said.

"Did you need to go to town for anything?" He asked.

"Maybe, but I'll just drive down on my own later."

"If you need to run a quick errand, we can go on my bike." He said.

Calista glared at the motorcycle. "Are you serious? I've never been on a motorcycle in my life." She gasped.

"How about riding in the sidecar?" He said. "Ride low and smooth." He grinned, an obvious invitation.

She opened her mouth to protest, then realized she had no good reason to say no. She threw her arms in the air.

"What the hell." She grunted, and went into the house to get her purse.

She slipped on her good shoes, a concession to dressing up, and joined him in the yard.

She slid her legs into the sidecar, a denim jacket over her shirt, clutching her purse between her knees, and peeked out from under the visor of her burgundy helmet, a match to Brandon's helmet and the gas tank on the motorcycle, gripping the padded bolster as he bounced down the clay driveway to the road.

He leaned down and called "Ready?"

She nodded. He turned onto the highway and picked up speed. He looked down and smiled at her, watching her reaction. Calista gripped the cushioned leather in front of her, holding tightly as she bounced along. She had been in a friend's little MG in high school a few times, racing down the back roads around Tillamook, but it felt nothing like this. She was terrified, lost at feeling so out of control.

Brandon looked over at her, seeing her apprehensiveness, and grinned. "Do this." He yelled over the sound of the engine. He lifted his free hand up over his head to demonstrate.

Calista slowly lifted her arms straight over her head. Brandon shifted gears and the motorcycle got up to cruising speed; Calista still kept her arms straight up. It felt incredible. She felt free, like flying, without a worry or care in the world, for the first time in a very long time. The yellow lines on the road whizzed past, racing up to meet her and disappearing under the wheels, and she felt that if she stood up, she could fly right now. She started to laugh, the pure joy of being out in the cool air and wind making her giddy.

Brandon looked down at her and grinned. Calista put her arms back down, tucked them inside the sidecar and out of the breeze, and sat back, enjoying the scenery. From this low down, the forest looked different than it did through the windows of her car. The occasional bump in the road, cushioned by the seat, gave her a thrill as they cruised along into Lincoln City.

Brandon rolled to a stop outside the diner. He got off the motorcycle, took off his helmet, and shook his head to let his hair shake free. He held his hand out to help Calista get up. She grabbed his hand tight, and for a brief second thought that she sensed something more in the grip. Maybe it was wishful thinking, maybe it was just his warm hands- maybe it was nothing, she told herself.

She shimmied up and stepped out of the sidecar, then bent forward and brushed her pants straight.

"So, where are you going to be?" Brandon asked her.

"I have to go to the newspaper and cancel that ad." Calista said. She smiled at that. "Then I'm going to order some paint for the cottages. I think we can spring for that much. How about you?"

Brandon looked over his shoulder at the post office. "I have to touch base with San Francisco. After that, do you want to meet in the diner for lunch?"

Calista smiled. "Deal. My treat though, all right?"

He shook his head. "I would never let a lady pay for a meal. It's on me."

Calista grinned. "I'm no lady. I'm your boss."

"Then I quit." Brandon said. Calista's face fell.

"For the next two hours, that is." He added. "See you at lunch."

She touched his arm, reassuring herself he was still there, and nodded. "See you shortly."

Calista crossed the street to the newspaper building, almost skipping as she went.

Brandon watched her go. She was very pretty, he thought, and very brave to try and save a crumbling wreck like the hotel. He hadn't been completely honest with her, though. He felt bad about that. Still, he had promised to do what he could for her, and he'd keep that promise if he could.

He walked past the diner, waved at the waitress he'd seen the day before, and headed toward the town's only hotel, just off the highway. It looked like any of a hundred generic road houses he'd stayed at; a shallow, wide lobby leading to a dark wood paneled desk, and patterned carpet that smelled faintly of French fries and cigars.

He smiled at the sad young man behind the counter. "Good morning." Brandon said.

"Hello. How may I help you?" The man asked, mechanically. He tapped his pen against the desk, looking Brandon up and down, trying to determine, it seemed, why he was here.

"Do you have a pay phone in the hotel?" Brandon asked.

The man pointed his pen at the far wall. Three telephones, clustered at the entrance to the bar, faced the window, away from the lobby. Brandon pulled some bills out of his pocket and placed one on the counter.

"Could I get some change, please?" He asked. The sad young man sighed and scooped the bill away, then counted out five dollars in quarters and poured them into Brandon's hands.

Brandon went to one phone and dialed a number. "Hello, operator. How much for this call?" He asked.

He pumped quarters into the phone for a few seconds, then said 'thank you' and waited.

The young man at the counter was bored. There was little of interest that happened in this town, and this stranger was certainly interesting. He listened to the conversation, as discreetly as he could.

Brandon listened to nothing, it seemed, then he brightened up. "Hi, Emily. How are you, sweetheart?"

He waited again. "That's great. Are you doing all right there, all by yourself?" Another pause. "Well, I'll come to see you at the end of the summer, you know."

He listened for a minute. "Yes, I will. I miss you too, honey. Bye."

He hung the phone up and walked past the desk. "Thanks very much." He nodded at the sad young man.

He walked back out of the hotel, the cloud-filtered sunlight making him squint. He crossed the street to a hardware store, just around the corner from the diner, and went in, browsing at the tools on the walls.

A man who looked like a caricature of a small town shopkeeper approached him. He was short, chubby, balding, with suspenders holding up loose pants and a plaid shirt under a khaki vest. The only thing missing was a fishing hat with lures on it.

"Hi there. Can I help you?" The man said, genially.

"Morning." Brandon said. "I've got a question- do you rent floor sanders and paint sprayers?"

"Don't have 'em here, but I can get 'em for you by Friday." The man said. "You just move into town, mister?"

Brandon shook his head. "I'm doing some work for Miss Blake at the Ocean Dunes Hotel."

The shopkeeper frowned. "You sure you want to do that, mister?"

"Why do you ask?"

"Well, it's not my business to say, but I hear from folks that her business isn't doing so well. If I was her, I'd take the offer they made her and sell up. She got some choices if she sells, but she got nothing if she loses her place."

Brandon handed him a written note. "Yes, you're absolutely right. It's not your business to say. Can you deliver these to the hotel?"

The man frowned. "Certainly, sir." He said frostily. "Of course, we will need a deposit on the equipment."

Brandon pulled his wallet out and slid a credit card toward the man. "You take these, I presume?"

The man looked at the credit card, curious. "This is a corporate credit card?"

"That's right."

"I've never seen a black American Express card before."

"Let's pretend it's a regular credit card, then." Brandon said, firmly.

The man entered the transaction and handed the card back.

He looked Brandon over. "Can I ask you a question, mister?" He sounded earnest now.

"Shoot."

"Why are you doing this? Everyone knows that hotel is a dead horse. Cali and Maisie are nice ladies, but we all know it's not going so good for them, and I can't see it getting any better."

Brandon smiled softly. "What would you do with the place, then?"

The man shrugged. "Glen at the John Deere deals in real estate. His wife, Jan, works at the diner? Anyway, he says he can get them out of there with some cash left over, let them get a fresh start."

"That's very commendable."

The man shrugged again. "He's just trying to help them out, I guess."

Brandon smiled. "Thanks for the chat. I look forward to seeing the equipment on Friday."

The man touched his arm. "What do you think about the hotel, then, mister? Don't you think they should sell?"

"I'm always suspicious when someone says they want to 'help me'. I'll let you know what happens. Thanks again."

He walked out of the store and thought about the conversation. He should mind his own business, he thought, and only do what he had said he'd do. Then again, he had never in his life kept his ideas to himself.

He heard a sound behind him. He turned around to see Calista, clutching the ad she'd retrieved from the newspaper. She smiled broadly at him.

"So, do you still want to buy me lunch?" She asked, cheerily.

He looked at her, deciding something. "Sure. How would it be if I could fix up that muddy road of yours?"

"That would be great." Calista said, puzzled. "What would that cost us, though?"

"Not much. A friend of mine owes me a favor. Look, meet you in the diner in fifteen minutes, all right?"

He patted her arm and walked back to the hotel. He headed directly to the pay phones and dialed a number. He waited for the operator's voice and plugged some coins into the phone.

"Hey Tim? It's Brandon." He said. The sad young man at the counter listened, as discreetly as he could.

Brandon paused for a moment. "Good, good, you too, man. Listen, can I call in a huge favor, big guy?"

Another pause. "Great, how are you set for excess gravel? In the middle of Oregon, along the coast?"

He laughed. "I got a mercy case, man. Lady needs some ruts filled. Hundred yards by three, whatever you got."

He listened for a minute. "Sure, that would be great. When's a good day?" He waited. "Yes, she is cute. That's not the reason, though. I'm just trying to score some good karma here, that's all." He laughed.

"Great. Here's where to drop it." He gave Calista's address. "Awesome. I owe you. My love to Tilly. Bye."

Brandon hung the phone up and went back out of the hotel. He opened the door to the diner and sat beside Calista, looking very pleased with himself.

She stared at him, trying to read his expression. "What?" She asked, finally.

"As I told you, I'm in construction. I have a friend who owes me a favor. Next week, Monday or Tuesday, he's going to drop off some gravel to fix your road."

Calista opened her mouth, speechless.

"What?" He asked. "Do you want him to cancel it?"

She shook her head. "That's like, a ton of gravel. Do you have any idea how much that would cost?"

"Of course I do. It's free for you. And it's closer to forty tons, by the way."

"How can you just ASK someone to give you that? Nobody does that."

"They do in my business." He picked up the menu. "What's good for lunch here?"

They ate their sandwiches, speaking only occasionally, then Calista announced she had to buy some groceries. Brandon called the waitress over and asked for the check. She grinned at him and leaned suggestively close.

"You want more coffee, too, hon?" She asked him, purring.

He smiled softly at her. "You know, I'd come here just to talk to you, even if the food wasn't this good. Yeah, I'll take some more coffee, thanks, love."

She beamed at him and poured his coffee, then straightened up and patted her hair, absentmindedly.

She sashayed back into the kitchen, looking over her shoulder at him.

Brandon watched her leave, then his expression went cold. "Say nothing for five minutes, would you?" He asked Calista, softly.

The waitress came back and handed him the check. He smiled warmly, pulled out his wallet and handed her a couple of bills. "That's good, keep the rest, hon." He said.

She picked up the bills and smiled back.

"So, your husband, Glen? I heard you say he sells real estate?" He asked casually.

She beamed. "Yeah, he works for Deere during the day, but he has his real estate job on weekends. Keeps him real busy. You lookin' to buy a place in town?"

He shook his head. "Must be tough though, a lovely lady like you, and he's off all the time working."

She blushed. "Well, he says we'll be doing fine, once the deal goes through. We'll be all set."

"The deal?"

"The casino that they're…" She stopped suddenly. "Sorry, I have to clean up out back." She ran off.

Calista watched the interplay without speaking, then she turned to face Brandon.

"What was that all about?" She asked.

"I rented some equipment from the hardware store, and he seemed to think that you should sell, that 'Glen' was doing you a favor by offering to buy the hotel."

"Yes, he's been after us to sell for a couple of months now. He says he wants us to come out of it all right, and not lose everything." Calista said.

Brandon sipped his coffee. "What about this casino? Is there one going in nearby?" he asked.

Calista shook her head. "I haven't heard anything about it. I figure I'd have heard if there was talk of that happening."

Brandon shrugged. "Maybe they didn't want you to hear, or maybe I'm just being paranoid. Let's see what shakes out." His expression didn't say that he believed that he was wrong, though.

They strolled back to the hardware store together. Calista's feet wobbled on the uneven sidewalk, her heels finding holes in the concrete. Brandon automatically wrapped his arm around her waist to keep her from falling.

She looked up at him, an odd look on her face. "Thank you." She said softly.

"Not at all. Thank *you*." He answered. They smiled at each other. He offered his arm, and she held it, steadying herself as they walked up the wooden steps to the front door of the hardware store.

The same rotund man was in the store. He stood up and met them, rocking slightly side to side as he walked.

"Hello again. Forget something?" He asked. He was looking directly at Brandon.

"Not at all. Miss Blake just needs some paint." Brandon said. Calista looked up at him, curious.

"Were you here earlier?" She asked, warily.

"Yeah, I was. I rented some equipment to sand and paint the cottages. I figure they could use a real freshening up."

Calista looked hard at him, trying to decide his reason for doing this. "Fine, I'd like to get a few gallons of house paint." She said.

She brought out three of slips of paper, paint color squares that she'd decided on, and asked the store owner how soon he could get them in for her.

He assured her they would be ready when the equipment was, and he'd make sure it was all delivered at the same time.

They went out onto the street. It was now well into the afternoon The sun had long ago crested the Coastal Range, the mountains to the east, and was now moving southwest, over the water. It was warmer than in the morning, too. Brandon took off his jacket and threw it into the sidecar, behind the seat. Calista also was too warm in a jacket, and folded hers up on her lap as she got comfortable in the sidecar.

Brandon handed her a helmet and squatted down close beside her, so only she could hear him.

"If you were going to build a casino between here and your place, where would you build it?" He asked.

Calista frowned. "Nowhere south of here, but there is Porter Point just north of incoln City, on Nestucca Bay. I can't imagine they'd let anyone build there though, it's right next to a state park."

Brandon smiled. "All right, let's go for a ride. You can show me around this part of Oregon."

He put his helmet on and fired up the motor. Calista hunched down, snug in the sidecar, and they rolled out onto the road and headed north. He called out to her occasionally, asking if they were going the right way, and she yelled back, smiling now, enjoying the ride.

They popped out of the Suislaw National Forest, past the town of Neskowin, and continued north. The road rose slightly, climbing up, away from the ocean and curving to the east. Brandon watched for traffic, looking carefully around, then Calista tapped his arm and waved for him to turn left.

He pointed at a road sign that said 'Wi Ne Ma Road'. "Here?" He yelled. Calista nodded.

He turned left, slowing as the paved road turned to gravel then branched left and right. He looked over to Calista for guidance; she motioned to the left, and he followed the road as it weaved back downhill, skirted a small lake then finally ended at a parking lot and a campground.

Brandon turned off the motor and got off the bike. He took off his helmet, shook his head and reached down to help Calista out of the sidecar. She shimmied up and out, brushing road dust off her shirt and pants as she stood. This procedure seemed to interest Brandon, she noticed. A lot, it seemed.

"Where would you build a casino here?" He asked.

Calista reached her hand out, automatically. "Come, I'll show you."

Brandon took her hand. Again, it seemed that his palm was warm, that there was emotion in the touch.

Maybe she was imagining it. Maybe it wasn't really there. Still, she was convinced she felt something.

They walked along a short path to a beach. Calista sat on a log, bent down and took her shoes off. Brandon watched this with great interest too, she thought.

"You may want to take those boots off. The sand gets really squishy." She told him.

He squatted down and unlaced his desert boots, then slipped off his socks too.

Calista pointed at the log. "We can leave these here." She said. She placed her shoes neatly by the log. Brandon laid his boots beside hers, his socks stuffed into the toes.

Calista rolled her pant legs up to her knees and Brandon rolled his up to his calves, then Calista said "Come" again and started walking. Brandon walked beside her, looking around at the scenery.

The beach went straight north, ending at a bay in the distance. To the left the ocean rolled in with big, slow waves that flattened out to grey splashes when they hit the shore. To the right, short sand dunes rose up and quickly became deep green farmland.

"This is really pretty." He remarked. "No cars, no people, no noise. I can see why you like it here."

Calista nodded. "Yeah, I don't get a chance to just bum around here very often. I'm usually doing stuff, you know? Either working on books or at the hotel. I loved coming here with my folks, though, when I was younger."

She pointed ahead, at a huge boulder on the beach. "My dad would set up a little barbecue right there, and my mom and I would play tag as he cooked. I used to collect things from the beach- glass, floats, driftwood, and take them home at the end of the day. Mom would argue that we didn't need all that junk, but dad would always side with me. To this day, though, I am not sure if those arguments were all staged for my benefit."

He glanced over at her. "So, did you play any sports in high school, or what?"

"You mean, because I'm blonde, was I a cheerleader?"

"No, you're too tall and curvy to be a cheerleader. Besides that, you can string long sentences together."

Calista laughed. "High jump. I was good at it, too, till, you know..."

"The 'endowments' began to sprout?" He asked, not looking at her chest.

"Well put. Then I was popular for just showing up."

They passed the boulder and continued up the coast. The beach was wide, flat, almost a hundred yards from the dunes to the water, and in the clear light Brandon could see up and down the shoreline for miles. He took a deep breath. The air was cool, crisp, salty from the spray that drifted onto the sand. He realized he felt more relaxed than he had in a very long time.

At this point, the beach ended. The bay curved off to the right, and narrowed to a thin path.

"That's Porter Point." Calista waved her arm. "The state park is a half mile beyond that." They walked some more. Calista tapped his arm and pointed.

"Look." She said. There was a farm off to the right, on a slope heading back to the highway, and scattered along the field facing the water were several yellow construction trailers.

She stood there, her hands on her hips, fuming. "How could they? Why would the Johansen's sell their farm for a stupid casino?" She spat. "They've been here as long as we have. This is insane."

Brandon looked at the trailers for a minute. "Those are field offices, used for site planning. They might be looking at something else, not necessarily a casino." He said. "Still, I can find out what's going on, if you like."

Calista looked up at him, amazed. "Full of surprises, aren't you?"

He smiled. "I try. Let's not jump to conclusions, though. Come on, let's go back."

Calista grinned and nodded. "Yeah, even if they did sell their land for a casino, it could take years before it gets through city planning."

"There you go. Think positive." He smiled. They walked back down the beach toward the motorcycle.

Brandon bent down and picked something up, examining it.

"What is that?" Calista asked.

He held it out to show her. "A dead crab."

She screamed like a schoolgirl and held her hands up, running away from it. "I HATE crabs."

He laughed out loud. "C'mon, Calista, it's just a crab." He walked slowly closer to her, and she screamed again and ran toward the water.

"OK, now you've done it." He giggled. He ran toward her, and she ran into the surf, up to her knees. He followed her, waving the limp crab in his hand.

Calista ran back and forth, trying to get around him. He dodged left and right, cutting her off, until she decided to go straight and ran into him, knocking him backwards into the water.

He fell flat on his back, sank under the water for a moment, then popped back out and sat up, a look of astonishment on his face. He sat in the water, shook his head in defeat, and waved his arms in surrender.

Calista felt terrible. She laughed out loud, but she still felt bad at what she'd done to him, and reached down to help him up. He took her hand and pulled her down into the water with him.

She gasped in shock, fell face first into the surf, then stood straight up and started to laugh again.

Brandon lay down again and did the backstroke, comically. Calista howled with laughter and just sat in the water. He sat up beside her and smiled.

"Thanks for this. That's the most fun I've had in years." He said.

"Me too." She said.

He stood up and held his hand out. "No tricks." He promised.

She gripped his hand and let him lift her up, then she shook herself like a wet dog and pulled at her soggy clothes.

Brandon was amused at her reaction, and looked at her shape under her wet things. She hadn't noticed, he thought.

By the time they walked back to the motorcycle, they were dry enough that they could ride home without catching pneumonia, but sand had gotten into places that made it uncomfortable to sit for long.

They raced down the highway, then down the clay road to the hotel, and Calista got out, gingerly. She shimmied to the steps of the hotel and turned to look at Brandon. She held her arms out at her sides.

"Thank you very much for lunch." She said. "And the swim." She giggled.

He bowed deeply. "The pleasure was all mine, ma'am."

She went inside and headed upstairs. She needed to shower and get the sand out of her clothes.

Brandon went back to his cottage and pulled out some clean clothes. He was wet, felt sticky, and wanted to get dry as quickly as he could.

He took his shaving kit out of his backpack, placed it on the vanity in the bathroom, and looked around for clean towels. There were none. Maisie had scooped them out and put them into the washing machine. He needed dry towels. He jogged quickly to the main house, knocked and went in.

"Hello?" He called. There was no answer. Upstairs, he could hear the shower running. Maisie was nowhere to be seen, so he looked out the window. She would know where the towels were.

The car was gone; Maisie had told him earlier that she might spend the afternoon with a friend in Tillamook. He still needed the towels. Perhaps there were some in the cupboard on the main floor.

He opened it up and looked. No luck- just placemats and tablecloths. He only had one option; he sighed and went up the stairs.

The bathroom door was slightly open; he could see shadows shifting as Calista moved in the shower.

There was a linen closet across the hall from the bathroom. Could he sneak over to it, get some towels and be back downstairs before she noticed? Possibly. But if she thought he was a peeping tom, it could get awkward. He decided on a more direct approach.

"Hello? Hi? Calista?" He yelled out.

The water turned off. "Hello? Who's there?" She called out tentatively.

"It's me. Your mom took all my towels. Do you have any in the closet here?"

There was a pause. "Yeah, top shelf. Found them?"

He opened the closet door and took two large towels out. He headed to the top of the stairs, around the corner from the bathroom door, out of sight of Calista.

"Got them. I'm headed back out." He called, and stomped loudly down the stairs.

He got to the bottom of the stairs and turned to head out to the cottage, when he heard a voice from upstairs.

"Hey!" Calista called. He looked up to see her; she was in a thick cotton robe, with a towel on her head.

She smiled at him. "I really enjoyed today. Thanks."

He looked up at her, long and hard. "Yeah, me too." He smiled. "We should do it again sometime this summer."

"Next time, we'll have a picnic." Calista grinned. "I'll make sandwiches."

Brandon nodded. "I'd love that. It sounds great." There was a tone in his voice that Calista couldn't quite read, somewhere between warm and wistful, almost sad.

He turned to leave. Calista felt she should say something. She wasn't sure why, but she felt she had to.

"Hey, do you have any idea what you'd like for dinner?" She called.

He looked up again and spread his arms wide. "Surprise me." He said. He went out of the house, and through the upstairs window, Calista watched him take the towels into his cottage.

She wondered what he thought of her, what he thought of the hotel, of her mother. He was well-spoken, seemed to not need money, and he hadn't asked her for anything, or tried to grope her, like some of the men in town.

There was a handyman that Calista had hired a couple of years before, a gruff, burly young man who whistled constantly as he worked. He had done what he was paid to do, but he spent a lot of time looking at Calista's legs, and he made a few comments that clearly indicated he was testing the water, to see if she was interested in him. Brandon wasn't like that; he talked more like a college professor than a handyman- and he bathed regularly, which made it easier to be around him.

Also, when Calista spoke to him, he looked into her eyes, actually listening to her, not staring at her shirt buttons, the way most of the men in Lincoln City did.

Maisie came back later in the afternoon. Brandon was off in the back part of the property, fixing a loose fence post. Calista decided to make meat loaf for dinner, and Maisie offered to cook roast potatoes to go with it. The two women worked in the kitchen side by side, silently chopping and cooking, a choreographed dance of movement borne out of a lifetime of working together.

They slid the pans of food into the oven, and Maisie leaned back, wiping her hands on her apron. She looked out to the back fence, at Brandon hammering a fence board up.

"He's very good." Maisie said.

"Yes, I think he's going to work out." Calista said, absentmindedly.

"That's not what I mean, and you know it, Cali." Maisie said, softly. "You've been alone too long, hon."

Calista stared at her. "Are you suggesting what I think you are, mom? Really."

Maisie shrugged. "I'm just saying, Cali, if I was thirty years younger, I'd ask him out myself. Heck, I still might, just for the fun of it."

Calista looked at her mother, incredulous, then burst out laughing.

Maisie poked her chin at the window. "It's a hot afternoon. Why don't you see if he needs a cool drink?"

Brandon looked along the board in his hand. It was warped, but he could flip it over and it would take most of the warp out of it. Once he did that, hardly anyone else would notice the twist in the wood. In any case, it made the fence look much better. Once he'd painted it, it would look almost new.

The sound of gravel crunching made him turn around. Calista came up to him with a thermos and plastic cups.

"Hi there, I thought you might like something cool to drink. We made lemonade." She said.

He smiled. "I'd love some, thanks."

She poured some lemonade from the thermos into a cup and handed it to him. She poured herself one.

"What are you doing?" she asked.

He waved at the grassy area. "People aren't just after a bed for the night, and they're not only paying for a place to stay. They're buying an experience. If you can give them peace and quiet, then they'll come back over and over. If you're only selling them a bed, they can get that at the motel down the way. There's no reason to come all the way out here."

Calista nodded. "So, why do you want to fix the fence?"

"When I drive in, it's the first thing I see at the end of the driveway. If I think the fences aren't being well maintained, then I'm going to assume the rest of the hotel is a wreck too, and you've already got two strikes against you."

Calista looked at the hotel from his point of view. She had never thought of it that way. He was right.

He took a sip of lemonade. "This is good. This isn't from a can, is it?"

"No, mom always makes it fresh, the old-fashioned way." She bent down to look at the board he had nailed on.

"What were you looking at just now?" She asked, curious.

"Sorry?"

"You were looking at the edge of the board. How come?" She repeated.

He guided her shoulders and pointed at the top of the fence board. "See there? There's a wow to the wood, and I was turning it so the post would take most of the wow out. Otherwise it looks really cheesy."

Calista tilted her head. "I don't see it."

He leaned in close to her and pointed at the wood. His face pressed against her cheek; she could smell sweat and aftershave in the air, and it gave her a quick, light thrill she hadn't felt in a long time.

"See there?" He said. "The board still has a twist to it, but it's not really noticeable now that it's nailed in."

Calista liked his face pressing against hers. She was still for a minute. "I see." She whispered.

Brandon leaned back slowly, and looked at Calista with an odd expression.

"Thanks for the lemonade." He said. "Sorry, I should get back to work." He glanced down at the ground.

Calista took the thermos and the plastic cups back to the house, puzzled. What had she said to upset him? Why did he get distant all of a sudden? She put it out of her mind and helped get dinner ready.

At six o clock, the sun was low over the trees, casting a shadow down the clay road. Even though it was still quite light, Maisie turned on the porch lamps and opened the windows, letting the evening breeze through the house.

Brandon had washed up and changed to clean clothes, and he sat at one end of the dining table, helplessly keeping his hands between his knees as Maisie and Calista busied about, bringing in food.

He watched in fascination as they served him meatloaf, potatoes, and grilled vegetables. Maisie said grace, quickly, and they all began to eat.

Brandon took a bite of his food and chewed slowly, thinking.

Maisie leaned forward and frowned. "Is there something wrong with the meatloaf?" She asked.

He shook his head. "I have to tell you, I have eaten at some of the best restaurants in the country. This rates right up there with any of them." He chewed his food again and nodded. "Yup. Honest."

Maisie smiled, pleased. Calista glanced at her and decided to ask the question that had been dogging her all day. She would do it in a roundabout way, so he wouldn't think she was grilling him.

"Mom, Brandon has arranged for us to get the driveway fixed." She said.

Maisie smiled. "That's lovely, dear. Can we afford it, though?"

"Apparently, he has friends who are willing to drop off a truckload of gravel for free."

Calista gave Brandon a cold smile. She still didn't trust him, somehow. This was too good to be true. And there was the strange look he gave her at the fence. What was he really after?

Brandon looked at her for several seconds. It seemed he was reading her mind, looking into her eyes and seeing her thoughts. He smiled softly and turned to face Maisie.

"Mrs. Blake, I have friends who are doing construction work in Oregon. As it happens, they're over in Depoe Bay, and they have some extra gravel they will drop off here. It's no big deal to them. I thought it would help the look of the place, that's all."

"Tell her about the casino." Calista said. She was still looking at him with suspicion.

He nodded. "I asked the gal at the diner- Jan?- why her husband was so eager to sell this place for you. She let slip that there are plans for a casino in the works. If that's true, then this property, hotel or no hotel, would be worth ten times what it is now."

Maisie put her fork down and leaned back. "Well, that certainly makes it interesting, doesn't it?"

She glanced at Calista then back at Brandon. "I'm afraid you'll have to forgive my daughter. She has a less charitable view of people than I do. What made you ask that about Glen? Not that I'm surprised, you understand. I've never held him in very high regard."

Brandon shrugged. "Look, I get it. I came out here; I've thrown my weight around and make these promises. That has got to be hard to believe, even with the best possible spin you can put on it. As I said before, though, I'm here for the summer because I see it as a challenge, not because I need the money."

Calista softened her look slightly. "You took a dislike to Glen pretty well right away. What made you think he wasn't being straight with us?"

He thought for a moment. "Can you tell the difference between a squirrel and a snake when you see them?"

She nodded.

"I smelled snake. He wasn't trying to help you; he was trying to devour you."

Maisie brought out apple pie for dessert, and over pie and coffee the three of them talked about other things the rest of the evening. After coffee, Brandon said that the next day, Thursday, he would start on fixing up cottage number two, then see what he could do once the rented equipment arrived.

He thanked the women for the meal, wished them good night, and went back to his cottage.

Calista and Maisie stood side by side, washing the dishes, and spoke little. Again, like when cooking the meal, they had done this most of their lives. Finally, Maisie shook her hands dry in the sink and wiped them on a tea towel. She leaned against the sink and studied Calista.

"So, Cali, what do you think of this fellow, Brandon? He has a thing for you, don't you think?"

Calista rolled her eyes. "Honestly, mom. You've said that a dozen times about guys that have been here. I think he's cute, and he seems to know what he's doing, but I don't know- he doesn't put out any kind of signal that I can read, you know?"

"Maybe he's just being a gentleman, not like that cretin we hired who kept trying to peek down your shirt."

Calista laughed. "Yeah, he was a real winner. Notice how he backtracked when his wife showed up?"

Maisie shook her head. "Well, this man does not have that feel about him. He seems like a genuinely nice man. You could do a lot worse, even if he does go around on a motorcycle."

Calista thought about the trip to the beach at Porter Point. She smiled at falling in the water, at coming home wet, at laughing with Brandon. Her mother looked in her eyes, reading her expression.

"Well, there is a spark there after all, isn't there, Cali?"

Calista stood up straight and frowned. "Leave it alone, mom." She went up to her room and turned on the radio. She would listen to some music for a while, then get ready for bed. Out her window, she saw a glow coming from the beach. It could have been anything; sometimes fishing boats moored just off the shore and cast nets for smelt, other times kids from the area had parties, but she thought the light was closer than that, and there was no yelling or screaming.

She pulled a sweater over her shirt and walked out to Brandon's cottage, wondering if he'd heard it too. He wasn't in- the door was open and he didn't answer her call. She continued on along the path by the back fence, over the rise of land and to the barbecue pit. She saw a figure sitting on a short log, its back to her, outlined by the red glow of the fire and the swirling sparks that zigzagged up in the smoke.

The figure turned around to face her. "Hi, I'm glad you came out to join me." Brandon said.

Calista sat beside him, on a short log beside his. "Why are you out here?" She asked.

He pointed straight up. "The Milky Way. Do you know how long it's been since I've seen the Milky Way?"

Calista looked up. "All right. So?"

He shook his head. "You don't realize what you have here, do you? I live in a city that's so noisy, so crowded, so.." He paused, thinking of the right word. "Bustling, busy, crowded."

"You already said 'crowded'." Calista teased.

"Well, anyway, you really should appreciate this place." He said. He reached down beside him and lifted up a stemmed glass, filled with dark red liquid.

"Would you like some wine?" He said.

Calista thought about that. "Do you have a glass for me?" She asked.

He smiled smugly and picked up a second glass. He handed it to Calista, then poured her some wine from a bottle between his feet. He raised his glass. "To our dip in the ocean."

"To getting our feet wet." Calista countered.

He nodded. "I'll drink to that." They clinked glasses.

Calista looked around. "Do you have a third glass, in case mom joins us?"

Brandon held up a third glass. "Yes. Confidentially, I was hoping I wouldn't need it."

Calista took a sip and looked down at into the glass. "This is really, really good." She sighed. "Where did you get it?"

"A friend of mine." Brandon shrugged.

"Let me guess- he has a vineyard, and he owed you a favor?"

Brandon watched her, amused. "No, no favor, he just has a vineyard."

Calista could feel the wine warming her up inside and it made her slightly giddy. "Of course you have a friend who owns a vineyard. Is he the same friend who's going to give us all that gravel?"

"No. a different friend." He sipped his wine. "Why exactly are you so hot and cold with me, Mrs. Blake?"

"Blake is my maiden name. I was Mrs. Shaughnessy when my husband was alive, but I went back to using my maiden name after he passed away." She looked away and sipped her wine.

"Sorry." He looked down at his glass.

Calista reached out and touched his arm. "No, it's not your fault. I should let you know, I'm not being intentionally crabby with you; it's just that we've had people- mostly men- try to take advantage of us. I guess we're a little gun-shy."

He smiled sadly. "No, I meant sorry about the 'Mrs. Blake'. I guess I was being a little snotty, too. It's just that you don't look like a 'Mrs.'."

"You mean I don't look like the kind of girl men would marry?" Calista teased.

He smiled. "Maybe this wine is making me foolish. No, I didn't mean that. I think you're very marriable."

She wrinkled her nose up. That one expression gave him a thrill. "Is 'marriable' a real word?" She asked.

"Probably not, but it sounded pretty good."

She drained her glass and held it out for a refill. He poured some more wine for each of them.

He looked up. The moon was now low on the southwest, sending a river of white light directly toward them. He sipped his wine and turned to face Calista. She was looking at him, reading his expression.

"What are you thinking?" She asked.

"How funny we all are, we silly people." He waved at the moon. "We've landed on that planet, and we know it's just a big dusty rock, we've even brought back some souvenir pebbles, yet when I see moonlight on the waves like that, I can't help but think that it's shining out there just for me."

Calista sipped her wine. "I used to think that if I could just run fast enough, on nights like this, I could run along the water and jump onto the moon. Not literally, you know, just one of those thoughts you get."

He took a sip of wine and leaned close to her. "Do you think that moonlight leads to romance?" He asked.

She shook her head. "Danger, danger. Do not go any further, danger ahead."

He nodded. "Yeah, time to turn in for the night, I guess."

He stood up and doused the fire with a handful of wet sand. The flames died down, and a cloud of steam covered them both. The firelight that had illuminated their faces was gone. Pale moonlight lit them now, just silhouettes of their bodies. Brandon held out a hand, Calista reached up and took it, then let herself be pulled upright.

She was standing just an inch or so away from him, now. She could feel the heat from his body through her sweater. She had an irrational urge to kiss him. She stepped back slightly, though, and took a breath.

"Goodnight, Brandon Cooper." She said.

"Sleep well, Miss Blake."

She walked back along the dark path, the moonlight behind her lighting the dusty trail enough that she could make her way back to the house. He waited a few seconds, watching her hips sway as she walked.

Behind her, she heard the clink of glasses and a squeaky sound as a cork went back into a bottle. There was something sad in that sound, something that implied an opportunity that had been missed.

She heard footsteps as Brandon followed her along the path, footsteps that faded as he turned to go to his cottage.

A glow behind her lit up the side of her house-Brandon turning on his cottage porch light. She turned and waved goodnight to him, then went home and up the stairs.

In her room, as she undressed for bed, she could see the light inside his cottage come on in the main room, then in the bathroom, then the main room, then the porch light went out, then finally the cottage went completely dark.

Calista stood at her window, leaned on the sill and looked up at the stars. He was right; she never really looked up at the night sky anymore; she took it for granted. Maybe she was taking too much of her life for granted.

That was enough philosophy for one night, she thought; besides, the wine was working its way through her, making her groggy. She crawled into bed and went to sleep.

In the darkened cottage, Brandon watched her look out her window. There, in the darkness of his room, she couldn't see him. Her face, in shadow when she looked down, lit up fully when she turned to look at the night sky.

He went to bed, lying on the covers, thinking about Calista. Something about her haunted him. Something about her looks, the way she moved, the shape of her thigh when she reached up, the way she smiled at him. She was not the most beautiful woman he had ever seen, far from it. She was certainly not nearly as pretty as his wife. He fell asleep.

Chapter Four

Friday had started off with cottony clouds coming over the ocean, drifting north with the current. They looked like big fluffy sheep, balls of white over a navy blue sea. By seven in the morning, Brandon had cleared all the furniture out of cottage number two, and covered it with tarps, out on the grass.

Maisie came out to meet him. Calista watched them from the kitchen, savoring her marvelous strong coffee, and tried to read their lips.

Her mother said something like 'what are you doing to the cabbage?' Probably 'cottage', she told herself.

Brandon said 'I want to sample floods (sand the floors, dummy) and faint the wells'. Paint the walls, right.

Her mother waved at the main house and said 'well, come and eek some bread fast'.

Calista chuckled at herself and busied about, getting a place ready at the table for him.

Brandon and her mother walked in a minute later, laughing about something.

He beamed at her. "Hey, good morning, how's the head?" He asked Calista.

She shot a look at her mother. "What? What did he tell you?"

Maisie smirked. "Nothing, really. Just a story about skinny dipping at Porter Point and getting drunk last night."

Calista glared at him.

He shook his head. "Not guilty, your honor. I only said we fell into the water yesterday, and that I needed some dry towels later. Then I said I kept a glass free for your mom in case she joined us on the beach last night. That's all- honest." He grinned.

Calista scowled at her mother. "You make me sound like a party animal. Honestly."

She turned to face Brandon. "Anyway, what would you like for breakfast?"

He shrugged. "Please don't go to any great effort. Anything you want to make, I'm sure it will be delicious."

Calista mixed up flour and eggs, then poured batter into a skillet. Within a few minutes she had a tall stack of pancakes on a plate for him. "Mom, want some?" She asked.

Her mother nodded. "Thanks, dear. Yes, I'd love some."

Brandon attacked his pancakes, savoring the taste and texture, then stopped briefly to catch his breath.

"These are great. Where did you get this recipe?" He said, sincerely.

Calista nodded at her mother. "We've made them this way for as long as I can remember. I'm glad you enjoy them."

"Heck, I might come back here next year for the food alone." He said.

Calista's heart sank. She hadn't thought about it much, but he would be gone in a couple of months. Even after just a very few days, she was getting used to having him around. She already missed him.

"Anyway, right after my second up of coffee I'll mask and tape up, then paint the cottage." He said.

Calista wanted to say nothing. "Can I help at all?" She said, involuntarily.

Maisie stepped in. "Yes, good idea, Cali. Why don't you help Mister Cooper tape and paint, or whatever it is he has to do? I'll do the dishes."

Calista sensed a setup, her mother pushing her toward this man, but she just frowned. "Fine." She said.

They gathered masking tape and old newspapers from the basement, then she followed Brandon to the cottage, keeping a slight distance. He looked over at her and smiled.

"Are you avoiding me this morning, Miss Blake?" He joked.

Calista shook her head. "Look, you're a nice guy, and I really hope you can help us, but you're going back to your real life in eight weeks, and we're still going to be here, all right?"

He nodded. "You've been let down a lot by men, huh?"

Calista glared at him, coldly, then she dropped the tape and newspapers she was holding.

"You were hired to do a job, not analyze my life. Please just do your job." She snapped. She walked away.

Brandon shrugged, picked up the supplies, and went on to the cottage. He dumped the paper and tape on the floor then walked back to the main house. Calista was sitting on the steps, her head in her hands, looking at her shoes. Brandon sat beside her, as far from her as he could. He looked at her and smiled.

She looked over at him. "What?" She barked.

"Nothing." He smiled again.

"Bull. What are you laughing at?"

"I'm not laughing."

"Yes you are, you're laughing at me. What's so funny?" She pressed.

He sighed. "I'm sorry if I hit a nerve there. All I meant was that you've obviously had a very hard time, and a lot of the heat for that goes to the men in your life. That's all."

"You sound like my mother."

"Well, she sounds a lot like my own mother, actually." He said.

"Does she live in San Francisco too?"

"No."

"Where is your mother, then?" Calista asked.

"New York."

"What does she do?"

"She works with a charity." He seemed slightly uneasy saying that.

"Which charity?"

"You wouldn't know it." He stood up. "Listen, as I say, I made you feel bad there. I apologize. Could you help me tape up the windows, please?"

He stood up and reached his hand out to help Calista up. She slapped his hand away and stood on her own, but her foot slipped and she fell forward, landing in his arms.

"Does this mean you forgive me?" He joked.

She smiled. "I can get a little sensitive at times- that's just me. I'm sorry too." She said. They walked to the cottage together. She had not seen a cottage this empty in years. The furniture, bed, drapes, carpets, everything was stacked outside. When Calista spoke, there was now an echo in the air. She looked at the walls; scuffs and scratches, from years of moved furniture and carelessly tossed luggage, had left a crosshatch pattern of lines and scrapes along the walls.

The lower walls, which had been hidden by night tables and headboards, were a different color than the rest, and the ceiling now clearly showed dark stains where heat from the lamps had sent dirt skyward.

Brandon walked around, sniffing. "Terrible smell in here." He said.

"I thought it might have been the carpet." Calista said. "But that's out on the lawn now. What could the smell be from?"

He sniffed and walked around, like a police bloodhound, settling on the bathroom sink.

"Here." He said. "I wonder- just a minute."

He went back into the main house, jogged down into the basement, and came back with a bag of plumbing tools and a plastic basin. He disassembled the drainpipe under the sink and dumped it into the basin. It smelled awful.

Calista covered her mouth with a handkerchief, and Brandon held his breath as he took the basin outside.

"Dear lord, what is that stuff?" She gasped, wrinkling her face up.

"Hair, shave cream, toothpaste." He said. "Years' worth of yuck."

He dumped the basin in the back yard and rinsed out the pipe with a garden hose. He inspected it, checking that it was clean inside, and reassembled the plumbing. The smell was gone.

"There." He said. "One down, four to go."

He stopped joking with Calista and gave her short, simple instructions to tape up the windows and light switches in the room, then he thanked her for the help and spent two hours nailing down every loose board on the cottage's porch.

It was noon by then, and Maisie had Calista ask if he could stop for lunch. The sun was high, the sky totally cloudless, and he was dripping with sweat. He took off his shirt, fluffed out his T shirt to create a breeze, then he said he'd be right in and went to change the T shirt. Calista followed him to his cottage, knocked on the door and walked in.

Brandon was in the washroom, splashing water on himself, and didn't hear her. She came a little closer to him and spoke loudly.

"Hi? Do you have any preferences for lunch, mom asked?" She called.

He came out of the washroom. He was shirtless, with a towel in his hand, and he scrubbed his face dry as he watched her. "Sorry?" He asked.

Calista opened her mouth to speak, then she noticed his muscles. He was lean, slim, but the veins in his biceps stuck out, and when he bent his arms to dry his hair, his back made a wide triangle, like she had seen in champion swimmers.

His waist was tight and flat, and Calista saw that there was a wide scar down the middle of his chest, the length of his hand.

"You were asking something?" He repeated.

"Lunch." Calista said. "Do you want a sandwich, or salad, or what?"

"Whatever you like." He said.

Calista nodded. She looked bashfully away and turned toward the door.

"Heart surgery." He said.

"Sorry?"

"The scar- it's from heart surgery. People always ask me about it. Men just think it's a cool badge of courage, women either think it's something they can nurse me back from, or it means I'm damaged."

Calista nodded. "I see."

"What about you?" He asked. "Do you think it's a fixable flaw, or a sign that I'm imperfect?"

He picked up a khaki T shirt from his bed and slid it on. It only made him look more muscular.

He ran his fingers quickly though his hair, casually smoothing it back. "So?" He asked.

"A sandwich, then?" Calista asked.

"No, I mean, am I damaged, or am I a fixer-upper?" He smiled.

She smirked. "I think it just proves that you do have a heart after all."

He nodded. "Touche'."

Maisie served homemade soup and sandwiches for lunch. Brandon ate heartily. He commented again on Maisie's cooking, and finished his soup almost before starting on the sandwich.

He leaned back at one point and shook his head. "What was in that stuff?" He asked.

"It's carrot and bean soup, an old family recipe. I'm glad you liked it." Maisie grinned.

Calista nodded at Brandon. "Ask him about his heart surgery, mom."

Maisie smiled politely and waited for him to talk.

"It's not that exciting." He said. "I had a bad valve, and they fixed it."

"You're fine now, though." Maisie said, with finality. He nodded.

"Well, that's that, then." Maisie said, closing the subject.

They had coffee and pie, then Brandon looked at his watch and sat on the porch steps, waiting for something.

Calista sat beside him, wondering what he was thinking. He looked down the long road toward the highway, as though someone was about to arrive any moment.

"What's up?" Calista asked at last.

"The stuff I rented should have been here by now. Along with your paint." He looked at his watch; it was just after one.

In the distance, a small flatbed truck turned onto the dusty road and lumbered toward the house, slowly.

"Right on time." He said. He stood up and waved the truck to a spot beside the main house.

He leapt onto the back of the truck and unchained some equipment. The truck driver got out and ambled over to join him.

"This stuff all for you?" The driver called.

"Yep." Brandon said. He and the man lifted down a series of machinery- motors and equipment, and three large pails of paint. The paint was the only thing Calista recognized; the rest of the items were totally foreign to her.

The truck driver had Brandon sign a delivery slip and drove off again. Brandon looked at the assorted bits and pieces like a child ready to assemble a train set.

He organized them, then he dragged one item that looked like a big vacuum cleaner into the empty cottage.

Calista followed him, curious. "What is that thing?" She asked.

"It's a floor sander. Let's see how this baby works on these old yellow pine boards." He put a sandpaper belt on the machine, plugged it in, slipped on a dust mask and started it up. It sounded like a hundred blenders going at once. Dust and smoke filled the air. Calista ran out of the cottage and went back to the main house, as her mother was finishing up the dishes.

"What's he doing out there, Cali?" She asked.

"Sanding the floors, he said. It's like Armageddon in there- smoke and dust everywhere."

Her mother smiled. "You like him, don't you?"

"He's an enigma, mom. I just don't understand what he's doing here."

"That's not what I asked, Cali."

Calista shook her head. "Let's see what happens for the rest of the summer, all right?"

An hour later, Brandon came back to the main house for a glass of water. Maisie pointed at the cottage.

"How are you doing in there?" She asked.

"Come and see." He said. He walked the two women to the cottage and stood just inside the door.

The floor was stripped of old lacquer and warped wood, and now looked as smooth and light as new. He pointed at one corner and spoke in an animated tone. "I got the baseboards off, stripped it to the walls, and now I'm going to vacuum and stain the floor. I should be done with this floor today, then when the floor's dry, I'll paint the inside walls tomorrow. It should be ready to rent out by Tuesday."

Maisie reached down and rubbed her hand along the floor. "This is smooth as glass." She said. "How on earth did you do that?"

"Fine sandpaper. This belt sander does a great job on the wood, doesn't it?" He said, proudly.

Calista smelled the floors in the cottage, now almost like a new house smell. She smiled.

"I'm impressed. This is terrific." She muttered. "Thank you, Brandon. We really can't thank you enough."

"Hey, that makes it all worthwhile right there." He said.

Just before dinner time, he called Calista and Maisie over to see how far he'd gotten.

Maisie surprised her daughter; she almost ran to see the cottage, and Calista trailed behind her, trying to keep up.

Brandon pointed to the work he'd finished. "So, the floors are done, and the urethane should be cured by breakfast. After that, I'll mask and paint the inside and outside of the cottage. As I say, I'll take Sunday off, but I should be done by Monday night or so, and we can call that unit completed."

Maisie took his arm and walked him back to the main house, chatting warmly. He was very proud of the work, he said, and it made him feel that it was time well spent when he could see a job through for a change.

"Don't you usually see a job through all the way?" Calista asked.

"No, not usually." He said.

"Why not?" She asked simply.

"I usually move on to other projects before then."

"You said you were a construction worker." Calista challenged. "Why wouldn't you stay till the job was done?"

"No." He said. "I told you I worked in construction, that's all, not that I was a construction worker."

Calista glared at him. "Then who the hell are you, Brandon?"

He smiled enigmatically. "I'm your man for the summer."

Maisie had made shepherd's pie for dinner. Brandon dug into his meal, talked pleasantly with Maisie, and avoided Calista's questions until coffee. Then he leaned back, looked at Calista long and hard, and finally shrugged.

"All right, now that you've fed me dinner, what do you want to know?"

"Why are you here?" Calista asked. Her mother looked back and forth between them but said nothing.

"I agreed to help you fix up the place." He answered. "Are you saying you want to fire me?"

"No, I mean- look, you have to admit that someone like you doesn't come by every day."

"I certainly hope not." He grinned.

Calista pointed a finger at him. "You're just playing with me now. I don't know anything about you. You're here, and you're helping us out, and we're grateful for that, but I have NO idea why you're doing it."

"You needed my help. I offered to help you." He said. He pulled his wallet out of his pocket. After his dunking on the beach, he had taken everything out to dry in his cottage. He retrieved a plastic card and handed it to Calista.

"My driver's license; I said I wanted you to check me out, now I insist you do it. Please."

Calista looked at the ID and shook her head. She handed it back. "No, that's not necessary." She said.

He didn't take it. "One trick con men use is to call someone's bluff, knowing they won't follow through. I would feel very much better if you would check me out, Miss Blake."

She stared at the license, read the address, on Jackson Street, as he had told her, and placed it on a sideboard. To make him feel better, and just because she was obstinate, she would go into town on Monday and talk to the police.

During dinner, Brandon mentioned to Maisie that he had enjoyed seeing the stars the night before. He still had a few bottles of wine he'd brought along, from his sidecar, he said. He invited her to join him at the fire pit.

Maisie glanced at Calista, who looked distinctly uncomfortable, and thanked him for the offer, but said she would be going to sleep early. Perhaps Cali would be interested in joining him?

Calista glared at her. "It's fine, thanks, mom." She turned to Brandon. "Thanks for the offer, but no."

He smiled. "Well, if you do change your mind, you know where to find me."

He thanked the ladies again for a wonderful meal and went back to his cottage. Maisie and Calista washed up, then Maisie said good night and excused herself to watch some TV before bed.

Calista tried to read a book she had started a long time before, but her mind kept going back to seeing Brandon, his shirt off, the veins in his muscles, the scar on his chest.

She put the book down and lay back on her bed. It was the first really warm night of the year. She was only wearing shorts and a short sleeved blouse, yet she was still warm. Maybe she should take a walk.

Yes, maybe a walk along the beach. Past the fire pit- it was nice there. She shook her head. He was out there- she just knew it. If she went back there again tonight, he might get the wrong idea about her. But was it the wrong idea? Did she really not feel the least bit attracted to him? She rolled over and tried to fall asleep. A faint sound came through the window; not a crackle or snap, like a fire would make, but a musical sound, like a small bird. She listened harder, trying to identify it.

It was a harmonica. She realized what the sound was, then wondered why on earth she was hearing a harmonica.

She was down the stairs and out the front door before she realized what she was doing. She was in the yard now, trying to decide whether to go back upstairs or to follow the sound. The harmonica started again, an old tune, one her mother would know. She walked toward Brandon's cottage, but the sound came from beyond it, out on the beach.

She walked slowly, as though making a sound might scare whoever was playing the music. She crested the rise in the dune and was almost at the fire pit before she saw him. He was sitting alone, like last night, but the fire was smaller tonight. He looked up, saw her, and waved. "Hey there, nice to see you again." He said quietly.

Calista sat across from him. "I bet you have a glass here for me tonight, too." She said.

He smiled, pulled a glass out from behind him, filled it with wine and handed it to her. She raised her glass and waited for him to raise his. "Bottoms up." She said.

"Enticing thought." He joked.

They sipped wine, silently, for a good minute. It made Calista's head spin. She enjoyed the feeling- it felt like being on a swing, like letting go, like not having to worry for the moment. Brandon sipped his glass slowly, examining the fire.

Calista smirked. "So, where did you learn to play harmonica?"

"Prison." He said, solemnly. He laughed. "Sorry, I couldn't resist that one. I was at a remote site for six months, and this was the only way to stay sane." He handed the harmonica to Calista. "Here. Try it."

She took it, turned it over so the writing was right way up, and blew into it. It sounded like a bad taxi horn.

She laughed, giddy from the wine, and handed it back. He shook his head.

"No, try again. You can do it. Here." He got up and sat beside her. He held the harmonica to her lips and kept it steady.

Calista giggled, embarrassed. She tried a few times to pucker up and blow into it, but then she would start to giggle again. Brandon smiled patiently and waited for her to calm down.

"OK, now, try to make an 'O' with your mouth." He said softly. She blew into the reed and a respectable noise came out.

"There, you see, it's not that difficult." He said. Calista took another sip of wine.

"I can't play that thing." She giggled. "It's the shape of my mouth- it's impossible for me to play it."

He looked at her, dead serious. "There is absolutely nothing wrong with the shape of your mouth." He said.

She got serious too, and leaned in close toward him. He was almost nose to nose with her. He sighed and held the harmonica up to her lips.

"Breathe out naturally." He said, softly.

She exhaled, and a series of musical notes filled the air. She smiled at that.

"There, that wasn't so bad, was it?" He asked. It was almost a whisper. He took a sip of wine. She leaned back, wondering why he had let an opportunity go by.

"Why didn't you try to kiss me?" She asked.

He looked at her sadly. "Because you would have let me."

"Am I that unappealing?"

He shook his head. "I have wanted to kiss you since the moment we met, back in the diner. Believe me, it took all my restraint to NOT kiss you just now."

She took his face in her hands and pulled him close. She kissed him, softly, passionately, letting out feelings that she had held in for years, feelings of love and lust and warmth all in one long kiss, letting them pour out on this near stranger.

He did not resist. He let her pull him close and press her warm lips against his, let her caress his cheek with her hair, let her face brush against his face.

The fire crackled behind them, warming them. Brandon knelt in front of her, wrapped his arms around her and kissed her fully, embracing her with his whole body.

He lifted her, effortlessly, and held her tight. They made no sound; the crackle of the fire was the only noise in their whole universe.

After a minute or so, he pulled back and breathed out, exhausted. "Ever go ice skating?" He asked.

She shook her head, puzzled.

"I think we're on VERY thin ice here, Calista."

"Are we?" She asked.

He nodded. "We're ready to fall in, feet-first. I'm not sure if we should just yet."

She smiled, a smile that was warmer, softer, than he had ever seen from her before. "Maybe we should call it a night, then."

"That's probably a good idea. I'm going to take a very cold shower- I'll see you at breakfast."

She laughed out loud. He stood up and held out his hand for her. She pulled herself up, careful not to bump into him.

He doused the fire, took her hand again and walked with her back along the path. She stopped as they got to his cottage, but he shook his head and nodded, indicating that he'd walk her home.

"It would be poor form to let my date walk home alone." He said.

"Was this a date?" Calista asked, wryly.

"Better than some I've had." He joked.

They reached the steps of the main house; Calista touched his arm. "Sleep well, Mister Cooper."

He reached down and kissed her, softly. "Pleasant dreams, Miss Blake."

He stood there, smiling at her, until she walked up the steps and closed her door, then he walked back to his cottage, whistling quietly to himself.

Calista crept up the stairs, not making any sound: her shadow was noisier than she was. At the top of the stairs, her mother's voice, clear and soft, came out of the dark.

"So, you went out there after all, did you, Cali?" She seemed amused, more than accusing.

"I heard music- he was playing a harmonica." Calista said softly. "And he gave me a glass of wine." She giggled.

She went into her room. "Goodnight, mom."

Chapter Five

At six thirty in the morning, Calista heard a sound like a powerboat in the yard. She squinted, trying to keep the noise away. The sound got louder, then softer, then louder again. She rolled over and buried her head in her pillow, but morning sunlight filled her room, and the sound was relentless.

She threw on a pair of shorts and a sweater, and stumbled downstairs. Her mother was already downstairs in the kitchen, flipping eggs in a skillet.

"Good morning, Cali." Her mother smiled. "Sleep well?"

Calista shrugged. "That wine of his really hits you hard. What's Brandon doing up so early, and so loudly?" She winced.

"Ask him yourself. He'll be right in for breakfast."

Maisie set a third place at the table for breakfast and poured coffee. On cue, Brandon walked in, humming to himself. He saw Calista and grinned.

"Good morning. You look well-rested." He smiled a disarming smile. Calista smiled back, despite herself.

"Good morning. What's all that noise you're making this early in the day?" She asked, wincing.

"A paint sprayer. You have to prime the feed hose before you can use it. Sorry about the noise." He grinned.

Maisie waved him over and patted the chair beside Calista. "You two need a good breakfast. Here." She said, firmly.

She put a plate of eggs and toast in front of Brandon, and the same in front of Calista. Brandon thanked her and started eating. Calista took a bite of her food and reached for the salt. Brandon's hand was there a split second later. His hand wrapped around hers, both clutching the salt shaker.

Their eyes met. Calista smiled slightly, and Brandon let go of her hand. His eyes never left hers. Calista pulled her hand slowly back and rested it in her lap.

Brandon leaned back and turned to face Maisie. "Mrs. Blake, would you excuse us for a minute?"

He looked at Calista. "Can I talk to you briefly?"

He held her chair out as she stood up. She was surprised by the courtesy. He took her arm and walked her out to the front porch. She went quietly, puzzled by this behavior.

He looked around to see that Maisie was still inside then leaned in close to Calista.

"Where exactly are we going, Calista?" He asked. The determination in his face was odd; not scary, or disturbing, just different than he had seemed before.

"What do you mean, Mister Cooper?" She asked coyly.

"Look, I'm not stupid. I'm not that bad looking, and I've dated a lot of women, all right?"

"Are you saying I'm one of the many you'd like to 'date'?"

He sighed. "No. you're different. Wait, no, that's a come-on line, 'I've never met a girl like you before', but damn it, Calista, I have never felt about a woman the way I feel about you. And the stupid thing is, I don't even know you. Now, would you please tell me if last night was just you testing the water, or a flash in the pan, or what?"

Calista nodded at the cottages. "You're going to be gone in August. You told us so. Doesn't that sort of limit our actions right there?"

"I could be gone then, yes. I could stay, though. But I'd need to know what I'm changing my plans for."

Calista shook her head. "You're making promises that are far too big. I enjoyed last night- more than I've enjoyed being out with someone in a very long time. But I can't pretend that this will last any longer than a couple of months."

She sighed and looked at her shoes. "When you read my ad, you said that 'a man for the summer' sounded like I was looking for a boyfriend. I'm not looking for a boyfriend. And I'm not looking for a fling, either. I like you- really- but please, let's not think that last night was anything more than it was."

He was not upset or sad, she noticed. He only stood there and smiled at her.

"Are you all right with that?" Calista asked. "Are we still all right with each other?"

He nodded slowly. "Yes. We're still friends, Calista. Come, our breakfast is getting cold."

They ate, sitting side by side, glancing at each other, saying little. Maisie busied about some more, staying out of the way.

After breakfast, Brandon thanked the women for the meal and went back out to the cottage. Calista stood in the kitchen, washing dishes, but jumped when Brandon started up a gas engine that backfired noisily.

Ten minutes later, Brandon was still at work. Calista had finished doing the monthly books for one of the farmers in town, and now she had nothing better to do; she wandered over to where Brandon was working and stood at the door, watching him. He was wearing a mask, goggles, and white fabric overalls, splashed with paint. He had a noisy gas engine running outside the cottage, drawing a bucket of paint into a hose that let him spray the walls a soft off-white color. It looked a lot better than the pale green the walls had been for the last thirty years. She leaned against the porch column, fascinated by the intricate ballet as he moved back and forth, covering the old paint in wide, smooth sweeps. When he'd finished, he came outside, turned off the engine, and peeled the mask and goggles off his face. He grinned at Calista.

"How does it look so far?" He asked.

"Amazing. It looks lovely." She sighed. "What are you doing next?"

He waved his arm at the wall. "Next I'll spray the outside, then I'll paint the deck, and by then the inside will be dry, and I can paint the ceiling. I think I should be done this cottage by Monday, maybe Tuesday."

For the first time in a long time, Calista felt optimistic. The way the place looked right now, just with a new floor and a fresh coat of paint, gave her hope that they could save the hotel after all. She smiled broadly.

"So, I'm doing all right after all, am I?" Brandon asked her, sincerely.

"It's terrific, yes, thank you." Calista said. She was elated, giddy with hope. She wrapped her arms around him and hugged him tight.

Brandon gasped at the emotion. "Wow. That was exciting." He grinned.

Calista shrugged. "You're doing us a tremendous favor. We appreciate it. Thank you."

He nodded. "OK, play time's over. Let's see how much more work I can get done today."

Solemnly, he placed newspaper on the outside deck, taped up the windows, and replaced the cream paint in the sprayer bucket with a putty color, then he sprayed the outside of the cottage. Within two hours, the outside looked like new, a pretty, beige tone, its fresh paint shaming the other four cottages, their faded yellow paint and twisted deck boards looking even worse now by comparison.

Calista asked if he could stop for lunch. Maisie had made chicken salad, and she had baked a pie for dessert.

Brandon ate lunch, sat quietly as Maisie served him pie and ice cream, then he dug in heartily, savoring every bite.

After he'd eaten, he checked walls of the cottage to be sure the paint was dry, and painted the porch decking.

By five o clock, the cottage was finished, save for painting the ceiling and replacing the furniture. Brandon looked up.

The sky was blue and cloudless; no rain in sight. The furniture would be safe overnight under the tarps. Calista just walked around, looking at the fresh paint, amazed at how much better the cottage looked.

Calista imagined how the other four cottages would look once he had finished. She was a young girl the last time they'd been able to repaint all of them; in the twenty years since, the weather had taken its toll on the hotel. This was turning out better than she could have hoped for. Even the smell of the fresh paint reminded her of being a little girl, of playing on the beach, of cycling to school with her friends. It reminded her of her father, when he had painted the cottages himself, his pipe clenched firmly in his mouth, when Calista watched him from the porch as he winked at her. This would not bring him back, but it could keep them going a while longer, keep his memory fresh, she thought.

Brandon walked around the cottage with a can of paint and a brush, making sure he hadn't missed any spots. Calista walked around it with him, thrilled with how good the building looked. She had lived around these buildings all her life, but for the first time, she felt very proud of them. They were around the back of the cottage, out of sight of the house. Brandon bent down to check the lower boards then jumped up to check the roof area. He stood up and dusted his pants off. Calista suddenly threw her arms around him and hugged him, passionately.

He didn't struggle. "What was that for?" He grinned.

"Thanks for the great work?" Calista offered.

"Bull." He said. "A handshake would do for that. You really are attracted to me, aren't you?"

Calista frowned. "It's complicated. I mean, yes, but, I mean, you're not going to be here for very long, are you? And I can't let myself get hurt anymore. You do understand that, right?"

"No, I don't understand. I have absolutely no idea what makes you tick." He shrugged. "That's what makes you so interesting."

He threw an arm over her shoulder and guided her toward the main house. "Come on, I smell your mom's cooking."

After dinner, over coffee, Brandon leaned forward and faced Maisie. "So, Mrs. Blake, what do you think of the cottage so far?"

"It's marvelous, son. You did a phenomenal amount of work in just a few days."

"Thank you, ma'am."

She shook her head. "We hired that fellow from Tillamook a couple of years ago, and he spent most of a week trying to cut a piece of wood to length. Then he would hang around the kitchen looking for food. I'm sure Cali has told you that we're quite vulnerable here- we're only two women."

He frowned. "Yes, she said that. Wonderful meal, as usual, by the way."

He stretched. "So, ladies, what is there to do on a Saturday night in Lincoln City?"

"There's a dance tonight at the fire hall." Maisie said. "Do you dance, Mister Cooper?"

"I do, yes. And please, call me Brandon."

He turned to look at Calista. "Do you like to dance, Miss Blake?"

Calista shrugged. "I haven't been to a dance in years."

"Great. I'm from out of town, and you're out of practice. It's a match made in heaven."

The inference was subtle, but Calista got it. Still, she hadn't been dancing for a long time, since before her husband died. It would be fun going out again, having a good time.

Brandon seemed to be reading her mind. "So, Calista, do you want to go?"

Calista threw her hands up in surrender. "Let me get a fresh pair of jeans on. I'll be right down."

She went upstairs to change. Brandon smiled as he watched her go up. Maisie was studying his face when he turned back to look at her.

"What are your intentions regarding my daughter, young man?" She asked.

"She's an enigma, Maisie. I can't figure her out."

"That she is. She's also very fragile. I don't want her hurt. Do we understand each other?"

He leaned forward and took Maisie's hand. "If you ever feel I'm doing something that could hurt her, tell me. I would never want to hurt her in any way, I promise."

Maisie nodded, satisfied. Calista came back downstairs, wearing jeans and a thin sweater. Brandon tried not to stare.

"All right, let's take the bike." He said. "It's a lovely night for a ride."

Calista slid into the sidecar and put her helmet on. Brandon fired up the motorcycle and bumped down the road to the highway. The night was cool, and the wind in her face made Calista shiver. She hunched down low, trying to stay warm.

Brandon saw what she was doing and pulled over. He took off his jacket and handed it to her.

"No, you need it." She protested. "You've got that...thing." She waved at his chest.

"I'm wearing a heavy shirt. You're going to freeze, dressed like that." He said over the engine's rumble.

She decided to accept his offer and pulled the jacket on. It still had his body's heat in it, warming her arms and back. It also smelled of his aftershave, the lingering sweat from the day's work and a faint smell of wood. It reminded her of him.

She wrapped it tight around her and smiled. He nodded approval and started off again.

They chugged into Lincoln City, rumbled past a half dozen pickup trucks and muscle cars, and parked across from the fire hall. Inside, forty or fifty people were dancing and drinking cola. The lone fire truck was out on the road, waiting forlornly, and a pair of speakers at one end of the hall blared out classic rock and roll- Chuck Berry or Little Richard or something.

Brandon held her hand and they crossed the road, running quickly even though there was no traffic.

He produced some cash and bought them tickets for the dance. The young woman who took his money smiled expectantly at him. She was hoping to dance with him too, Calista thought. They wandered into the hall, found a quiet corner and waited for the next song to start.

A burly young man in firefighter pants and a t shirt which read 'LCFD' worked the stereo system, switching the music to a jazzier selection. Brandon grabbed Calista's hand and dragged her to the middle of the floor. They danced a swing dance, twirling and pivoting smoothly, as though they had done this a hundred times before. The music changed to a thump-thump rock song, and Brandon changed his style, moving her around the floor to this tune too.

They danced for a half hour, then he bought them soda and they rested up for a few minutes.

The man in the firefighter pants turned the lights down, and switched to a romantic slow tune. Brandon smiled at Calista.

"Come, they're playing our song." He said.

They danced close, his arm around her waist, her head resting on his shoulder. She sighed, content.

"Are you all right?" He asked her, worried.

"I'm great, thanks. I haven't done this in forever, that's all." She sighed again. The dance ended, everyone clapped politely, then the man in the firefighter pants announced a short intermission before the next number.

Brandon asked Calista if she wanted anything more to drink.

"No, I'll just wait here till the music starts up again." She smiled. She sat on a stool and looked around, nodding at people she knew.

Brandon chatted with a man who had seen his motorcycle. The man also had a motorcycle, and asked about the sidecar. They spoke pleasantly for a minute, then the man left to talk with someone else.

A large man, wearing a lumpy suit and sporting a stubble of beard, walked across the dance floor and straight over to Calista.

"Hey, Cali, how ya doin'?" He asked. His voice was smooth and warm, but Brandon sensed something wrong with the tone.

"Hi, Glen. You haven't met Brandon, I don't think. Brandon Cooper, Glen."

The two men shook hands.

"So, Glen, how's everything?" Calista asked politely.

"Doin' well, Calista. Say, have you thought any more about that offer to help you out? I tell you, you got to jump on these things before they get away from you."

She smiled softly. "Yes, I have thought about it, Glen. I'm not selling."

He frowned. He looked concerned, but Calista sensed that he was angry. Most people wouldn't see that part of his expression.

"Are you sure about that? After all, I can't guarantee that you'll get near as much for the place in a month, you know?"

"Yes, Glen, we're fixing the hotel up, so we can run it for good." She replied. Brandon said nothing. He just stood off to one side, watching.

The big man scowled. "Calista, be reasonable. We're all trying to do what's best for you here, you know?"

"By all, do you include the casino people too?" She asked. Her face went hard. The man scowled. He glared at Brandon.

"You're the dork that was asking my wife all them questions, right?" He pointed a fat finger at Brandon's chest.

"Hey, she brought it up first. I figure that Miss Blake should know all her options before she decides, that's all." Brandon shrugged.

The man rushed up to Brandon, glared at him and made a fist. "You're sticking your nose into other people's business here, fella. You better watch what you say or else."

Brandon smiled at the fist. "Are you threatening me, just for painting someone's house?" He asked.

The hall was dead quiet. Everyone watched the two men. The big man looked around, embarrassed, and turned to Brandon again. He leaned close, nose to nose with Brandon. "This isn't over." He hissed. He walked out of the hall.

Calista and Brandon danced for a couple more sets, then both said they were exhausted and agreed to go home.

Calista swung Brandon's hand in hers, playfully, as they walked across to the motorcycle. Brandon stopped and looked at the motorcycle's tires. Both tires were flat.

"Well, that's just childish." Calista said. "Why would he do something like that?"

Brandon sighed. "Believe it or not, I expected something like this. This is not the first time I've gotten under someone's skin."

Calista squatted down and looked at the tires. "What do we do now?" She asked.

"Let's take a cab." He said. They asked at the fire hall if he could park the motorcycle there for the weekend, then pushed it slowly over into the parking lot and called a taxi.

An old man in a station wagon showed up and agreed on a price to drive them home.

The man drove silently down the highway as the pair sat in the back seat.

Calista stared out her window and fumed, angry at the vandalism. "That Glen is such a jerk! He thinks he can push people around. He messed with the wrong girl tonight, I tell you." She snarled.

Brandon just smiled at her.

"What?" She snapped.

"You're even more beautiful when you're angry." He said. "How do you do that?"

Calista sneered. "Don't you ever get mad at people?"

"Sure, when it's warranted. But not at people like Glen. He's not worth it."

The cab driver glanced in the rearview mirror and chuckled. Brandon caught the look and leaned forward.

"Say, mister, do you know Glen, the fellow from the John Deere?" He asked.

The driver nodded. "Sold us a house and a piece of land a year back."

"Decent sort of man, would you say?"

"Couldn't tell you." The cabbie shrugged. "I can only say how he was with us, is all."

"Did everything go all right for you?" Brandon asked, casually, winking at Calista.

"Not sure if it's true, but I hear he sold our old place for twice what we got. Can't prove it, you understand."

Brandon leaned back. "So he's a certified weasel. All right. That makes this easier."

"Makes what easier?" Calista asked.

"Paying him back for the tires." Brandon smiled.

The cabbie turned off the highway and drove down the road to the hotel. Brandon paid him and watched the cab's taillights fade as he left. The house was dark. Maisie had gone to bed, and there was thin a cloud covering the moon. The whole yard was lit by a diffuse grey moonlight. Brandon took Calista's hand in both of his.

"I want to thank you for a lovely evening." He said. "Mostly. All in all, it was still a better than average evening."

Calista laughed. "Thank you too, sir. I hope we can go dancing again soon. I really enjoyed myself."

"Sounds like a date. We should do it again this summer, yes?"

Calista stretched up and kissed him quickly on the cheek. "Good night." She said.

She stood there for a moment, considering what to do next, then she threw her arms around him and kissed him hard, passionately; she placed her hands on the back of his head and pulled him closer still as she kissed him again.

He didn't move as she kissed him. She let go and stood back, watching his reaction.

He stepped forward, so fast she almost jumped, and wrapped his arms around her. He pulled her close, his hands around her back and her waist. He kissed her, softly, moving his hands up and down her back, making her shiver. She reached around and slipped her hands under his shirt, her fingers slipping over the sweat under the flannel, touching his warm, smooth skin.

A long minute later, he stood back. "I think I better say goodnight." He said quietly. "Before I end up saying good morning."

She smiled. "Sleep tight, Mister Cooper." She turned and walked slowly up to the main house.

"Good night, Miss Blake."

He watched her move, the shape of her hips as she climbed the steps, the sway of her back. He turned to go to his cottage.

"Hey." Calista's voice called, behind him. He looked back, just in time to see her toss his jacket to him.

"Thanks again for a lovely evening. Good night." She said. She opened her door and disappeared.

He folded the jacket and lay it over one arm. It smelled of Calista- her perfume, the smell of her skin, was still on the lining. That made him smile. He went to bed.

Sunday morning, Maisie made pancakes and sausages for breakfast, a family tradition, she said.

Brandon savored his food, eating slowly, and chatted about the dance, the fire hall music, and how much fun it was.

Calista mentioned that the local motorcycle shop would be open later in the day to fix his bike.

Maisie looked at him, puzzled.

"We had to cab it home." He smiled. "Someone flattened my tires."

"Who on earth would do that?" Maisie asked.

"Glen." Calista said, simply. "He got very upset when I told him I wouldn't sell this place."

"Ah." Maisie said. "I see."

Brandon shrugged and finished his coffee. "Anyway, now that the lacquer has had a chance to dry, I'd like to see how the cottage turned out."

Maisie and Calista followed him to the cottage. There was a faint smell of paint in the air, mixed with fresh varnish. When they opened the door, both women gasped. The walls were pristine, a crisp cream color, and the floor looked like new wood. Brandon crouched down and passed his hand carefully over the planks.

"No ripples, no bumps. It looks pretty good, if I do say so myself." He grinned.

He stood up. "Next, I'm going to mask the walls and roller the ceiling. That will be tomorrow, of course. I'm goofing off today."

They walked around the small living room, listening to the echo as they spoke, then they filed into the bedroom and bathroom, and examined the walls and floors again. Maisie rubbed the floor, as if to convince herself it was real.

"So, did it pass muster, Mrs. Blake?" Brandon asked proudly.

"This is exceptional, son. I've said it before, but we can't thank you enough. Can we, Cali?"

Calista nodded. "Thanks again, Brandon." She looked sadly down and walked out of the cottage.

Calista walked around the porch of the cottage, examining the boards casually, rubbing her foot against the crisp new paint. Brandon excused himself, leaving Maisie in the cottage, and went outside.

"Something wrong, Calista?"

She shook her head. "No. You've done marvelous work. Very, very good work, and very quickly, too."

He looked at her, as though looking at her green eyes for the first time, seeing a sadness in them.

"You feel bad because I'll be finished faster than you thought." He said simply.

"You could be out of here in three weeks at this pace." She shrugged.

"I said I'd be here until late August." He said. "There's plenty to do around here to keep me busy."

"Really?" She asked, brightening.

"Sure. Besides, you owe me another dance."

"You got it. Next time, we'll take a cab both ways, though." She joked.

Later in the morning, Calista drove Brandon into Lincoln City. The motorcycle shop was open, and the owner had already heard about the incident, he told them.

Calista smiled at Brandon. "Life in a small town- it's like living in a fishbowl, sometimes." She said.

Brandon nodded. "Not a problem. Did you get a chance to look at my bike?"

The owner shrugged. "Yeah, it's just a pair of tires- the rims are all right. You want to come back in an hour or so?"

"Sure." Brandon said. "See you soon."

Calista said she had some groceries and supplies to get, and Brandon offered to go with her and push the shopping buggy. They zigzagged the aisles of the local grocery store, talking and joking about nothing in particular, just enjoying each other's company.

A slightly plump woman in a velour track suit stopped them at the cereal section and introduced herself.

"Hi, I'm Nadia." She stuck her hand out at Brandon. He politely extended his hand, and she clutched it firmly.

"I hear you're living out at the Ocean Dunes Hotel, with Calista, is that right?" She asked, suggestively.

"I'm staying in one of the cottages while I work on the hotel." He corrected. "Miss Blake and her mother hired me to do some work on the place."

"Really?" There was a sharp, disbelieving tone in her voice. "You're *just* a handyman, then?"

"Oh, no. I also have a FABULOUS fashion sense." He lilted. "These ladies have given me free rein with fabrics and colors, just like my place in San Francisco. It's super."

The woman wrinkled her nose in disappointment. "Ah. I see. Well, it was nice to meet you, Mister, Mister...?"

He rested his hands backwards on his hips. "Call me Brandon. I just go by Brandon. It's my professional name, you know- like 'Madonna' or 'Cher'."

The woman grunted something and pushed her buggy around the corner. Brandon looked over at Calista. Her face was scrunched up, contorted, like an arrested sneeze.

She waited until the woman was out of earshot, then she started to snicker. She snickered quietly for almost a minute, with tears running down her face, then she took out a handkerchief and mopped her eyes.

She looked at Brandon and snickered again. She shook her head. "God, that was priceless." She said.

"What, me having her think that I don't like women?" He asked, smirking. "I thought I was helping you out there."

Calista put a hand on his arm. "Gosh, I love that about you. Thanks, Brandon."

He looked at the hand, then blushed visibly. "You're welcome."

He glanced at his watch. "Ah. Can you excuse me for a few minutes? Something I have to do."

He walked down the street to the hotel, asked the same sad young man for more change, and went to the same pay phone in the corner of the floor. He dialed a number and waited for the operator's voice.

He plugged a handful of quarters into the phone and listened. "Hey, sweetheart, how are you doing?" He smiled.

"You are? That's great, Emily. How's Oscar?" He waited. "Yeah, they grow so fast, huh? Is he behaving himself?"

He laughed. "Well, they often will, at this age. Look, I'll call you later in the week, all right? Talk to you soon, honey. Bye."

He hung up and looked at the phone for a moment, smiling to himself. He turned around to leave, and almost bumped into Calista. She was glaring at him, stone faced.

"Are you all done with your call?" She snapped.

"Yes, thanks." He nodded.

"And how *is* Emily?" She asked, icily.

He smirked. "Emily is fine, thank you."

"Perhaps I could meet her some time." Calista said, with a voice that could slice glass.

"Yes, perhaps you could. I'm sure she'd like that." He smiled, enjoying a private joke.

"Emily is nine years old." He said, softly.

Calista snorted. "And exactly who is this Emily?"

"She is my daughter." He said simply.

Calista looked down sadly. "Oh, I see. How is your wife?"

He shrugged. "She's fine, thanks. Actually, she's pregnant."

Calista's heart sank. "I should offer you my congratulations then."

He shook his head. "You'll want to speak to her husband about that. They got married three years ago."

Calista blushed and covered her face with her hands. "Oops." She said. "Well, that was embarrassing."

Brandon laughed. "You're not the first person to make that mistake. Come on, I'll buy you lunch."

They sat at a booth in the diner, by the window. The waitress apologized profusely for Glen's behavior and brought out their food very quickly, then offered them free pie and coffee. Calista hunched down, still embarrassed at her gaffe.

Brandon winked at Calista and smiled at the waitress. "Look, Jan, you're a really nice girl, and Glen's behavior is not your fault. Let's just put this down to him being a little overzealous, all right?"

She beamed at him and nodded. She busied about again, zipping in and out of the kitchen.

Calista leaned forward and whispered. "Don't you ever get upset with people?"

"You already asked me that. Only when it makes sense to get upset."

She leaned back. "Why did you never tell me about Emily?"

"You never talk about your husband. Some things are better kept private. Some wounds don't heal."

"Fair enough. Who is Oscar- her little brother?"

"Oscar is a cocker spaniel puppy. He was a birthday gift from her stepfather." Brandon frowned.

Calista felt she was getting close to a very sensitive subject now. She rested her forearms on the table and leaned forward. Brandon glanced at the vee of skin showing above her shirt buttons, then he looked up into her eyes and smiled.

"So," she said. "What do you do for a living, when you're not giving things away for free?"

He took a sip of coffee and looked out the window, thinking. "Count Otto Von Bismarck." He said.

"You are descended from a German Count?" She asked.

Brandon laughed. "Von Bismarck said, basically, that you shouldn't see how either laws or sausages were made. Take that as the guide for how I get things done."

"Are you in the Mafia or something?" She asked.

"Nope. My family has run a perfectly legitimate business for the past three generations."

Calista sighed, frustrated. "Well, I'm stumped. I have no idea how you got here, and why you've stayed. I guess I should just be glad you're willing to help us out."

"That's the spirit." He smiled. He looked at his watch. "My bike should be ready to go by now, I guess."

Calista finished her coffee and stood up. "Ah. I have your driver's license." She said. She handed it over to him.

He leaned back. "Did you check me out with the local police?" He asked.

Calista shook her head.

"OK, you talk to them and I'll go pick up the bike. See you at your car."

She shook her head. "It's really not necessary. I do trust you, after all."

"I insist." He said, firmly.

Calista walked the two blocks to the small building that housed the Lincoln City Police Department. She explained that this man was working on her hotel, and he'd offered his ID to assure her that he was not a fugitive.

They seemed impressed, and ran his license through their computer. They told her that he'd had a parking ticket a year before, but nothing else. She felt better about that, so she headed back to the motorcycle shop and walked in.

The man who owned the shop told her that Brandon had already paid for his repair and left.

"Of course." She said. "My fault, he said to meet him at my car."

"Yeah, man, I've never seen one of those before." The man said.

"One what- a sidecar?" Calista asked.

"Credit cards. He had one of them fancy charge cards. The kind movie stars got."

Calista thanked the man and walked back to her car. Brandon was cleaning the visor on his helmet as he waited for her.

She gave him a puzzled look. "What?" He asked.

"What kind of credit card do you have, exactly?" She asked.

"A company one." He shrugged. "Why?"

"Apparently it caused quite a stir at the bike shop, I'm told."

He wrinkled up his nose, thinking. "You're wondering about my reason for spending time here. You're thinking I must have some ulterior, nefarious motive for being here?"

Calista nodded. "Why else would you be here?" She said.

"Did you ever consider that it was because I think you're very attractive?"

She shook her head. "There are plenty of cute women out there. Willing, elegant women, society women, models, actresses, not plain country girls like me."

He chuckled. "I know. In San Francisco, they're everywhere. But I was never attracted to plastic people. That's why I came back to see you, after I had passed through here. That's why I wanted to help you. You're not plastic."

Calista smiled softly. "Smooth talker." She said.

Brandon reached down into the sidecar and brought out a second helmet. "Here. Leave your car for now, OK? Let's go for a ride."

Calista put the helmet on, almost without thinking. "Where are we going?" She asked.

"Back to the scene of the crime." He intoned in a Boris Karloff voice.

He drove north along the highway, to the turnoff for Wi Ne Ma Road, then down that same road to the campground by the sand dunes. Brandon produced a cardboard box- a small case of beer- and tucked it under one arm.

"When did you get that?" Calista asked.

"Back at the grocery store, just before we left town."

"You're getting tired of drinking your wine?" She joked.

"When you feed seagulls, you bring bread. For this trip, you bring beer." He said.

They carried their shoes and walked barefoot to the beach, like before. This time, they walked holding hands, swinging their linked fingers as they did.

"Is this a date, then?" Calista asked. "Because if it is, I expect dinner and a movie, you know, not just beer."

"Sounds like a fun time." Brandon chuckled. "Right now, though, this is a business trip."

They walked along to the end of the beach, where the sand gave way to scraggly grass, then to thicker, lush grass and finally rolled up the hill and away from the beach. The construction trailers were still there, a handful of yellow, bus-sized boxes scattered along the field.

Brandon put his shoes on and climbed through a gap in the fence. Calista followed him.

"Don't say anything, all right? Just follow my lead." He whispered.

He walked confidently to a trailer with an open door and stuck his head in. "Hi there? Hello?" He called.

A gruff, burly man in an orange safety vest and hard hat stomped down the three steps of the trailer and faced him.

"Yeah? What do you want?" The man grunted.

Brandon smiled a disarming smile. "Hey there. It's a hot afternoon. I just thought you guys might be thirsty."

He handed the case of beer to the man. The man's face softened immediately.

"Gee, thanks, mister, that's real nice of you." The man said. He looked around furtively and put the beer inside the trailer, out of sight of anyone who might walk by.

Brandon stuck his hands in his back pockets, trying to look as goofy as he could. "So, how's it coming?"

The man leaned against the trailer and pulled a package of cigarettes from his shirt pocket. He offered one to Brandon, who politely shook his head. The man smiled at Calista, and she shook her head, too.

He popped a cigarette into his mouth and lit it. "Well, I tell ya, the ground looks good for the building, but I think it's kinda wet for the underground lot, you know? Still, we get enough preload and drainage in, we should be all right."

Brandon laughed. "I don't know about any of that stuff. All I know is that we can't wait till it's built." He nodded at Calista. "We're looking forward to seeing the place all finished, you know?"

"You folks with the Johansen family? I don't remember meeting you before." The big man said, carefully.

Brandon shook his head. "We're second cousins, from Iowa. Me and my wife, we're just here to say hello to our people, that's all."

The man took a drag on his cigarette and shrugged. "Whatever. They'll be packed and gone as soon as this deal closes, no matter what. You want to go through to the farmhouse and say hi?" He motioned up the hill.

"Yeah, we'll drop by later." Brandon smiled again. "Right now, though, we're just going for a walk on the beach." He said goodbye to the man, and Calista mumbled something.

Brandon and Calista went back through the gap in the fence, and walked slowly along the beach back toward the motorcycle.

"Very smooth." Calista said. "What was that whole charade all about?"

"They're building something big. You don't need drainage and underground parking for a barn. Plus, he said 'preload'; that's a large pile of heavy sand you dump temporarily to squish down the soil so you can build tall buildings there. That sounds like a large casino to me." He stopped and looked out at the ocean. A long, low wave started down at the south end of the beach, grew larger and curled up, breaking softly against the tall rock at Porter Point.

Calista arched her head back and breathed deeply: it felt good, smelling the salt water and seaweed in the air.

Brandon watched her, intently, as she curved back and slowly straightened up.

He was staring into her eyes as she looked over at him. "What?" She asked, puzzled.

He wrapped his arms around her and kissed her, passionately. A full minute later, he pulled back and smiled.

Calista's mouth fell open, a surprised expression on her face. "What was that for?" She gasped.

"You looked like you needed a kiss." He smiled. "I just gave you one."

They walked back toward the motorcycle, hand in hand. As they reached it, Calista saw a figure, a large man, pacing in circles beside the sidecar. A few steps on she realized it was Glen, the real estate salesman. He did not look happy.

They were now within twenty feet of Glen; Brandon casually, almost imperceptibly, pulled Calista behind him as they got to the bike. Glen stopped pacing and stood still, his feet apart, a look of anger on his face.

He had a piece of wood in his hand, a log about the size of a baseball bat.

He pointed it at Brandon. "You! You stupid idiot!" He barked. "Why is your nose in my business? Huh?"

Brandon smiled and shook his head. "We're just out for a walk on the beach, mac. What business is that of yours?"

Glen waved the wood in Brandon's face. "You think I'm some kind of dummy, don't you? I tell you, nobody messes with me and gets away with it."

Brandon's smile disappeared. "Look, you may be a big fish in this little town, but right now you're swimming in the shark pool. Why don't you put the stick down and walk away? I'll even let the tire thing slide. How about it?"

Glen's nostrils flared; he poked Brandon in the chest with the log. "You think you can scare me? I don't scare, no sir."

"Good, neither do I." Brandon said. "Now that we've established that, how about I buy you lunch and we both walk away from this right now?"

Glen snorted and turned red. He poked the log into Brandon's stomach. "I'm telling you to stay out of my affairs. Understand?"

Brandon's face went hard. "Don't do that."

"Why? Does this irritate you?" Glen laughed and prodded Brandon again.

"Please stop doing that. Right now." Brandon said. He didn't seem afraid or upset, just very firm.

Glen laughed again and poked him another time.

Brandon moved in close to Glen, and everything became a blur. Glen flew over Brandon's shoulder and landed on the ground with a thump. Brandon now had the log in his hand, and held it high over Glen's head.

Glen whimpered and covered his face. "Don't! Don't hit me!" He begged.

"Say please." Brandon said. He lifted the log higher over his head.

"No, please, please don't hit me." Glen whined. He curled up in a ball.

Brandon threw the log away. "You're quite a bully, aren't you, Glen? How does it feel when you're the one being bullied for a change?"

Glen stood up and brushed himself off. He wiped his nose and shook a finger at Brandon. "This is not over, you know. This is not the end of this, I tell you."

Brandon walked up to him, face to face. "It better be. I'm civilized, but my friends will be here soon, and they're not."

Glen scurried away to his car, and drove off in a cloud of dust.

Brandon helped Calista into the sidecar and started the engine. They rode back to her car and he followed her on the highway back home. Calista said nothing on the ride back to town, little when she got into her car, and finally, when they pulled to a stop at the hotel, she looked at her shoes and sighed. She looked up at Brandon.

"I've never seen anyone do what you just did." She said. "Where did you learn that?"

Brandon grinned. "In the army. I don't usually need it in construction, though. Those guys are way smarter than Glen."

Calista shook her head. "Men." She sneered.

Chapter Six

Later that afternoon, the sun moved west, slowly sinking over the dunes, and a breeze blew in from the beach, carrying the smell of mussel shells and seaweed. Maisie called Brandon for dinner. He had washed up and put on a clean shirt and fresh jeans. He looked elegant even in those casual clothes, Calista thought.

Maisie filled serving plates with food, while Calista set the table, and Brandon stood off to one side. Maisie placed dishes at the table and said that a friend of hers, her bridge partner, had heard gossip about a 'dust-up' with two men on the beach. She looked up at Brandon. He shrugged sheepishly, hunched his head down and ate silently.

The evening sun streamed into the main house through a west window, painting the opposite wall with a square of orange light. As the sun sank behind the trees, on its path over the ocean, the light moved higher, then shadows of the far trees poked up onto the wall, like a phantom forest in the living room.

Over coffee and dessert, Brandon reminded the women that within a day or so, the gravel trucks would stop by to fill the holes in the roadway. They were excited about that, they told him.

After dinner, Calista went up to her room to read. Maisie called a friend on the downstairs phone and chatted for a long time. By nine thirty or so, Maisie was tired, said goodnight to Calista and went to bed.

Calista lay on her bed, trying to read her book, but her ears were listening for a harmonica on the beach. It didn't come. She had an irrational fear that whatever was wrong with Brandon's heart had come back. Maybe he was feeling sick, or he needed someone, in his cottage, but there was nobody who could hear him. Maybe he was calling for her, desperate.

No, that was irrational. Why would she even imagine that could ever happen? Forget all about it, she thought.

Two minutes later, she had a sweater on, and was picking her way down the path to the beach. Brandon's cottage was empty, the front door open. There was a nearly full moon, and the sand on the path glowed a reflected pale grey moonlight.

Cresting the rise before the fire pit, she saw orange fireflies- cinders winding up and dying in the cool air. By the time she could see the fire pit, Brandon was already looking up at her, smiling. He reached behind him, pulled out a wine glass, and held it up for Calista. She sat across from him and took it.

"Hi. I was hoping you'd come." He smiled. He reached back again and produced a bottle, a white wine this time. He poured some into Calista's glass and put the bottle down. He raised his own glass in a toast.

"To a wonderful summer." He said.

Calista clinked glasses and nodded. "To summer." She said simply. She took a sip, frowned and looked into the glass.

"Oh, wow, this is good." She said. She took another sip. "This is really, really good."

Brandon grinned. "Thanks. I'll pass on the compliments."

She examined the glass. "Your friend's vineyard again?" Calista smiled.

He nodded. "I have a blanket here, in case you get cold. Are you warm enough?"

He stood slightly and slid a travel rug out from under him, offering it to Calista.

She shook her head. "I'm fine, thanks, it's warm enough by the fire."

He looked up at the clear skies, admiring the stars, then he pointed excitedly at a moving point of light.

"Look, a falling star. Make a wish." He said.

Calista looked up too. "That's just an airplane- it's the commuter plane from Newport, flying up to Seattle twice a week."

Brandon smiled again. "OK, then, just pretend it's a piece of cosmic dust burning up in the atmosphere. Make a wish."

Calista pursed her lips and closed her eyes. "OK. Done." She said. She took a deep drink of wine.

"What did you wish for?" He asked her.

She laughed. "I can't tell you that. If I let you know what I wished for, it won't come true."

He leaned forward and poured her more wine. She leaned forward to meet him halfway, their noses almost touching.

Calista's mouth opened slightly, as though she was about to speak. Brandon looked down at her lips, tilted his head to one side, then softly, gently kissed her. He leaned back and smiled.

"Wow." He said. "This could get to be habit-forming."

Calista looked at his face, illuminated by the fire light. There was something about him, like a lost child, a sad boy in the face of this man. The expression on his face wasn't a leer, like the men in town gave her, not the ogling looks they gave, but something much warmer, much deeper.

A wave of lust rushed over her, warming her from her hips to her neck. It was now or never, she told herself. She put down her glass and threw her arms around Brandon's neck. She hugged him tight, kissing him harder, longer than she thought she possibly could. He leaned back slightly and put his glass down too. He stared into her eyes, as if to make sure they were both thinking the same thing, and smiled.

His arms wrapped around her back, caressing her spine and running up and down from her neck to the base of her spine. She huffed, winded and excited, and struggled to undo the buttons on his shirt. He leaned back and let her pull his shirt over his head. She wrapped her arms around him again and kissed him, her hands feeling the warmth of his back.

It had been years since Calista had been intimate with a man. A brief fling with one local farmer, not long after her husband died, had left her feeling even more unloved and alone than before. He had treated her like a tramp; she could have been any woman- it didn't matter to him. This experience with Brandon was different, though.

Brandon's hands were still moving up and down her back; they slid under her sweater, his hands caressing her skin. Deftly, he slipped his fingers under the catch of her bra and undid it. With one smooth, graceful gesture he peeled her sweater and bra over her head at once and tossed them behind him.

He pulled her to him, chest to chest. Her breasts rubbed against him, exciting him. He looked down and kissed the base of her neck, moved down and slowly, gently kissed the space between her breasts, then moved back up and kissed her neck again. He kissed all the way up her neck to the underside of her chin, then he took her face in his hands and kissed her lips, softly.

He fell backwards onto the sand. It had been warmed by the campfire, and felt soft against his shoulders.

Calista stood over him, undid his belt and pulled his jeans off his legs. He lay back and let her move at her speed. She fumbled with the knot keeping her shorts up, then let them fall and sat on him, her hands on his shoulders.

He stretched up and kissed her. "You know we've reached the point of no return, right?" He said.

She smiled softly. "Damn the torpedoes."

They made love in the sand, rolling over and over by the light of the campfire. It was not rushed, it was not perfunctory. It was two people who were completely entangled in each other's embrace, completely oblivious to everything else. Her hands traced the outline of his chest, the shape of his muscles, the curve of his shoulders wrapping around to his biceps. She ran her fingers around his waist and caressed his back, the sand and sweat sticking in places around his waist.

He kissed her all over, warmly, softly, not with the urgency and roughness she had known before, but with admiration, with appreciation.

Afterwards, Brandon sat on the log, still nude, with Calista on his lap, holding her glass, sipping her wine again. They had the travel blanket wrapped around them for warmth. She rolled her glass back and forth between her palms and looked down, thinking. Brandon studied her expression.

"A penny for your thoughts?" He asked.

"This was wonderful." She said, softly. "What comes next?" She looked up at him.

"You mean, will we make this an ongoing experience, or was it a one-off?"

She shook her head. "I mean, what happens when summer's over?" She leaned back and stretched. In the light of the fire, her breasts stuck out while the rest of her was in shadow.

"If I were to go back to living in San Francisco, I could get here in just a few hours." He said, hopefully.

"Is that what you want? To have me as a long-distance girlfriend when you're lonely? Would that be all I was?" She said.

He shook his head. "No. I told you, I could date a different girl every week back there, but you're not like any of them."

She clutched her knees and hunched forward. Even through the blanket, the curve of her back was exciting for him. She shrugged.

"Sorry; look, I've been alone for a very long time, and I guess I mistrust men as a rule." She said softly.

He rubbed her spine softly. "That's a good rule." He sighed. "Look, Calista, what would you like from me? Tell me."

She looked straight at him. "Respect. I don't want you thinking I'm just some easy girl you picked up. That's what I want- respect."

He nodded solemnly. "That's fair. In return, I want something, too."

"What?" She asked, puzzled.

"Your assurance that this evening will in no way hurt our friendship."

She smiled broadly, and held out her hand. He took it in his. It was an incongruous sight, two naked people under a blanket, shaking hands.

"Agreed." She said. "Want to get dressed yet?"

He smirked. "Not particularly. Do you?"

She shrugged. "I'm fine like this." She lifted up her glass, waiting for him to fill it.

He poured some wine into her glass and raised his to make a toast. "To this night." He said.

"And to more nights to come." She replied. Their glasses clinked.

They sat there talking, watching the fire crackle. He told her some of his life story, things about him that fascinated her. He had married his college sweetheart, a girl from a 'good family', and they'd had Emily. It was a match heartily encouraged by both families, and it should have worked out, but his wife met someone that she 'liked better', he said. He blinked away a moist eye and sipped his wine. He was vague and evasive about the family business, but more open when he spoke about himself.

"What about you, miss?" He said formally. "What's your life story?"

He casually caressed Calista's thighs, as she sat with her knees together, her ankles off to one side.

"I was born and raised here. My father taught school in Tillamook."

"You told me- he liked the Greek classics, hence Calista." Brandon said.

"You do remember- yes, he did. His salary helped keep this place open." She waved a hand back at the hotel.

She wrapped the blanket tighter around her shoulders and took another sip of wine.

"Ed was from Portland, and he was a teacher, like my father. He moved to Tillamook to teach, and I met him through dad. He was a good guy, well liked." She downed her wine, and Brandon refilled her empty glass. She took it gratefully.

"Anyway, one day I was in town, working on someone's books- I forget whose- and I didn't get back to our place till dinner time. Ed never came home. We thought he'd had car trouble or something, so we didn't think much of it at the time, because he sometimes had meetings or work that kept him late, but then the police called us. Apparently the school janitor found him beside his desk. They told us he'd had an aneurism, that he died in seconds, and there was nothing that anyone could have done to help him."

"Was it hard for you, having him go that way?" Brandon asked.

Calista shrugged. "It would have been much worse if he'd passed away at home. I don't think I could have stayed on if he'd died here. Anyway, the insurance money helped keep us afloat a while longer. Truth is, though, we haven't had a good year in over a decade. That's why I was so glad you offered to help us. Beside the other benefits, that is." She smiled.

He looked out at the dark horizon, toward the ocean, away from the house. "This place is really beautiful, you know. You should be able to attract people who want to stay here for just the peace and solitude, if for no other reason."

Calista shrugged. She wrapped an arm around his neck and kissed his cheek. "That's what we're trying to make people see. We need to save the hotel. It's more than just our home, more than just a business. If it goes, then we could see the whole area turned into crappy condos and cheap strip malls."

"That would be a sin." He said.

He looked at his watch. "You should get some sleep. If I'm right, tomorrow will be a very busy day."

Calista sighed and picked up her clothes. She brushed seaweed off her sweater, shook sand out of her bra- to his amusement- and got dressed. He slid his pants on and put his shirt loosely over his shoulders. They doused the fire and walked, hand in hand, back to the main house.

Calista stopped at the base of the stairs, turned and kissed him. "Good night, Mister Cooper." She said.

"Sleep well, Miss Blake." He answered.

She nodded and walked slowly up the steps. "Hey." He called, softly.

She turned to look at him.

"There's no way I can talk you into sleeping over at my cottage, huh?" He grinned.

She looked over her shoulder at the main house and shook her head. "One step at a time." She said, quietly.

He nodded and waved goodnight to her, then walked back to his cottage, humming softly.

Calista went slowly up the stairs to her room. She crept softly past her mother's door, waiting for the voice that she knew so well. She didn't want to hear her mother's voice tonight, calling out to her. If her mother asked her why she was out so late, she wouldn't be able to lie.

She made it all the way to her door and opened it, cautiously. A sound behind her made her freeze. Then she realized she was only her mother rolling over in her sleep. Calista went to bed and lay there, thinking.

What had she done? Why would she give herself so easily to this near stranger? Still, she felt more alive, more joyful inside, than she had in a long time. She was too excited to sleep. Maybe she *would* sneak out to his cottage. They could make love again. He would still be awake, she was sure of it. She would just wait a few minutes until she was still sure her mother was deeply asleep, then she'd sneak out and crawl into his bed. She could almost imagine what it would feel like, slipping under the sheets with him, caressing his body, having his damp skin arching over her. She would just wait a few minutes, then she'd go out there. She could stay awake that long.

She woke with a start and went to her window. There was a lot of commotion in the yard. Three large dump trucks, filled with gravel, were lined up in a row, engines running. Six men in orange vests and blue overalls were standing in a cluster, talking to Brandon. He gestured to the road as it met the highway, made two parallel lines with his hands and pointed back toward the cottages. That's when he glanced up and saw Calista. He smiled briefly, then looked down again and kept talking to the men.

Another man, better-dressed than the rest in a windbreaker and slacks, glanced up at Calista. He saw her, stared for a moment, then went back to speaking with Brandon. The men nodded and headed back to the trucks. The man in the slacks said something to Brandon, then made a gesture and wagged his thumb up toward Calista's window.

Brandon grinned sheepishly and shook a finger at the man. The man roared with laughter and smacked Brandon's arm.

The trucks suddenly went silent, and the men climbed out of them, walking towards the main house.

What were they doing now? Where were they going? She scrambled to her closet, threw on a pair of jeans and a sloppy, unflattering sweatshirt, and hurried downstairs.

Maisie was in the kitchen racing back and forth, moving frypans and coffee pots everywhere.

She glanced up at her daughter. "Hello, Cali. You didn't sleep too well, last night?" She asked.

Calista thought of something to say that was not a lie. "I was out at the fire pit, having some wine with Brandon. I guess I had a little more than I should have." She shrugged.

Her mother looked straight at her and stopped dead. "Be careful, all right?" She said. She went back to her cooking.

"What exactly is happening out there, mom?" Calista asked.

"We're making breakfast for these men." Her mother said simply. She pointed to a frypan. "You make the pancakes."

Calista helped her mother cook. She poured pancake batter, flipped eggs, and brewed coffee. At one point she had a pause in the action for just a few seconds, and realized she had no idea what time it was. She glanced up at the clock. Seven fifteen- hardly late in the morning, yet these men looked wide awake, hungry for a meal.

By seven thirty, the six men from the trucks, the one in the slacks, Brandon and the two women were seated around the big dining table, the one the women never used.

The men ate vast amounts of food and drank gallons of coffee, grunting happily throughout the meal. Calista and Maisie stopped eating several times to refill cups and plates, despite protests from the men that they could get it themselves.

Before eight o clock, they were still at the table, but everyone had slowed to a crawl, stuffed. The man in the slacks, who Brandon identified as his friend 'Tim', looked more like a banker than a construction worker. The other men listened intently as he told them what to do. Calista only understood some of it; grading and dumping, then terms that she didn't understand; all the while he was gesturing with a pen and making sketches on a scribble pad.

The men seemed to know exactly what he meant. They nodded and headed back to their trucks. They stopped and individually thanked Maisie and Calista for breakfast, then Calista again heard the thunder of their trucks as they started the engines.

Within an hour, they had emptied all the gravel from the three trucks in a handful of mounds up and down the roadway. Calista worried that the road looked far worse than it had before. The men parked their trucks in a line off to the side of the property, and three of them walked out to the highway, talking amongst themselves about how nice this was, how this would be a great place for a vacation.

They disappeared around the corner and returned a minute later, backing a long flatbed truck down the driveway, with a monstrous bulldozer on it. Within five more minutes, they had unloaded the bulldozer. Soon after that, the bulldozer roared up and down the path to smooth the gravel down to a flat surface. Calista's heart raced. This was wonderful- people could now drive in without being bounced around.

Brandon and 'Tim' were off to one side, talking happily and laughing. Tim had a walkie-talkie, and he called instructions into it, listening to a crackly response and giving more directions.

Maisie finished cleaning up the breakfast dishes and came out to see the work. She beamed at the driveway and patted the gravel, as if to be sure it was real.

"My goodness, this is impressive. I can't thank you boys enough." She said. "This is quite remarkable."

Brandon nodded at Tim, who nodded back and called something into the walkie-talkie. The bulldozer went back onto the flatbed, and two men chained it down.

“Nice work, guy. I owe you.” Brandon said.

“Hey, you know I never do a half-assed job. Let me finish, before you thank me.” Tim said, smiling at Brandon.

The truck left, and another flatbed truck rolled in to take its place, with a massive steamroller on the back.

In less than an hour, the steamroller traveled up and down the roadway a few times, packing the gravel down hard.

Tim walked over the path, zigzagging, feeling for soft spots and irregularities. “Not bad, not bad if I say so myself.” He said.

Brandon said something technical, and both men nodded. Calista walked on the packed gravel, marveling at the smooth surface.

Tim patted the roadway. “If it rains this week, it should settle hard as rock. Either way, you’re way better off than you were before.” He smiled.

The other men sauntered back, checking out their handiwork. They grunted and mumbled approval.

Maisie looked at her watch and lifted her head up to address them all. “Listen, it’s a bit early, but if you can all wait, we would be honored to make lunch for you gentlemen.” She said, hopefully.

One of the men, older and burly, called out. “Take your time, sweetheart. We’ll wait.” The rest laughed.

Maisie grabbed Calista's arm and shooed her into the kitchen. Maisie worked at breakneck speed, getting steaks and ground beef and chicken out of the fridge.

She set up a deep fryer and cut up potatoes, then covered the big stove with pots and pans as the potatoes cooked.

Brandon, meanwhile, took Tim and the other men on a tour of the cottage he was fixing up. They discussed paint, materials and construction methods, then the men wandered through the path, over the rise and looked at the ocean.

Within forty-five minutes or so, Maisie had finished cooking up burgers, chicken and steaks, and piled them high on plates on the dinner table again. She had a mass of French fries steaming beside the other food, with fixings and beverages. She rushed out to the top of the stairs and called out "Lunch!"

The men piled in quickly, but in an orderly rush. They took the same seats as before, thanked Maisie for the meal, and hunkered down to eat. Plates levitated over each other, as the men swapped and sampled everything on the table.

One man, the burly one who had spoken before, turned to Maisie. He looked like a wrestler, with massive arms and a thick neck. He smiled politely. "I got to say, sweetheart, this is absolutely the best meal I've had in years."

The others grumbled agreement. Maisie put a hand on his shoulder and grinned. "Thank you, son, I'm glad you like it."

He made a circle with his finger at the ceiling. "So, later this year, could I rent a couple of cottages for a week or two?"

Maisie frowned. "Of course." She said, surprised. "We can rent them by the night or by the week."

The man shook his head. "No, I mean, if I wanted to bring my family here, what would you let them go for?"

Maisie opened her mouth to speak. Brandon placed a hand on Maisie's arm and she stopped.

"What do you think is reasonable?" Brandon smiled.

The man shrugged. "I dunno. A thousand dollars a week?"

Maisie gasped. That was more money than they saw in a good month. She stared at Brandon, stunned.

"I mean, that's for EACH cottage, you understand." The man added, quickly.

It occurred to Maisie that he'd misunderstood her reaction; he thought she felt insulted at the offer.

Maisie smiled and reached her hand out to the man. "You have a deal." She said.

The man wrapped three of his fingers around Maisie's hand and shook it gently. "Done. We'll be here the last two weeks of August- me, the wife and four kids." He grinned.

Maisie sat back and sighed. The morning was turning out even better than she could have imagined.

An hour later, the men were packing up their tools and sweeping out the beds of the trucks, ready to drive away.

Heading toward them on the fresh gravel, Calista and Maisie saw a familiar car- Glen's car. Behind him was a black and white sedan, with 'Oregon State Police' painted on the doors.

Glen got out of his car, straightened his belt and stomped over to Calista and Maisie, ignoring Brandon completely. A young police officer got out of the other car and followed Glen, sheepishly.

Glen shook his finger in Maisie's face. "You're doing construction without a permit, and I'm going to see you get fined for that." He snapped.

Tim, Brandon's friend, sauntered over and smiled a disarming smile. "Is there some sort of a misunderstanding here? Can I help sort this out?" He said.

Glen sneered at him. "You stay out of this. This is between Maisie and me."

Tim's smiled vanished. "What construction are you talking about, exactly?"

Glen laughed. "Roadwork. You're constructing a road without a building permit, without permission. So, either you dig up this gravel and leave right away, or this officer will arrest you all."

Tim glanced at the police officer. He seemed distinctly uncomfortable at being there, but was obviously trying to do his duty.

Tim nodded and said "Excuse me for a moment." He went to his truck and grabbed a stack of papers, then he handed the stack to the police officer.

"Here you go. State permit for dumping. State permit for road leveling, and state permit for infrastructure improvements. It authorizes me to fix roads anywhere in Oregon. I'm dumping gravel to fix this road. Will that do, officer?"

The police officer smiled, relieved. He read the permits and handed them back to Tim.

"I'd say that works for me, sir. Sorry to have bothered you folks." He turned and walked toward his car.

"Officer?" Maisie called. "Would you care for some lunch? We were just eating."

The police officer glanced at Tim and Glen and touched the brim of his hat. "Thanks, ma'am, possibly another time."

He got into his car and left. Glen was fuming. He stuck his hands on his hips and glared at Tim.

"What kind of an idiot do you think I am?" Glen snapped.

"I don't know. How many kinds of idiot are there?" Tim said. The other men laughed.

Glen snorted and poked his finger into Tim's chest. "I am fed up with you city folks thinking you can butt into our business out here. I am sick to death with it." He poked Tim's chest again.

Tim sneered at Glen's finger. "Yeah, Brandon told me about you. I see he wasn't exaggerating."

Glen glared at him. "You think you got trouble from me now? You have no idea."

From nowhere, the burly man's hand appeared and grabbed Glen's shoulder, spun Glen around and stared at him.

Brandon noticed with amusement that the man was almost a foot taller than Glen.

"What did you call me?" The man growled. Glen's face went white.

"I didn't call you any.."

The big man pushed Glen backwards with one hand. "You can't say things like that about my wife."

Glen staggered and walked slowly backwards. "Listen, you got me all wrong, fella. I never said anything..."

The big man grabbed Glen by the jacket and lifted him off the ground. He carried Glen, the smaller man's legs dangling in midair, to one of the dump trucks, and slammed him against the door. Glen was clearly terrified.

"Next time I see you, I will break you in half." The big man said, and dropped Glen on the ground.

Glen fell down on all fours and crawled, then ran, to his car and drove off.

The big man chuckled. "Gee, did I scare him, do you think?"

The other men roared with laughter.

They carefully watered down the gravel, then they washed up and climbed onto their trucks. Maisie spent the time baking dozens of muffins, and made sure each man had a quantity to take home. They all accepted them gratefully.

The burly man shook Maisie's hand again, carefully, and bowed slightly. "Ma'am, my family and me look forward to seeing you this August." He smiled.

"I'll lay in a lot of food." Maisie joked.

The man laughed, and the crew left. After the last truck had pulled out, the dust had settled and the noise was gone, the place seemed strangely quiet.

Calista stood by the house, her hands on her hips, shaking her head. "You know, this is still unbelievable." She said.

She looked up and down the roadway, admiring the work the men had done.

Brandon grinned at her. "Come, let's inspect the road." He said. He looked over at Maisie to join them.

She shook her head. "You two go on. I have a pile of dishes to do." She went into the main house.

Brandon held his hand out for Calista. "Come." He repeated.

Calista smiled and took his hand. They walked down the road, looking for rough patches and dips, kicking loose pebbles out of the way. The road looked better than new, and Calista was delighted.

"So," Brandon asked, "Do I pass muster?"

"What do you mean?"

"Have I come through for you then, or what?" He asked.

"Amazing." Calista smiled.

"Want to spend another evening by the fire?" He asked coyly.

Calista stopped dead. "You're not implying that I owe you sex because of the roadway, are you?"

He grimaced. "Ah. I hadn't thought that it might sound like that. Sorry. Forget it."

They walked all the way to the highway, then turned to look down the gravel drive, down to the house and cottages. The driveway was now a smooth, clear path; the red mud had been covered by pale grey gravel, a long flat road that pointed directly to the house.

"Very nice." Calista said, simply. She smiled at Brandon, reached up and kissed his cheek. "Very nice." She repeated.

Brandon walked her back down to the house, still holding her hand. He looked up and frowned.

"You know, there is one thing that's bothering me." He said. "The bed in the cottage is really uncomfortable."

"Don't you ever give up?" Calista asked. "Honestly."

He laughed. "No, this is a completely different topic. It feels like the bed is a hundred years old."

"The bed frames are old, but we replaced the mattresses a while ago." Calista protested.

"When?" He challenged.

Calista frowned, thinking. "Let's see. I was in the eleventh grade, and..."

"Hah! I was right. You need new beds."

"Let me guess. You have a friend?" Calista asked.

He laughed. "Yes, 'I have a friend'."

They went into the main house; Brandon produced a little book and opened it to a page. He dialed a number and asked for a person called 'Billy'. He waited politely, then his face lit up.

"Billy? How are you doing, you useless sack of skin?" He yelled.

There was a pause, then he laughed. "Yeah, I love you too, man. Listen, I got a favor to ask you."

"OK. So, who are you revamping this month?" A pause. "Fine. Can you throw some castoffs my way?"

He listened then said "One sec." He put the phone down and looked at Maisie. "How many beds are in the main house?"

"Four." Maisie said, puzzled.

"Does each room have a queen-sized bed?" Brandon asked, matter-of-factly.

Maisie nodded. Brandon turned back to the phone.

"Good. Save me ten sets, OK?" Brandon said. He listened for a moment. "Great, those too, man. Listen I owe you."

He gave the man the address of the hotel and spoke with him for a moment more, then hung up.

"All right. He will drop off ten beds, plus twenty night tables and ten tallboy dressers, in dark oak finish.

They should be here Thursday. Would that be alright with you?"

Maisie stared at him. "Why would he give you all those things?" She asked. "They must be worth a fortune."

"A hotel in Portland is renovating. They're basically throwing out their old furniture, and they replace mattresses every six months. I've stayed there; it's good quality stuff, and I'm sure you'll like it for this place."

Maisie thought for a moment. "But with the main house and five cottages, we only have nine beds."

"One set is a spare. You can keep that stuff in the basement." Brandon smiled. "Besides, ten is a nice round number."

Calista shrugged. "Sounds good to me."

Brandon grinned and said he wanted to finish off the first cottage. He went out, pulled on his overalls and masked up the walls with tape and plastic sheets. Then he covered the floor with tarps and got out a long roller and paint bucket. He was about to paint the ceiling when he noticed a figure in the doorway.

He turned to see Calista, watching him with great interest. She grinned. "How are we doing?" She asked.

He nodded. "Good. I should have the ceiling done this afternoon, then we can put the furniture back in, and this one will be wrapped up, at least until we get the new furniture."

"No, that's not what I mean." She said. "I mean, I'm talking about our conversation earlier?"

He smiled. "You mean, was I actually trying to extract sexual favors as payment?"

She laughed. "Seriously. Look, I really like you, and it seems you like me too. I'm just trying to figure out where we're going with this, you know?"

He put the roller down and peeled the plastic gloves off his hands.

"OK. Time to talk seriously." He sat cross-legged on the floor. "Yeah, I really, REALLY like you. You're a very open, very welcome breath of fresh air. You're also very attractive. Do I think there's a spark there? I'd like to think so, but tell you what; if this was just a summer romance, where we shook hands and said goodbye in August, would you feel any differently about me now?"

Calista leaned back and thought about that. "Well, that's honest, I guess. I don't know. Can I think about it?"

"Sure. Meanwhile, take a step back. I need to do the ceiling." He put on the plastic gloves again. Calista stepped out of the cottage and watched him work. He moved smoothly, fluidly, covering the main room ceiling in a crisp white paint, then moved into the bedroom and bathroom and did the same. In an hour, he was finished and packing up the tools.

He snapped the lid closed on the paint can and smiled at Calista. "So, what do you think?" He asked.

"It looks terrific. It makes the whole cottage look brand new," She smiled.

"No, I mean, about us, what do you think?"

"Ah, that." She sighed. "I honestly don't know. Look, what if last night was a one-time thing, would that be all right for you?"

"Honestly, no, it wouldn't."

Calista winced slightly. "Really? You expect to have sex with me again, then?"

"No, what I want is to make love to you. As a matter of fact, I'm having a tough time keeping my hands off you right now."

He looked over Calista's shoulder and stood back slightly. Maisie walked from the house to the door of the cottage.

"My, this looks wonderful, I have to say. Brandon, you've certainly given this cottage a fresh lease on life."

He nodded. "Thanks, ma'am. I'm glad you like it."

Maisie frowned. "You wanted that man to say what he was willing to pay for the cottage before I told him our rates. Why?"

"I figured you've been underpricing these cottages, even before they've been fixed up. I wanted you to see that."

Maisie shrugged. "Sometimes we don't appreciate what we have right in front of us, I suppose."

He glanced at Calista. "Yes, you're right. We should appreciate what we have right here."

Maisie was inspecting the ceiling and didn't see the look. "Anyway, I have to go into Lincoln City for some groceries. The fridge is absolutely empty. Is there anything you need?"

Brandon shook his head. "I'm fine, thanks. I should have the furniture in and this cottage ready to go by the time you get back."

Maisie shook her head. "Nonsense, take the day off and rest up. You've more than earned it."

She took another look at the cottage and walked to the car, singing to herself.

Calista watched her mother drive on the fresh gravel, cruising over the smooth surface as the car gathered speed.

She looked down at the floor of the cottage, thinking.

"So, what's on your mind?" Brandon asked, curious.

"Drive me into town, I want to show you something." Calista said.

Brandon helped her into the sidecar, fired up the motorcycle and rolled down the fresh gravel road.

Calista directed him toward Lincoln City. They rode along the highway, enjoying the fresh, crisp air. Calista lifted her hands up high, letting the wind blow her arms back. It felt like when she was a little girl, riding her bicycle. She felt young again.

Just south of Lincoln City, she pointed to a narrow road on the west side of the highway. Brandon turned in, slowing to a crawl as he navigated the snaky, undulating path. He accelerated to crest a low rise in the land and slowed down again as he realized where they were.

There were rows and rows of tombstones, lined up like chairs in an auditorium. Calista motioned for him to keep going, toward the middle of one row, then waved for him to stop. He rolled to a halt and shut the engine off.

Calista struggled to climb up, lifted her leg out of the sidecar and stood on the short grass beside the road.

Brandon slid off his motorcycle seat to join her.

"What did you want to show me?" He asked.

"My father and my husband. They're both buried here." Calista said, simply.

She reached a hand out. "Come."

She led Brandon along to a small granite headstone, surrounded by a semicircular patch of gravel. The headstone had the name "Edward Shaughnessy" chiseled on it, and two dates. He had died at age thirty-two.

Calista picked some spikes of tall grass away from the base of the tombstone and smoothed the remaining grass down, then she tamped down the soil around the stone.

"You've been widowed for six years, then." Brandon commented. "It must have been a tough time for you and your mom."

Calista shrugged. "When dad died, he went slowly, of the disease, but mom at least had me and Ed. When Ed died, it was sudden, and we lost everything that kept us going. We have been in a slow decline ever since. That's why we're so grateful for your help." She brushed the soil from her hands.

Brandon shrugged. "It's the least I can do. Where is your dad buried?"

Calista poked her chin and walked a short way to another, similar tombstone. This one was slightly worn, and the name on it, Nathaniel Blake, had a pair of dates below the name that said he had died in his late fifties.

There was an inscription below the dates. 'Love is but a single soul inhabiting two bodies- Aristotle'.

"He couldn't get away from quoting the classics, huh?" Brandon smiled.

"Are you making fun of him?" Calista frowned.

"Not at all. It says a lot about his character. I think I'd have enjoyed talking with him."

Calista walked to a hillock a few yards away, and stood at the top of it, looking toward the water.

Brandon came up beside her. "This is a nice view. I wouldn't mind being buried here myself." He said, softly.

Calista scowled. "That's not funny." She said, curtly.

"No, I'm serious. If I had to spend eternity in one spot, this would a good spot to spend it."

Calista shrugged. "We already have plots for my mother and me, next to dad and Ed. At least that's taken care of. Can we talk about a cheerier subject now?"

"Hey, you brought *me* here, remember?" Brandon grinned. "Come on, let me buy you coffee."

They drove into Lincoln City and parked at the diner. Brandon rolled to a stop behind the State Police cruiser that had visited the hotel, and he helped Calista out of the sidecar.

They walked into the diner, Calista wondering what kind of reception the waitress would give them. They sat at the front counter, a seat away from the state trooper. He was finishing a sandwich and trying to avoid eye contact with Calista.

The waitress did a slight double-take and smiled sheepishly at Brandon, then hunched her shoulders and crouched close to Calista.

"Hon, you know Glen has always been kinda fiery." She whispered. "You shouldn't take much notice of him, though. He's a little high strung, but his heart's in the right place."

Calista smiled a plastic smile. "Yeah, I guess he's just doing what he thinks is best, but he got it kind of wrong today."

Brandon went around her and sat beside the state trooper. "Hey there, we meet again." He said, cheerily.

The trooper, relieved at the warm reception, relaxed visibly. "Hi. Nice to see you too." He grinned. "Did you get everything settled OK, mister?"

Brandon smiled a warm smile. "Brandon, please. Sure, I realize Glen was just trying to be a good neighbor for the good of the county, is all. He has to do that, with his real estate work and everything."

The trooper seemed to see this as a welcome escape route. He beamed at Brandon.

"You know, I guess you're right. I'm sure we can put it down to him being just overly keen to uphold the law." He said.

Brandon nodded, solemnly. "Yeah, I suppose if you look at it that way, he's only trying to be a good citizen here."

The waitress, of course, absorbed all this and smiled broadly. She seemed delighted that Brandon had given Glen an excuse for his actions.

She offered Brandon some free pie, and spooned ice cream to go with it. He munched happily, sharing it with Calista.

The waitress watched this intently, her mouth open.

Brandon excused himself and went to the restroom. The waitress hunched close to Calista, her elbows on the counter.

"So, Cali, you and mister tight jeans, huh?" She purred.

Calista turned bright red. "What do you mean, Jan?"

The waitress stood back and held out her two pointer fingers, pressing them together side by side.

"You know, the mattress mamba, the horizontal bop, the wild thing? How is he, Cali? Worth the drive?"

Calista sat up straight and pulled back her shoulders. "I have no idea. It hasn't gotten to that point."

"Yet." The waitress added. "Not yet, you mean. Keep me posted, hon." She patted the counter.

Brandon came back from the restroom, paid for the food and shepherded Calista to the motorcycle.

He handed Calista her helmet and smiled. "Now, it's my turn to show *you* something." He said.

Chapter Seven

He rode north, away from Lincoln City, and east, away from the ocean, toward the mountains. She sat back and let him steer through the twisty, turning road, past small clumps of houses, lone gas stations and miles of forest.

Calista had been on this road perhaps a half dozen times in her life. Most of the time, she drove up and down the coast, staying close to the water. The air was cooler here, where the trees shaded the road from the sunlight. Puffy clouds built up overhead, filtering the light and giving a deeper hue to the green leaves. After almost an hour on the road, Brandon stood up on the foot pegs and pointed to something off to the side, away from the road. Calista looked where he was pointing.

It seemed to be a big shopping mall- a sprawling building with a massive parking lot surrounding it. Brandon turned right at a broad driveway and rolled to a stop near a main entrance. There were rocks stacked higher than Calista's house, forming a backdrop for a waterfall with a handful of fountains gushing around it. A wide covered portico at the entrance to the building had a pair of smaller fountains flanking it, leading to a glass wall and through that to a huge foyer.

Brandon stowed the helmets in his saddlebags and held Calista's hand as they entered the building.

Calista read the words 'Evergreen Casino' carved in a large section of tree trunk by the main entrance. She had never been in a casino before; this would be another new experience.

Brandon seemed to know where to go. He nodded at a man with a navy blazer and a name tag that said 'Security', then led Calista through the foyer to a restaurant, set around a massive aquarium. They sat down, and an eager-looking young woman with thick black hair and dreamcatcher earrings handed them menus.

"Good afternoon." The woman grinned. "Would you like to start with something from the bar?"

Brandon shook his head. "Not for me, thanks. Calista, would you like anything to drink?"

Calista shook her head. The woman smiled again. "Take your time. Just let me know when you're ready to order."

She walked away. Calista leaned forward. "Why are we here?"

Brandon grinned. "They're building that casino up at Porter Point. I bet it's going to be just like this one- it would be a good way to get employment for the locals. There's gaming tables here, a hotel with shows and a dance floor, the whole enchilada. It's good for the economy, but in your case I think it's probably going to be too close to other places like this one."

"That's why Glen wanted to buy our place- because our land values will skyrocket once it's built?"

"Yeah. He's a moron, but he's not stupid."

Calista laughed and opened her menu. "What's good here?" She asked, then she looked at the right side of the page.

"Do you see these PRICES? Is this right?" She hissed. "Brandon. Did you see them?"

He glanced at his menu and smiled at her. "Welcome to the great big world, Calista. Choose whatever you'd like to eat."

They had a leisurely lunch, with a decadent crème brulee and cappuccino for dessert. Calista was groggy from the food and giddy from the coffee. Brandon gave the waitress a credit card then scrawled an amount for a tip. The young woman beamed at the number. They walked around the casino for a while, looking at the gaming tables and the rows of slot machines, then wandered an arcade lined with gift shops.

Brandon looked at his watch. "It's four thirty. Do you think we should head back?"

Calista shrugged and nodded. They made their way to the front entrance, but stopped; out in the parking lot it had started raining, globs of water pelting down in random splashes on the road.

"One sec." Brandon said. "Let me cover the bike till this rain lets up."

He ran out, dug a large plastic sheet from his saddlebag and slipped it over the motorcycle and sidecar, tucking the sheet under the fenders. The rain got heavier, a steady downpour, and he ran back inside.

Calista watched people scurrying around in the parking lot, putting the tops up on convertibles, closing sun roofs and opening umbrellas as they rushed to stay dry.

Brandon shook himself like a wet dog and took off his jacket. "Well, we're stuck here till it lets up. What would you like to do?" He asked.

"How long do you think it will rain for?" Calista asked. "I should let mom know we're OK."

They found a pay phone and Calista dialed the hotel. Her mother answered; "Ocean Dunes Hotel, can I help you?"

"Mom, it's Cali. I'm in Grand Ronde. Brandon took me out for a motorcycle ride, but we're trapped here till the rain stops."

"Hi, dear. Why are you all the way over there?" Her mother asked, worried.

"He was showing me the casino; he said it's like one they want to build at Porter Point."

Her mother sighed. "The weatherman says it will rain all night. You might be stuck there till tomorrow."

Calista looked at Brandon and smiled. "Don't worry then, mom. I'll be fine. If it keeps raining, I'll stay over here and see you in the morning." She hung up.

Brandon's eyes widened. "What?" He asked, hopeful.

"We may be stuck here overnight. The rain won't let up till morning, mom says." Calista shrugged.

Brandon smiled softly. "Well, Miss Blake, what would you like to do?"

She smiled sheepishly. "I've always wanted to gamble in a casino- just for fun. Do you suppose we could play a game or two?"

Brandon stood beside her at the blackjack table and explained the rules of the game. He bought a stack of ten blue chips, and bet for her. Luck was on Calista's side; after a half dozen hands, she had increased her chip count to fifteen. At that point the novelty wore off and she left the table. She gave ten chips back to Brandon and clutched the remaining five in her hand. She looked at them, curious.

"How much are these chips worth?" She asked.

Brandon smiled. "A hundred dollars." He said.

She gasped. "I've been playing with twenty dollar chips?" Calista couldn't imagine being so reckless with money.

"No, they're a hundred dollars EACH. You just made five hundred dollars, Calista."

Calista stared at the chips. The tiny clump of plastic in her hand would keep her hotel going for weeks.

"Are you serious? That's amazing." She gasped. She looked over her shoulder at the blackjack table, hopeful.

"Don't." Brandon said. "You were lucky once, but the odds always favor the house. Come, let's find a room for the night."

He took Calista's arm and walked to the registration desk. A young Native man with a bolo tie and ponytail greeted them cheerfully and said that they had rooms available, but only on the golf course side of the building, which were at a premium.

"That's fine." Brandon nodded.

"Will you require one room or two?" The man asked, completely unemotionally.

Brandon glanced at Calista. "One room, thanks."

"Would you prefer one king size bed or two queens?" The man continued.

"Two queens, thanks."

"That will be three hundred fifty dollars per night." The man said, matter-of-factly.

The young man took Brandon's credit card then returned it, along with a key on a large brass tag.

"Penthouse floor, room five twelve." He said. "Take the elevator to the top floor, and turn left. Enjoy your stay."

Brandon nodded thanks and escorted Calista into the elevator. She was staring down at her feet, thinking.

"Something wrong?" Brandon asked.

Calista offered him the casino chips. "Here." She said.

Brandon looked at them in her hand. "I can't take those, you won them. They're yours."

"You bought me a hundred-dollar lunch, and a three-hundred-dollar room. It's the least I can do."

He shook his head, and Calista sadly put the chips into her purse.

The elevator stopped, and Brandon steered Calista down the hall to a room with '512' in brass on the door. He unlocked it and ushered her in. The room was huge; a couch and easy chair took up one corner, two sumptuous beds were flanked by night tables, and opposite them a fireplace was bracketed by picture windows overlooking a golf course.

Out on the course, a dozen men were out, hunched over in the pouring rain, swinging clubs and dragging golf carts.

Calista walked around, exploring the room. There was a large bathroom, of course, done in black tile with a luxuriously deep black marble tub and a separate shower stall in frosted glass.

She sat on one of the beds and sighed. "Look, I don't like feeling that I owe you sex because you bought me lunch."

Brandon shook his head. "Is that what you think? You think I just brought you here for a naughty night? I didn't arrange the rain, you know. I only wanted to show you what you're going to have for neighbors when they build a casino at Porter Point."

"Still, you seem quite prepared to take advantage of the situation." Calista countered.

Brandon frowned. "I'm sure the hotel has a limo. I'll get them to drive you home, then." He picked up the phone.

Calista stood up. "No, don't. Please." She pleaded.

He put the phone back down.

She looked up at him and sighed. "I'm sorry." She smiled. "I'm just out of my depth here, I guess. Why don't you watch TV or something? I'm going to take a bath."

Calista lay in the tub, her eyes closed, the warm water all the way up to her chin. It was glorious. She felt weightless, floating, carefree.

She could hear Brandon in the bedroom ordering dinner, reading from a menu and repeating items occasionally. "Hey, would you prefer wine, or beer with your dinner?" He called.

"I'm not sure. What's for dinner?" Calista called back.

"It's a surprise."

"OK, surprise me, then." She called.

Brandon finished ordering, then said "Fine, that's in half an hour, thanks." and hung up the phone.

He went into the bathroom and rested his chin on the edge of the tub. Calista opened one eye and looked at him.

"What?" She asked.

"Really? Do you have to ask? I'm alone in a bathroom with a beautiful naked woman and all you can ask is 'what'?" He smirked.

He scooped up a handful of water and poured it over her chest, slowly. Calista tilted her head back, letting the warm water flow over her. Brandon leaned forward and kissed her, gently. Calista felt a thrill at that.

The bathtub felt like her own private swimming pool. She grinned and held her breath, slid under the water for a few seconds, then popped back up. She opened her mouth to say something, but Brandon wasn't there. She couldn't see him. Where was he?

"Brandon?" She called.

He came back into the bathroom. "Here." He said. He held up a pale grey bathrobe. "We don't want you catching cold."

Calista stood up, casually, and slipped her arms into the robe. It was a thick terry, and she pulled it tight around her, feeling warm and cozy. Brandon reached up to a chrome rack and pulled out a large bath towel. Wordlessly, Calista leaned forward and he toweled her hair dry.

He tossed the towel aside and handed her a new one; she wrapped that around her head and padded through into the bedroom. She lay on the bed, her arms stretched out to her sides, looking at the ceiling.

"I could really get used to this." She sighed. "I have never had anything that felt this luxurious."

"Don't you ever get away from your place? Don't you go somewhere nice on vacation every so often?" Brandon asked.

Calista shook her head. "The hotel takes up all our time. Don't get me wrong- I love our place- I just sometimes wish I had some space in my life all to myself."

Brandon slipped a finger into the vee formed by the bathrobe, and moved it down along her chest, exposing her cleavage. Calista watched him, amused.

"Having fun?" She asked.

"God, yes." He said.

He leaned down and kissed the bottom of her neck, slowly moved up and kissed his way to the underside of her chin, then tilted her head back slightly and kissed her softly on the lips.

Calista wrapped her arms around his neck and pulled him close. She kissed him, passionately, then slipped one arm out of the robe and pulled at the other sleeve to take it off her shoulders.

"Gee, and you didn't even ply me with wine this time." She joked.

A knock at the door startled them both. Calista quickly pulled the robe back on and sat up, sheepish. Brandon opened the door.

A thin man in a white cotton jacket mumbled something then wheeled a cart into the room, stopping by the foot of one of the beds. Brandon pulled some bills from his pocket, handed them to the man and thanked him.

The man grinned broadly, bowed several times and backed out of the room, closing the door behind him.

Brandon turned back to Calista. "So, do you want to eat first, or what?" He smiled, but it was almost apologetic.

"I don't know. What did you order?" Calista asked, curious.

He lifted a large chrome cover. "Sandwiches." He said. He put the cover back down.

Calista grabbed his shirt and pulled him close. "They'll keep."

They made love. Not like at the campfire, where they had to be careful of rocks and sand, careful to be quiet. They moved all over the bed, groping, kissing and fondling, exploring each other's bodies.

The muscles in Brandon's arms bulged as he lifted his body up into the air, his back glistened with sweat, and his thighs, drenched in perspiration, slid easily against Calista's legs. Calista finally pinned Brandon to the bed and straddled him, her hands gripping the headboard, their bodies slapping together noisily as they made love.

Brandon had his hands around her waist, guiding her, caressing her backside, reveling in the feel of her skin. As they finished, Calista slumped down and fell on him, smiling. Brandon stroked two fingers up and down her spine, tracing the line of her body from the curve of her bottom to the back of her neck.

They lay there for a long time, just holding each other. A long time later, Calista rolled off him, turned onto her stomach, shimmied to the foot of the bed, and reached for the food.

Brandon slid under the sheets, popping out comically beside her. She looked at him and laughed.

"Listen," he said, suddenly serious. "I have something very important to tell you."

Calista sat up, cross-legged. "What?" She smirked.

He looked at her naked body. "No, don't do that. Don't make this even harder for me to say." He said.

Calista pulled at a corner of the sheet and covered herself. "Do you have something contagious?" She asked, worried.

He chuckled. "No, nothing like that." He sighed. "Do you believe that two people find each other because they're meant to find each other? Do you believe in fate?"

"Are you saying that you think we were destined to meet?" Calista asked.

"Maybe we were, yes. The thing is, right now, the way I feel about you…" He sighed again, composing his thoughts. "The way I feel about you; I have never felt that way about a woman before- not even when I got married. Yet the moment I first saw you in the diner, I knew that I wanted desperately to know you better." He was trembling, Calista realized.

"Well, now that you do know me better, what's next? What happens after you go back to San Francisco?" She asked.

"I don't know. I have no idea what I'm going to do next. Up until the day I met you, I was determined to just work in my family business. But now, I have absolutely no idea what I'm going to do next."

Calista wrapped the sheet tighter around her. Instead of simply covering her up, it revealed the outline of her body. Brandon looked her up and down, admiring her shape.

"What?" She asked. "What is it?"

"How about you? How do you feel about me, Calista?"

"Let me think about it. I'll tell you when we get back."

He laughed and held his hands up. "You have me. I am your prisoner." He said. "Let's eat."

The rain fell much harder now. The golfers, even the hardier ones from earlier, bundled up and ran for cover. The manicured greens and sand traps, the tees and the fairways, splashed with pooled water. The windows of the hotel room were streaked with dark raindrops, long slashes of water striking at an angle, muffled by the thick glass.

Calista munched on her sandwich, then frowned and looked down at the bread.

"Something wrong with your food?" Brandon asked.

She wrinkled her nose. "What's in this?"

"I think that one's lobster salad. Is there a problem with it?"

"We could never afford lobster." She took another bite. "I could really get hooked on this, you know."

He grinned. "Glad you like it."

She reached for a beer, her robe falling open and his eyes lingered on the curve of her breast.

She seemed not to notice. "Enjoying the scenery?" She asked, casually.

He grinned, slightly embarrassed. "Yes, very pleasant." He said.

She glanced up and grinned, amused. "You." She chuckled.

Brandon chewed absentmindedly on his food, looking out to the south, over the golf course. In the distance, the mountains were barely visible through the rain. A line of dark cloud moved over the sky, and the rain, impossibly, got ever heavier.

A strobe of light hit the ground, flickered, then hit the ground again. Ten seconds later, a sharp crack of thunder, like an exploding bomb, rumbled the windows.

Calista jumped. She hadn't seen the lightning, and the thunder took her by surprise. She looked over her shoulder at the window, trying to see to the far side of the golf course, but the rain was too thick, and the field faded to grey in the streaked glass.

Another blast of lightning, then after a shorter interval, another crack of thunder. This time, she jumped less.

"It's getting closer." She said. "Hopefully it will pass over us soon. What do you think?"

Brandon nodded. "Yeah, in any case, we're nice and cozy in here, right? At least, as soon as the room warms up a bit."

He stood up. "I'll get the fire going." He said. He pressed a switch on the wall and a blue gas flame rose up in the fireplace. He slid a control beside the switch, and the flame grew brighter.

He turned off the lamps in the room. The evening light outside was softened by the rainfall, and took on a green color as it reflected off the wet fairways. Calista shimmied down off the bed and sat cross-legged in front of the fireplace. She held her hands out to the heat, then playfully opened her robe and let the glow warm her. She pulled the robe close to her again, enjoying the warmth trapped in the fabric.

Brandon sat beside her and leaned close. "Are you feeling happy?" He asked.

"Hmm. Yes." She said. She turned to look at him, puzzled. "Why would you ask that?"

A third blip of lightning and a crack of thunder struck beyond the hotel, into the forest; the storm was passing.

"Because I'd like to know that you're happy." Brandon said.

Calista lay on her side, then stretched out to feel the heat along her body. "Why wouldn't I be happy?" She asked.

"I'm in a gorgeous hotel, with a gorgeous man, and he's helping to make my home gorgeous, too."

Brandon chuckled. "Actually, that brings up another thought I had."

Calista rolled casually onto her back. "Hmm?" She asked.

He lay on his stomach beside her and caressed her shoulder with his fingertip.

"Your mom's car." He started. "It's on its last legs. Did you want a newer one?"

Calista sat up. "I love that old car." She said. "My father bought that car when I was very young. it has a lot of sentimental value to me."

Brandon sat up too, and leaned back on his elbows. "All right, then how about if I could get it fixed up for you?"

"You have a friend." Calista smirked.

"I have a friend, yes."

They watched TV for a while. Calista started to blink more slowly, then her eyes closed altogether.

She opened them again with a start and stood up. "I have to wash my briefs." She said.

"What?" Brandon asked.

"My underwear. I should wash my briefs, and they'll need to dry out in the bathroom. I didn't bring fresh ones."

He stood up. "Give me ten minutes. I don't suppose you brought pajamas either?"

She shook her head.

"I'll be right back." He said, and left the hotel room.

Calista was alone. She was almost never alone. She walked around the room, opened all the dresser drawers and cupboards, then sat on the bed.

Almost unconsciously, she picked up the phone and dialed a number. Her mother answered.

"Hi, mom, it's me. I just wanted to let you know that we're still stuck in Grand Ronde. Brandon booked us into a hotel here, so I'll stay over, and I'll be back tomorrow, all right?"

Her mother sighed. "Is everything OK, Cali? Are you alright?"

Calista was taken aback at the question. "It's fine, mom. What do you mean, am I alright?"

"He's a very attractive man, Cali. You know exactly what I mean."

Calista wondered just how much she should say. She thought for a moment. "He's being a real gentleman. Nothing is going to happen later, I don't think." That part at least, she told herself, was true.

Her mother chuckled. "Too bad. I was hoping to hear some good gossip."

Calista smiled. "If anything develops, I'll let you know tomorrow. Good night, mom."

She put the phone down and went back to watching TV.

A few moments later the door opened, and Brandon came in holding a paper shopping bag.

"What's this?" Calista asked.

"Beware of geeks bearing gifts." He said.

"You mean 'Greeks'." Calista corrected.

"You didn't meet the store clerk." He quipped. He handed her the shopping bag.

Calista opened it and examined the contents.

She pulled out a toothbrush and a travel-sized tube of toothpaste, then reached into the bag again.

She found a pair of pink satin briefs, with 'Feeling Lucky?' embroidered across the back, and a long, hot pink tee shirt with a stylized cartoon of a donkey, that read 'I lost my ass in the casino'.

Calista held the shirt up, amused. "Is this my colour, do you think?"

Brandon smiled. "Works for me."

She slipped on the briefs and opened out the tee shirt.

Brandon stared at her, like a dog watching a rabbit. "Wow." He muttered.

Calista smirked at the comment. The men in town often ogled her, leering, whispering behind her back, but this was different. Brandon wasn't trying to imagine her naked, and he wasn't trying to peek down her blouse. He was simply admiring her for the way she looked.

Calista lifted the tee shirt high over her head and wiggled, letting the cotton slide over her hips. She tugged the hem down until it reached her knees. When she let go it shrank back up to mid-thigh.

Brandon watched her, grinning. "I still say 'wow'", he said simply.

Calista smiled at him, a look of amusement on her face. "Thank you, kind sir." She said.

"Do you have something to wear tonight, too?" She asked.

He shook his head. "Nope. I prefer sleeping in the buff." He said.

He looked at the two beds. "So, which bed do you want to sleep in?"

"Aren't we sharing?" Calista asked, amused.

"I certainly hope so, but which one would you prefer that we shared?"

Calista looked back and forth at the beds. "That one." She pointed. "It's closer to the fireplace."

Brandon glanced at his watch. "It's ten thirty- let's get some sleep, then. Tomorrow, we'll get back early, provided the rain has stopped."

Calista slid under the sheets. They were smooth, luxurious, wrapping her up in soft texture. They were unlike the simple cotton on the beds at her hotel. This bedding was fine linen; it was crisp, smelling of lemon and roses. She leaned back and let her head sink into the fluffy pillow, soaking up the experience.

Brandon casually took off his shirt and jeans, then padded into the bathroom to shower. He came out a few moments later, toweled his body dry, and tossed the damp towel through the bathroom door. He turned off all the lights, pulled the drapes open wide, and turned off the fireplace. Outlined against the dull grey glow of evening light, she could see his muscled legs and arms, arching down as he moved things away for the night, and she realized just how much she craved the physical closeness he gave her, how much she had missed it in her life. He shimmied under the sheets beside her, and threw an arm over her waist.

She looked over at him, watching his eyes open and close slower and slower. He sighed and pulled her close to him, then he leaned sleepily forward and kissed her shoulder.

"Good night, miss Blake." He mumbled.

She kissed his forehead. "Sleep well, Mister Cooper."

Calista woke up, slowly. Her first thought was that there was a strange smell. It was not unpleasant, just unusual. She opened one eye and realized the smell was Brandon, asleep beside her. Under the warm blanket and linen sheets, his body gave off the aroma of the hotel soap.

He had one arm draped over her chest as he lay there, his hand touching Calista's side, just under her armpit.

She opened her other eye and looked around the room. Brandon must have gotten up in the night and closed the drapes; they were pulled shut, blocking out the morning light. Calista slid toward the edge of the bed and tentatively placed one foot on the floor.

The carpet was thick, cushy under her feet. She pressed a switch on the wall and the fire came to life. She knelt in front of it, her hands in front of her, warming herself in the blue glow. She looked down and smirked at the drawing of the donkey on her shirt, its sparkly paint shimmering in the firelight.

She heard Brandon stirring behind her, rolling over in bed. For a brief moment, she thought that this could be permanent between them, that he would always wake up beside her, he would always be there, always in her life. Then her heart sank. The sadness she felt, realizing that he would be gone soon, that this couldn't go on for long, nearly brought her to tears.

She heard fabric rustling behind her and looked back. Brandon was sitting up, cross-legged, smiling at her.

"Good morning." He said softly. "Sleep well?"

She nodded, climbed back onto the bed and slid under the covers. The warmth still trapped in the sheets felt marvelous.

"I slept like a baby." She said.

She lay on her back and put her hands behind her head. He leaned forward and kissed her, very softly.

"So, are you hungry?" He asked.

She rolled her eyes. "Oh, gosh, yes."

He got up and pulled the drapes open. There were cotton-ball clouds over the mountains in the distance, but the morning sun had already dried out the golf course. Men and women were clustered in groups of two or four, polishing clubs and talking animatedly, waiting for their tee times.

"Do you want to eat in the restaurant, or up here?" Brandon asked.

Calista sat up and hugged her knees. "You pick." She said.

He scratched his head. "More free coffee in the restaurant. Do you mind eating down there?"

She shook her head. They got dressed, then Calista carefully folded up her new tee shirt and old briefs and put them in a bag. Brandon handed the room key back, they found a table in the restaurant right beside the massive aquarium, and read their menus.

Calista's eyes widened. "Eggs Benedict with crab? I've never heard of that." She said.

"Do you want that? If you don't like it, I'll eat it." Brandon smiled.

Calista grinned. "I do want that. And I want the buckwheat pancakes, too."

They ate breakfast, talking like any other young couple, sharing each other's food, holding hands as they drank their coffee. Brandon looked out the window as the busboy took away the last plates, and nodded to Calista.

"Look. It seems like blue skies all the way to Portland. Are you ready to head back?"

She looked over her shoulder at the mountains in the distance. The sun was now high in the southeast, warming the hills to the west, and clouds of mist rose up like steam from a kettle, as the morning light dried the fields.

She had mixed feelings; she was glad that she would be home again soon, but already slightly sad at leaving the luxury of the hotel.

"Yeah, let's go." She sighed.

Brandon waved over the waitress, paid the bill and held Calista's chair out as she got up. Even this small polite gesture surprised her. None of the men in town would ever be so gracious as that, not ever, especially once they'd gotten what they wanted from a woman.

He held her hand as they strolled along the long marble corridor, swinging her arm gently. She cashed in her chips; he refused to take the money from her, and she grudgingly put the cash in her purse. They uncovered his motorcycle, shook the tarp dry and put on their helmets. In another minute, they were trundling down the casino's driveway towards home. They turned onto the highway, and Calista listened to the click-click-click of Brandon changing gears as he accelerated, along with the thumping of the engine on his bike. It seemed a familiar sound now, something she knew well.

The morning sun climbed higher and shone over the road. Even between tall trees that lined the highway, the asphalt sent heat up to warm Calista. She sat back in the sidecar, bouncing over the ripples in the road, feeling the wind in her face. Brandon hunched forward, grimacing slightly in the breeze, and occasionally looking down to smile at her.

They headed west through the National Forest, then joined the Pacific Coast Highway and pulled into Lincoln City.

Brandon stopped at a gas station on the north edge of town and filled the tank. He looked around, casually nodding, as people always seemed to smile at a sidecar, careful that he didn't spill fuel on the bike's paint.

A rough voice off to one side made him look up. It was Glen, the real estate man. Brandon stiffened, ready to get physical, but Glen sauntered over, his head down low.

"Say, listen, Mister Cooper, I just wanted to say how sorry I am about our misunderstanding back at Calista's place." He said it softly, almost mumbling.

Brandon smiled a wide, open smile. "Hey, Glen. Look, I know that you're just looking out for your family, I get it. But if it makes you feel any better, I feel as bad as you do about that incident. I'm just trying to make sure that Miss Blake and her mom have a nice place to live, you know?"

Glen looked back at his truck; Jan, the waitress from the diner, was glaring at him, waiting for him to say something else.

He wiped his hands on his pants and held out his right hand for Brandon. "Anyway, no hard feelings, right?"

Brandon smiled and nodded, then shook Glen's hand firmly. "Let's consider it a 'welcome to Oregon' prank."

Glen nodded meekly and shuffled back to his truck. Jan waved at Calista and Brandon, then glowered at Glen as he started up and drove away.

Calista shook her head. "Do you believe that speech?" She muttered.

Brandon's smile faded as they left. "I don't believe it for one slimy second." He muttered.

"What was that all about, then?" Calista asked him.

Brandon shrugged. "I smell a skunk. He wants to keep you away from whatever he's doing."

Calista turned around to look behind her. "Do you think it has something to do with that casino they're building at Porter Point?"

"I'd bet hard money on it. Tell you what, let's just concentrate on making your place look good, all right?"

Chapter Eight

Brandon spent the following days working on the second cottage. He lay a broad tarp on the ground beside it, stacked all the furniture in a pile and covered that with another tarp. He sanded, painted, patched the floor and ceiling as he had with the first cottage, and repaired rusty hinges and sticky windows. The first night it rained hard, hitting the tarp that protected the furniture like a drummer in a rock band. The next morning, the sun rose in a clear blue sky, and the ground dried up by noon. The rain had helped to set the driveway- it was now as hard as concrete. Calista came over to watch him after breakfast, fascinated as he reached up to cover the ceiling in paint, taking one long sweep after another to cover the stained beige with a brilliant white.

He took a step back and checked his work, satisfied with his work thus far. He leaned on his long paint roller and looked behind him at Calista, her hands on her hips, admiring his work.

"So, it's all right, is it?" He asked. "It's beautiful." She said.

"No, you're beautiful. It's just very nice." He corrected.

She grinned and threw her arms around his neck, then she leaned up and kissed him passionately. He wrapped an arm around her waist, hugging her close. A sound made them look, a gasp, coming from the house.

Maisie was at the base of the steps, her laundry basket in her hands, her mouth open in shock. She put the laundry carefully down on the lowest step and walked slowly toward the cottage.

She turned to face Calista and grabbed her arm. "Dear, would you excuse us for a moment?" Maisie said.

Calista opened her mouth to explain, to protest, to say something. Her mother tightened her grip and shook her head.

"Go." She said, firmly. Calista closed her mouth, looked guiltily at Brandon and walked back to the main house.

Maisie turned to face Brandon. "Mister Cooper, what are your intentions toward my daughter?"

He thought for a moment, then he pulled a large handkerchief out of his pocket and spread it out on the top step of the cottage deck.

"Would you sit down please, Maisie?" He asked.

Maisie sat. "Well?" She asked.

He sat beside her and knitted his fingers together, hanging them between his knees. He looked down, thinking.

"Calista is a very special woman." He started. "For me to meet a woman like that, a woman who likes me for just being me, is astonishing. And to meet one as beautiful as she is, and who hasn't been spoiled by the world, is unbelievable."

Maisie sat back, studying him. "She's all I have. She's the only person I have in the whole world. I will do anything to keep her safe from you, or anyone else who wants to take advantage of her. You do know that, don't you?" She said.

"I do know that. You should also know that there's nothing I would ever do to hurt her, but she knows that I'm only here for the summer. Whatever time we have, whatever we mean to each other, it's going to end then." He said, sadly.

Maisie looked down at her shoes. "We've had lots of men come through here, wanting things from us, one way or another. They think we're pushovers. I have had to protect her from all of them since our husbands died. Do I have to protect her from you too, Mister Cooper?" She looked up.

Brandon looked at her, her deep blue eyes unmoving as they read his face. He smiled and took her hand.

"I swear to you that I am not here to take advantage of either of you in any way. Whatever happens between Calista and me will be her choice alone, and not mine." He said.

Maisie's expression softened and she smiled slightly. "I believe you. But if you're lying to me…"

He grinned and kissed her cheek. "That's not going to happen. Ever."

He stood, holding her hand to help her up. She got to her feet, brushing dust off her skirt.

"Dinner is at six. I assume you'll eat with us?" She said, matter-of-fact.

"I'll be there." He said. "Now, if you'll excuse me, I need to get back to what I was doing."

He finished painting the ceiling on the cottage, cleaned up the equipment, and peeled off his coveralls. He looked out toward the main house; he was nervous about going in for dinner, torn between wanting to spend every possible moment with Calista and feeling guilty about it when he was around Maisie. He washed up at his cottage, pulled on a clean shirt and a fresh pair of pants, then went up the steps into the main house right at six o'clock.

Maisie was setting plates out, placing cutlery carefully on top of folded cotton napkins, arranging the table as though someone special was coming to visit. Calista was in the kitchen, bent over, staring into the oven. Brandon admired the curve of her hips and legs, trying not to be too obvious.

Maisie smiled at him, as though the earlier conversation had never happened, and waved him to a spot at the middle of the table. "You sit here, Brandon." She said. There was another place set beside his, and a third place set across the table from them.

Brandon sat, politely. "Isn't there something I can do to help?" He asked.

Maisie shook her head. "No, dear, it's fine. We have it in hand." She turned toward Calista. "Cali, you sit, too."

Calista glanced nervously at her mother, wiped her hands on her apron, then took it off and sat across from Brandon.

Her mother waved casually at her. "No, dear. You sit beside Brandon. That's my spot."

Calista got up slowly and sat beside Brandon. He seemed amused by this. He rested one elbow on the table, his head on his knuckles, watching Calista's expression.

Calista leaned in close to him. "What's so funny?" She whispered.

"Nothing. Nothing at all." He smirked. "What's for dinner?"

She glanced at her mother in the kitchen. "Casserole." She whispered.

"My favorite." Brandon said, dryly.

"No, mom only makes casserole when she's angry." Calista explained.

Brandon sat up straight and put his hands between his knees, like a school child. "Oh, I see." He grinned.

Calista glared at him. "It's not FUNNY! She's really pissed at us." She hissed.

She glanced over at her mother then she shook her finger at him. "This is your fault, you know."

Brandon shook his head. "No, don't do that, Calista. Don't try to make me regret how I feel about you."

Calista scowled. Maisie brought through a wooden board, then a steaming casserole and placed it on the board.

"There." Maisie said, sitting down. "Who wants some carrots and cauliflower?"

Brandon leaned forward. "Can I say something first?"

Maisie nodded. "Certainly, dear."

Brandon sighed and looked out to the cottages, thinking. "I have not lied to you. I took this job to make your place better, to help you out. The other motivation for me to do that was to be around Calista as much as possible. I told you earlier, Maisie, that she's the most extraordinary woman I've ever met. All I can tell you is that I will never do anything to hurt you or her in any way."

Calista smiled at him, held his chin and gave him a kiss on the cheek. Maisie glanced back and forth between them. "So, is that a yes on the carrots?" She asked. Maisie leaned forward and carefully scooped food onto everyone's plates. They ate in near-silence,

Calista watching Maisie and Brandon as though one of them might explode at any moment.

After dinner, Maisie sat Brandon on the sofa, brought out an old photo album and described old family pictures to him. She told him about her husband- Calista's father- and how they had made their home here before Calista was born. She pointed to school photos, family trips, the memories of a lifetime.

She turned the page and pointed to the station wagon. "This was the only new car Nathaniel was ever able to afford. We've kept it partly because of expense, but mostly in his memory." She said.

Brandon sat up. "About that car," He said. Calista's eyes widened.

"I have a friend who's great with older cars. Would you mind if he took a look at it, and see what it needs to fix it up? He'd enjoy doing it, I'm sure."

Maisie stared at him for a moment, then shot a quick look at Calista and back at Brandon. "Why would he do that?" She asked.

"As I say, he likes older cars. Your car needs some work done, and this is a way for him to have fun while helping you out. If you'd rather not, though, I understand. It's just that it's going to break down soon if you don't have the work done."

Maisie leaned back, thinking. "How long would this take? I need that car to get around."

Brandon nodded. "Leave it with me, then. I'll talk to him later tonight."

Brandon thanked the women for dinner, excused himself and went out to his cottage. Calista helped her mother with the dishes, silent, then finally she couldn't take the silence any longer. She put down her dish towel and turned to face Maisie.

"Mom, what's going on with you two? Why are you and Brandon acting so strange?" She asked.

Her mother sighed, dropped her head and turned to face her. "How was your night at the hotel?" She asked, simply.

"Lovely. We had great food, we had luxurious accommodations overlooking the golf course, and the bathtub was sheer bliss. What else do you want to know?"

Maisie shook her head. "It's none of my business. You're a grown woman, it's none of my business. I just don't want to see you hurt, all right?"

Calista leaned back, amazed. "Is that it? You're wondering if I'll wither away once he's gone? Or are you afraid I'll run after him?"

Maisie hadn't thought of that possibility. Her mouth dropped open. Calista shook her head.

"No, mom. That's not what's going to happen. No matter what transpires, we both know it ends in August, period. All right?"

Maisie's expression softened, and she bumped Calista's shoulder playfully. "He has a very cute backside." Maisie said.

Calista smirked. "He does at that."

At eight thirty that night, Brandon was out on the dunes, feeding wood onto a small campfire. He played 'Moon River' on his harmonica, watching golden sparks float slowly up into the sky. He took a sip of wine, savoring the taste as it swirled around in his mouth. A sound behind him made him look: Calista was picking her way along the path, holding a flashlight as she walked. His face brightened at seeing her, but she glared at him and shook her head slowly. He saw a second figure trailing behind her- Maisie.

He stood up as the two women approached him. "Hi, what a lovely surprise to see you." He said.

Maisie wrapped her cardigan tightly around her, smoothed her skirt and sat on one log. "I've heard you playing music out here before." She said. I always wondered what made you choose the harmonica."

He held the instrument up. "It's too hard to keep a trombone in my pocket." He joked.

He lifted up a pale bottle. "Would either of you ladies care for a glass of wine?" He said.

Maisie smiled. "I would, very much, yes."

Brandon reached around behind him and produced a glass. He filled it halfway then handed the glass to Maisie.

"Miss Blake, would you like some wine too?" He asked.

"Yes, please." Calista said.

He brought out another glass, filled it and handed it to Calista. He held up his glass. "To a starry evening." He said.

Maisie nodded. "To clear skies." She said. She took a sip and smacked her lips. "My, this is very good."

Brandon glanced at Calista. "So I've been told."

Maisie turned toward her daughter. "Do you remember when your father used to take us out here on summer evenings, just the three of us, and we'd cook frankfurters and drink hot chocolate?"

Calista smiled sadly. "Dad would always burn them. I can't remember eating a hot dog that wasn't mostly charred."

Maisie chuckled. "Then he'd point to the stars and tell you the stories about how they got their names. He could never get enough of teaching."

Brandon reached back and picked up a small dry log, then set it carefully on the fire. "When I was nine, I went to visit my grandfather, at his ranch in Arizona." He said.

He took a sip of wine. "I spent the whole summer with him; one week we took horses down the Gila River and camped out at night all along the way. It was really nice, just us, the horses, and my grandfather telling me stories about the old days."

Maisie leaned forward. "Do you miss him?"

Brandon shrugged. "Very much. He was more of a father to me than my actual father, in some ways. He had a perspective on things that my dad didn't get until later in life."

He took another sip of wine. Overhead, a thick cloud hid the moon. Brandon looked up, curious at the sudden darkness. In the distance, out over the ocean, he heard a sound like a rolling bass drum. Thunder, echoing over the waves, reverberated off the main house and bounced back toward the beach.

Calista looked up, too. A drop of rain fell on her cheek and she winced, surprised by the water. Another drop fell, then a symphony of raindrops splashed onto the grass around them, getting louder and harder by the second.

Brandon stood up. "Time to go inside, I guess." He said. He picked up the bottle and kicked sand onto the fire. Another roar of thunder, stronger and closer, boomed out over the water, then a brilliant flash of lightning, a blur of white light that froze an image of the three people, then the rain started in earnest.

Brandon kicked at the campfire; the rain had now soaked the sand, smothering the flames. Maisie turned to head back to the main house, covering her head with the sleeve of her cardigan. Calista hunched her shoulders, aimed the flashlight ahead of her and followed her mother along the path. The rainfall turned into a deluge. Maisie squealed and kicked her feet up, racing to get under cover. Calista shuffled quickly behind her mother, trying to not trip her as they both raced back to the house.

Brandon ran to the house with them, watched them walk up the steps to the door, then held up the bottle.

"Sorry about the inclement weather. Perhaps we can do this again when it's dry?" He said, smiling.

Maisie nodded. "That would be nice. Thank you for the wine, by the way."

Brandon started to leave then turned back. "Ah. May I use your phone?" He said.

Maisie waved him up the stairs. Brandon sprinted up, pulled out a small address book and looked something up.

He dialed a number and waited a moment. "Hey Jerry, It's Brandon." He said. He waited another minute. "I'm good, man. How's business?"

He listened a moment more. "Listen, I got a favor to ask. It's not for me, it's for friends who need help. How do you feel about old Pontiac wagons?" He paused.

"Yeah, it's- I don't know- maybe thirty years old? Anyway, it's crying out for some love. What can you do for me?"

He listened. "Right, suspension, tune up, muffler, brakes, the standard bit. And they need a loaner, if you can spare one."

He scribbled something down. "Sure. When?" He nodded, listening. "Perfect. Here's the address."

He gave the hotel's address, spelling the name of the highway. He smiled, listening to the other person say something. "Great, terrific. Listen, I still owe you one, all right?" Calista heard a soft voice on the other end of the phone. "No, you're a good man, Jerry. Talk to you." Brandon said. He hung up.

"So, in a couple of days he'll come by with a car you can drive while he fixes your wagon, so to speak. Is that alright with you?"

Maisie looked at him, puzzled. "Who is this person?" She asked.

"He's a family friend who loves old Pontiacs."

Maisie rubbed her hands on her skirt and shook her head.

"I'm not sure about this. You're certain he doesn't want to be paid anything?"

"He wouldn't say no to a basket full of muffins. Look, he has restored a dozen classic cars for our family. We've given him a fortune in business. He has told me for a while that he wanted to give me something as a thank-you. This serves us both well. What do you say?"

Maisie shrugged and nodded. Brandon grinned. "Great. That's settled, then."

Brandon looked out at the yard. The rain now fell in thick waves, drenching the grass. He hunched his shoulders, said good night to the women and rushed out to his cottage.

He shook off his coat, flapped it at the door for a moment to get the heavier water off it, and hung the coat on the edge of the bathroom door. He inhaled deeply. This cottage smelled moldy, he thought. After he was finished the second cottage, he'd move into that one, then redo this cottage next. If he could think of someone that had good used plumbing fixtures, maybe he could replace the sinks and tubs, too. Then again, the old ones had character, so maybe Maisie and Calista would prefer to keep them.

Maybe he could get them refinished? He shook his head. Too much thinking for one night. He took off his clothes, washed his face and climbed into bed. At least the new mattresses would be here soon, and he could get a better night's sleep then. He closed his eyes and fell asleep.

He dreamed of a woman he once knew. She had dated him, briefly, after his divorce. She was a jazz singer, with long brown legs and short blond hair, but she seemed more interested in his family and their connections than in him. He rolled over. The jazz singer was in his bed, suddenly. He smiled at how real the dream felt, and rubbed his hand up and down her side, enjoying the fantasy. This woman's hips were not as broad as the singer's, though. He opened his eyes, slowly. Calista was under the sheets with him, a look of amusement on her face.

"Wha…? When did you get here?" He said, groggy.

"Not quite the reception I'd hoped for, but hello to you, too." She giggled.

He sat up. "What time is it?"

"Almost eleven. Mom never drinks, and the wine really knocked her out." Calista giggled.

Brandon lifted his head up and looked out. "Is it still raining?"

"Pouring- cats and dogs." Calista said. "And the campfire's dead. What can we do for amusement?"

Brandon wrapped his arm around her waist and pulled her close. They made love. Not wild, free, like in the hotel, and not careful, hurried, like on the beach, but softly, carefully, as though Maisie might hear them from the house. Afterward, Calista took a quick shower. She came back, wrapped in a towel, and sat on the bed.

"That's kind of pointless, isn't that?" Brandon asked. "You're going to get drenched if you go back now. Do you want to stay here until the rain lets up?"

Calista looked out at the yard and sighed. "If I wait here, I'll fall asleep, and mom will find us together. She already guessed we've been intimate, and I don't want to give her anything more to worry about."

Brandon smiled. "I think that's a lovely way to express it."

"What?"

"Intimate." He repeated. "That's a beautiful way to describe what we have together."

Calista unwrapped the towel and pulled it around both of them. She kissed him softly and leaned back.

"Thank you. That was a very sweet thing to say." She said. "Sorry, I've got to go."

She reached down to her clothes by the bed, pulled on a sweater and shorts, slid her feet into rubber flip-flops and opened the door, silhouetted against the grey light outside. Brandon leaned up on one elbow and watched her.

"Hey." He said. "Can I count on us doing this again?"

She looked over her shoulder, her legs and back turning in a graceful curve that stayed burned in Brandon's memory. "We'll see." She said. She hunched her shoulders against the rain and ran back to the main house.

She crept up the stairs, silently, listening to be sure her mother was still asleep. The slow soft breathing from Maisie's room and the odd nearly silent snore told Calista that she was. Calista got into her own bed, feeling warmth and a rush of exhilaration from making love with Brandon, unlike how she had ever felt before, even after making love to him at other times. She slid deep under her covers, remembering every moment in delicious detail. She fell asleep.

Eight in the morning, and Calista was still in bed. Maisie was downstairs; Calista could hear the oven closing and pots clunking on the stove. She looked out her window at Brandon's cottage. There was no sign of him. She casually looked out to see where his motorcycle was, but it wasn't anywhere she could see either. That was odd, she thought.

Calista threw on a sweater and jeans and came downstairs. Her mother looked up at her and smiled.

"Hello, dear. You certainly slept in this morning."

"Hi, mom. Yeah, I guess the wine hit me pretty hard last night." Calista hoped it would sound convincing.

Calista looked around. "Where's Brandon?"

Maisie frowned. "Isn't he in his cottage?"

Calista walked out across the yard toward Brandon's cottage. The rain had made the grass soggy, and a gentle breeze over the beach gave the air a faint smell of seaweed and sand. It brought back all the memories she had of making love with Brandon. She knocked at the door of the cottage, mostly for Maisie's benefit, and opened the door.

"Hi? It's me." She whispered. She looked around- he wasn't there. She went into the bathroom; his razor and hairbrush were missing.

"Hello?" She called, worried.

She opened the small closet door- his clothes were gone too. Now she felt a sense of panic. She rushed around to the back of the cottage, where his motorcycle was parked. It wasn't there.

Calista felt like the sky had just fallen down on her. She ran her fingers through her hair, trying to make sense of what she was seeing, and she looked around, desperate, hoping that she was somehow missing some important clue. He had gone. He hadn't left a note, he hadn't said anything to her, he was just gone.

Calista rubbed her fingers up and down on her hips, an instinctive act to make herself feel better, and pressed the palms of her hands against her cheeks, warming her face. She breathed deeply, gasping for oxygen, so as not to get nauseous from the panic. She scrunched up her face, trying not to scream out loud, trying to keep some control.

He had left her. He had been nice to her, he had made love to her, had said warm endearing things to her, then he had left. In the back of her mind, Calista felt the same way she had when her father had died, then later when Ed had died. The men in her life had left her, because despite what she had felt for them, it was not enough to keep them there with her.

Calista ran back to the main house and stopped dead in the middle of the kitchen. "Mom, he's gone." She said, softly.

Maisie put down the plate in her hand and let her arms fall to her sides. "What?" She asked, softly.

"He's gone. All his stuff is gone. His motorcycle is gone. He didn't leave a note, or clothes, or anything."

Maisie walked slowly over to her and put her arms around Calista. "Oh, my dear. I'm so sorry for you." She said.

Calista rested her head on her mother's shoulder and cried for a long time.

That evening, Maisie spent a long time with a friend on the phone, talking about what they might do if they had to sell the hotel. She said that at least a new owner could see what was possible, now that they had a new road and two of the cottages were restored. Hopefully that would raise the sale price to where Maisie could afford to buy a house near Portland or Salem.

Calista said, when she had stopped crying, that she would be glad to live in a town, maybe get an apartment, work in an office, something like that. She didn't sound too convinced about it.

The next day, Calista mowed the lawn, laundered the sheets from Brandon's cottage, and hung them on a line to dry. It was an hour after she brought them in that she remembered he had fixed her clothes dryer, and she didn't need to hang out the laundry anymore. She drove out to a neighbor's farm; they had dairy cattle, and Calista did their accounts every month, in exchange for milk, cheese and eggs. She worked quietly, letting her mind focus on a ledger page, blocking out the pain she felt.

That evening, her mother spoke on the phone with the same friend for hours more. The friend had lost her husband the year before, so the two women commiserated, telling funny stories about their husbands to keep their spirits up.

The next morning, the sun shone brightly. The clouds were gone, and a brilliant blue sky warmed the yard. Calista was still brooding, upset that he had gone so abruptly, without any warning or explanation. She ate breakfast, made her bed, and took a shower. She swept the front porch, mechanically, just as she did most mornings. She was trying to decide whether she should find someone to finish Brandon's work, or see if she could do it herself. After all, if that thoughtless bastard could do it, she could too.

An unfamiliar car rolled down the driveway, slowly creeping toward the house. Finally, a bit of good luck- a guest. She put on a smile and waited for the car to stop, ready to greet the visitor.

The car's door opened, and a wiry, scruffy man got out. He had a shaved head, tattoos on his arms and neck, and a gold tooth where one of his canines should have been. He had a slight sneer, as though he was smelling something bad, and he looked around nervously, as if waiting for someone, it seemed.

Calista was scared. He looked like a thug, and she and her mother were nowhere near anyone who could help them.

The man walked slowly up to Calista. She backed away from him, her hands tucked behind her back.

The man nodded. "Hey there. Are you Calista?" He asked. His voice sounded like a scratchy record. Calista nodded.

"I'm Geraldo. Call me Jerry. Nice to meet you." The man said. "Where's your wagon?"

Calista frowned. "Wagon?"

The man nodded. "Yeah. Brandon asked me to take a look at your Pontiac?"

Calista's shoulders softened. "You're his mechanic friend?"

The man smiled, his gold tooth a foot wide in his face. "Yeah. He said you got an old Pontiac wagon. I dig old Pontiacs."

Calista waved at the back of the house, where their car was parked. The man walked around and stood at the front of her car, examining it.

He opened the doors, checked latches and hinges and floorboards, then he popped the hood and looked at something deep down in the engine.

"Your air conditioning isn't working, is it?" The man said.

"No, not for years. And the car overheats if we drive too fast." Calista added.

The man nodded. "Good. Give me a week. The body's in good shape, and the mechanicals are ok, it just needs some basic work. Can I get the keys for it?"

Calista shrugged. "We can't be without a car, though. We need to get into town for groceries and things."

The man held out his car keys. "Here you go, you can use mine."

Calista looked out at his car. It looked like one she had seen in an old movie once, all chrome and shiny black metal. It had a thin white pinstripe going from front to back down the side, and sparking whitewall tires. "What kind of car is that?" She asked.

"It's a fifty-six Chieftain. Like I told you, I like Pontiacs. Be careful, though, she's got gobs of power. Got a good stereo, too, and cold air. You can use her till I get back."

Calista went into the kitchen and got her car keys. Maisie came in from the living room, curious.

"What is it, dear?" She asked.

"Brandon's friend is here to fix our car, and he brought a car for us to use in the meantime."

"Oh, my. That's wonderful. That reminds me." Maisie said.

Calista went out to the porch, clutching her keys. The man had his hands in the back pockets of his jeans, looking at the dunes beyond the fence.

"Brandon told me about this place. You guys got any vacancies in September?" He asked, casually.

"Yeah, I think so." Calista said, carefully.

"We got a big family anniversary this summer; maybe we could rent all five cottages for a couple weeks?" He said.

Calista tried to not look stunned. "Sure. Let us know when you'd need them." She smiled.

He grunted agreement.

"I don't suppose you know where Brandon is right now?" Calista asked.

The man waved at the road. "Yeah, he stopped for gas, but he should be right along."

Calista's heart thumped. She hoped the man couldn't hear it. Her mother came out of the house onto the porch and rested a large wicker basket full of muffins on a step.

"Hello, I'm Calista's mother, Maisie." She held her hand out. "I'm pleased to meet you, mister...?"

The man grinned. "Jerry. Everyone just calls me Jerry." He took her hand. "Pleased to meet you too, ma'am."

Maisie handed him the basket. "Brandon said you might like these to bring back to your garage?"

He took them carefully and inhaled the air over the basket. "Yeah, well, maybe one or two will make it back." He joked.

He took Calista's car key and placed the muffins in her car. "See you in a week." He called out, and drove off.

Maisie wandered over to the man's car, curious. She peered in the window, then gingerly opened the door and sat behind the wheel.

Calista walked over to join her, still not quite believing what had just happened. This car smelled like new; the seats were pristine, the paint gleamed, the glass was clear, with none of the scratches or cracks in the windows their car had.

A sound from the road made her step back. Maisie was still in the car, touching controls and opening the glove box. Calista saw a figure turn onto their drive, a motorcycle with a sidecar, rolling slowly along the fresh gravel, and a familiar figure on the motorcycle. He stood up on the foot pegs as he got closer, smiling at Calista through his helmet visor.

He rolled up to his cottage and shut the motor off, then he threw a leg into the air and got off the bike.

Calista was stunned. Up until five minutes ago, she thought that he was gone for good. Now, he was back, smiling, as though nothing had happened.

Brandon waved hello to Maisie and dragged a duffel bag out of the sidecar and into his cottage. Calista followed him, away from Maisie's view.

Brandon threw the bag onto his bed and turned to face her. "Hey, Calista, I missed you." He said. He reached out to hug her.

She slapped his arm away and glared at him. "How DARE you? Huh? How DARE you?" She spat.

"What?" He asked, puzzled.

"What? That's rich. You disappear in the middle of the night, right after we…" She looked to see that Maisie was out of earshot and whispered. "Right after that night together, with no note, no explanation, NOTHING, and you say 'what'?"

He smirked at that. "When I called Jerry, he told me he was going to come by today. I thought I told you. In any case, I tried to call you here a few times, and the line was busy. You should get a second line, or an answering service or something."

Calista wrinkled her mouth. "Mom was talking most of the night to a friend of hers. It's still your fault. You should have left a note. Why did you go, anyway?"

He pointed at the duffel bag. "I needed fresh clothes, and more wine. Plus, I had some things to do. Do you forgive me?"

Calista rubbed her face, frustrated. "I thought you'd left us. I thought you were gone for good." She moaned. "Do you understand how much it hurts me, to lose a man in my life?"

Brandon stared at her, shocked. He hadn't thought of it that way, obviously. He put his arms around her, but she pushed him away.

"No, don't. Don't touch me. Don't try to apologize." She said. "You went away without telling us you were going away. Why would you do that?"

"I'm sorry." He said. "I just realized that I needed to do some things, so I headed out early to get back as soon as I could. You're right, though. I should have left you a note."

Calista's eyes were wet. She blinked hard to keep from crying, but she tried to look at Brandon through her tears.

He brushed her cheek gently with his thumb, wiping it dry. "You know the worst part?" He said softly.

Calista shook her head.

"You're even more beautiful when you cry. That's such a pity." He smiled.

Calista snickered, despite herself. "You're hopeless." She said.

Chapter Nine

Brandon spent the next day putting finishing touches on the second cottage. He cleaned up the paint, scraped old caulking off the windows, flushed gunk out of the plumbing, then prepared to work on the third cottage. He moved his things into one of the renovated ones, stowing his duffel bag by the bed. He stayed awake as long as he could that night, looking out across the lawn at the main house, waiting for Calista to come, hoping she would tiptoe across the grass to join him. She never came. He fell asleep.

The following morning, he ate breakfast, smiled pleasantly, but said little. He pulled old furniture out of the third cottage, stacked it carefully outside, and walked through it, mentally noting down what to do next.

A sound of feet behind him lifted his spirits. He wanted to wrap Calista in his arms, to give her a hug and kiss. He turned to greet her. It wasn't Calista, it was Maisie.

"So, how is the cottage coming?" Maisie asked him.

"It's coming along fine. I should be done this one by the end of next week." He said.

Maisie looked at the walls and ceiling, nodding. She turned slowly and stared at him. "What exactly happened between you and Cali?" She said, sadly. "She seems lost, all of a sudden."

"I think she felt abandoned when I left." He said. "I can understand why. She has been abandoned twice before, as she said."

Maisie dragged over an upturned plastic paint bucket and sat on it. She wrapped her hands around her knees, hugging herself, and sighed.

"When her father died, I was devastated, and she was, too. She and Nate were very close; she was just like the son he never had. Losing him left a hole in her heart that I just couldn't fill. After she met Ed, she got happy again- she came back to life. It was a cruel twist of fate that took Ed away from her too."

Brandon knelt beside her and put an arm over her shoulder. "I have deep feelings for her. You must see that. I can't imagine what will happen when summer's over. I guess we'll see when that time comes...."

Maisie sighed. "Just don't hurt her. Please. She's not as strong as she seems."

Brandon thought for a moment and shrugged sadly. "I guessed as much. Look, there is no way in the world I'd knowingly hurt her. I realize she felt abandoned when I left just now, but there were things I needed to do, and they couldn't wait. I'm sorry that I forgot to leave a message. I'm sorry I hurt her."

Maisie stood up and waved her hand at the cottage. "We're in your debt for everything you've done so far. There's no way we could repay you for all this. But you're in Cali's life now, and I can't bear to see her hurt, that's all."

Brandon looked at the walls, making a mental note of every crack and stain. "I understand. Look, even after I've gone, how about if she had something to remember me by, something that would give her comfort?"

"What do you mean?" Maisie asked, curious.

Brandon frowned, thinking. "Leave it with me." He said.

Maisie went back to the main house and busied about, cleaning and getting food ready for lunch.

Brandon scraped old paint off the walls of the cottage, removing blistered and jagged flakes with a spatula. He worked in silence, thinking about his conversation with Maisie, wondering if he could have acted differently with Calista.

Maybe he should have let her know he had to go back, maybe he should have told her why he had to leave, maybe...

A sound behind him brought him back. Did Maisie have another question for him? He turned around.

Calista was standing in the doorway, her arms hanging at her sides, with a sadness in her face he hadn't seen before.

She shook her head. "Why did you go?" She asked softly. "Why?"

He put down the spatula. "There were things I had to do. I'm sorry, there are things that I needed to do that just won't wait."

Her eyes filled with tears. "You never said anything. Why didn't you say anything?"

He slid over the bucket that Maisie had sat on, and Calista sat down on it.

He took her hand in both of his and looked into her eyes. "Look, I won't ever do that again, all right? I promise. I will never, ever leave again without telling you that I have to go."

Calista looked up and smiled softly. "Pinky swear?"

He grinned and held out a hooked little finger. "Pinky swear."

She grasped it with her little finger, then pulled him toward her and kissed him softly. "OK." She whispered.

Out in the yard, they heard a grinding noise, gears chattering and gravel moving. Calista got up quickly and went to the doorway of the cottage. A large truck wobbled down the driveway, rolled to a stop outside the main house, and three men jumped down from the cab. One of them, a short man with a baseball cap and overalls, ordered the other two to open the back of the truck. Brandon walked toward them.

"Billy! How are you, man?" He bellowed. The short man put his hands on his hips and stood still, waiting.

As Brandon approached him, he threw one arm around Brandon's neck and pulled him tight. Calista though he was going to kiss him, or choke him. She couldn't tell which.

"BC! You old pirate! Fancy finding you out here in the middle of nowhere."

Maisie came out of the house, wiping her hands on her apron. She walked straight up to the man. "Hello, I'm Maisie Blake. And you are?"

The man took off the baseball cap and held his hand out. "Bill Russell. Not the basketball player. Pleased to meet you."

Maisie shook his hand. "Hello. What brings you out here, Mister Russell?"

The man poked his chin at Brandon. "He asked me for a favor. Actually, it saves us a trip. Where do you want them, BC?"

Maisie turned to look at Brandon. "Where do we want what?"

Brandon grinned. "Replacement beds and dressers. Billy brought you some, for the cottages and the main house. Remember I told you that he'd come over here this week?"

Maisie smiled broadly. "That's wonderful. Can we help you at all?"

The man shook his head. "No, we got it, ma'am. Where would you like everything?"

Brandon waved at the first cottage. "We can stack the mattresses and dressers in there for now."

The man grunted and said something to the other two men. They pulled mattresses, cardboard boxes and flat bundles of wooden bed frames out of the truck and stored them in the first cottage. The furniture filled the small space. Maisie watched this all, mesmerized, then turned to the first man. "Excuse me, but would you boys like some lunch?"

The man looked at Brandon. Brandon nodded and opened his eyes wide. The man turned to Maisie and smiled.

"Why, that's very nice of you, ma'am. We would love some lunch, thank you."

Maisie grinned. "If you can give me about twenty minutes, we can all eat together, if that's all right?"

The man nodded. "Did you want us to replace the mattresses in the cottages, then, while we wait?"

Brandon stepped forward. "That would be great, Billy. The main house could use your help first, though."

Maisie glanced back at the main house steps. "Yes, you could do the four rooms in the house. Would that be alright?"

Calista stepped forward. "I'll take the sheets off for you." She said.

The men waited as she stripped the linen off the beds, then with military precision they pulled the old mattresses out and placed the replacement ones in their place. The short man took two large cardboard boxes and handed them to Calista.

"These are the sheets that go with the beds. They're basically new, but the hotel was changing its color scheme, so they wanted them gone." He said, shrugging.

Calista opened a box and ran her hand over a sheet. It felt like silk, luxurious and warm, just like the sheets in the casino hotel. She couldn't say that out loud, though. She mumbled something and took the boxes upstairs.

The men took the old mattresses from the cottages and stacked them in their truck, along with assorted other castoffs, then they closed the truck door and locked it.

Maisie stepped onto the porch and called everyone in for lunch. She had placed a large bowl of salad, a stack of sandwiches and pitchers of milk and lemonade on the table. The three men shuffled nervously until Maisie told them to sit down and help themselves. Everyone began to eat.

The short man, Billy, stopped after a particularly large mouthful of food and tuned to Maisie. "This is very good, ma'am. So, are any of your cottages free this summer?"

Maisie glanced at Brandon. "We're filling up for late August, but I'm sure we could find space for you." She smiled.

Brandon patted his mouth with a napkin, so nobody could see him grinning. Calista glanced over at him and smirked.

"What would you want for a cottage for two weeks?" The man asked. He shot a look at Brandon. "For a very special friend, you understand."

Maisie nodded. "We could let you have it for five hundred dollars."

The man grinned. "Five hundred a week? Done. I'll call you when we got the dates firmed up."

Maisie's eyes widened. She had meant five hundred dollars in total, not for a week.

Her shoulders drooped slightly as she relaxed. "Of course, for that you would also get breakfasts." She added.

The man leaned back. "Wow. Where is the ocean from here?"

Maisie waved her hand toward the door. "It's just a hundred feet down our path to a sandy beach. We also have a fire pit that's very popular in the summer; this beach is famous for surf fishing, as well."

The man looked out the door, listening for sounds from the beach. "I'm going to take a walk out there after we eat, if that's OK?"

Maisie smiled. "Please, by all means."

After lunch, the men offered to install the dressers in the house. Maisie and Calista rushed to empty the old ones and watched dumbfounded as the men whisked them away and put in the new ones.

Maisie put their clothes away, remarking how these drawers slid noiselessly and smoothly, not like on her old ones.

Maisie gave the men a basket of muffins. The short man, Billy, walked down to the beach, munching happily as he went, and came back a few minutes later.

"This is great. No crowds, no traffic. I love your fire pit, too. Yeah, I got your card, I'll call you and set up a date, all right?"

Maisie reached out her hand. "We would be pleased to have you as a guest." She smiled.

The men all thanked her for lunch and piled into the truck. It rumbled down the drive, turned onto the highway and disappeared. Brandon watched them go, his hands on his hips. "So, that was exciting." He muttered.

"Yes, it certainly was." Maisie said. "Calista, would you mind helping me with the linens?"

Cali smiled at Brandon and followed her mother into the house. Brandon went back to scraping the paint in the third cottage. He worked on autopilot, not thinking at all about the work he was doing. His mind was on Calista. He hoped that she had forgiven him for leaving. He hoped she would still make love to him. He wished he didn't have to leave later in the summer. He wished life could be different, but he couldn't tell her why he had to leave. Not just yet, anyway.

Calista and Maisie unpacked the bed linens. They were crisp, clean, smelling of lavender and starch. The women made the beds then stood back and looked at the finished work. Calista slipped off her shoes and lay on the bed in her room. She reached out her arms, side to side, and closed her eyes.

"I'm going to sleep for a week." She sighed. "You should try this, mom."

Maisie lay down beside her and stretched herself out. She groaned a contented groan. "Good heavens, this is nice. Why on earth would they throw these out?" She said. She rolled onto her side and closed her eyes.

"Turn out the light, Cali, I'm taking a nap." She joked.

She sat up and patted the blanket, as if to make sure the bed was still there, then she got up again.

"I think you should thank Brandon for getting us these things. Don't you agree, Cali?" She said.

Calista understood the statement. She nodded and went out to the cottage where Brandon was working.

He had his back to the door, scraping old flakes of paint from the baseboard, when he heard footsteps on the porch. He assumed it was Maisie again. He straightened up to greet her, and saw Calista in the doorway, leaning against the frame.

He had never seen anyone looking so seductive, even just lounging in the doorway like that. He wiped his hands on his pants and wiped his face with the inside of his elbow.

"Wow, it sure gets warm doing this." He said.

Calista's eyes dropped, as she formulated what she wanted to say. "We just wanted to thank you for the beds and dressers." She said softly. "They're very nice, extremely comfortable."

He shrugged. "It's nothing. I just figured it was an easy solution to your problem, that's all."

Calista shook her head. "No, don't say it's nothing. It's not nothing. You have resources that we couldn't imagine, and you can do things we could never do. As my mother said, we can't thank you enough for what you've done for us."

Brandon smiled. "Does that mean you forgive me for taking off earlier?"

Calista shrugged. "Did you want to tell me why you had to leave in such a hurry?"

He thought for a moment. "Not just yet, but I promise I'll tell you soon."

Maisie came out from the main house, a stack of linen in her arms, and called out to Calista. Calista turned to look and Maisie tilted her head, beckoning. Calista excused herself and followed her mother to the cottage that had Brandon's things in it.

The women made the bed and loaded clothes in the new dresser, the room now looking like a tasteful bedroom somewhere in California. Maisie took a step back and admired the layout.

"Well, this is certainly more impressive now." She said. She caressed the dresser with her fingertips, the smooth oak finish feeling sensual to her touch.

They arranged the new night tables and placed their lamps on them. Somehow, even their old lamps looked newer, now.

Brandon was lost in thought, scraping old paint off the walls. As the sun went over the dunes, Calista came over to see how he was doing. He was still deep in thought, humming a tune to himself, and didn't notice her in the doorway until she moved and blocked the light.

He turned to look at her and smiled. She tucked her hands behind her and shrugged. "That looks like a lot of work." She said. "What are you doing, exactly?"

He waved a metal scraper at the wall. "Whoever did this used the wrong paint. It bubbled and flaked, so I'm scraping it off before I paint over it."

Calista nodded and looked at the walls. "I see." She said. "We had a fellow do the painting for us, years ago, but he did a terrible job. We didn't want him back."

Brandon wiped his forehead and nodded. "I don't blame you. He mixed different types of paints together, probably just some old junk he had lying around, and it was not very good."

A tap-tap-tap sound made Calista look behind her. Large raindrops, globs of water hitting the patio like popcorn in a pan, came down without warning. Brandon put down the scraper and ran to cover his motorcycle. He made sure the tarps over the furniture on the lawn were secure, then he went back into the cottage and put away his tools.

"Looks like a good afternoon to take a break." He smiled. "Want to go get a burger or something?"

Calista gave him a sheepish smile. "Yeah, let's go." She said.

They, asked Maisie if she wanted anything, then took Jerry's Pontiac out and headed down the driveway.

Calista hadn't been in the car before. She looked around, curious. "What is this thing?" She muttered.

"It's called a resto-mod. It looks like an old car on the outside, but it has a modern suspension, engine, air conditioning, stuff like that. How is it?"

Calista ran her hand over the seat, admiring the fabric. "Very nice. Is this what our car will look like?"

"Do you want it to? I can ask him to do this to your car." Brandon offered.

She shook her head. "I'm just happy that he wants to fix it for us, that's all."

Brandon turned onto the highway and stepped on the gas. The acceleration pinned Calista against the seat, and she gasped at the sensation. Brandon smiled at her reaction.

"You're not used to being in a performance car, then?" He chuckled.

Calista shrugged. "Our car was never very quick to begin with, but it's still nothing like this car."

"Jerry is a hot-rodder. He'd soup up a lawn mower if he got his hands on it."

They headed north towards Lincoln City, the windshield wipers slapping away the rain, the motor now a quiet purr as they drove.

Calista wrapped her hands around Brandon's free right arm, hugging him tight. He glanced over at her and smiled.

"So, do you have anything special you need to do this afternoon?" He asked.

"Not really. Is there anything special you have in mind?" She asked, suggestively.

He thought for a moment. "Yeah. Let's have some fun. The piece of land next to yours is for sale, isn't it? I saw the sign."

Calista nodded. "The Parsoner lot. They've been trying to sell it for a while, but they've had no takers."

"Any idea what they want for it?" He asked.

"Sixty-five thousand, I hear, but they'll take a lot less. Freda and Barry want to help their son buy a house. I do their farm's books, and I know they're not doing so well. They're a little better off than us, but not much."

"Let's kill two birds with one stone." Brandon grinned. "It'll be fun."

They rolled to a stop outside the diner in Lincoln City, the engine rumbling as it slowed to idle, then cackling and ticking after Brandon turned off the ignition. Brandon turned to face Calista just outside the door to the diner, and spoke very softly.

"Whatever you do, just let me do the talking, and for heaven's sake, don't laugh."

Calista frowned, puzzled. Brandon went into the diner, Calista following him to the counter. She sat beside him, looking over at him to see what he was up to, but he seemed to be ignoring her. The waitress, Jan, came out from the kitchen, the swinging door still flapping long after she was up front. She grinned at Brandon and leaned her elbows on the counter, almost nose-to-nose with him.

"Hey, hon, what can I get you?" She purred.

Calista felt a flash of jealousy, but said nothing.

Brandon smiled at Jan, reached slowly out and caressed Jan's forearm with his finger. "Well, hello to you too. I think we'll just have a couple of burgers and coffee. That ok with you, Miss Blake?"

Calista grunted something. Brandon's eyes never left Jan. "Yeah, sounds great, Jan. take your time. I plan to stay in town all afternoon, anyhow." He said.

Jan grinned like a schoolgirl, glanced at Calista, then frowned, slightly embarrassed. "Coming right up." She said. She disappeared into the kitchen.

Calista scowled at Brandon. "What was all that about?" She hissed.

He leaned her way, ever so slightly. "Ever go fishing? I was baiting the hook." He whispered.

Jan reappeared with two coffees, and set them down. "Careful, they're hot." She warned.

Brandon ogled her. "I'll say." He joked. Jan giggled and went back into the kitchen.

Calista leaned close again. "Now I KNOW you're up to something." She whispered. "What gives?"

Jan came back out with two burgers on oval plates, and set them down. Calista started eating hers, silently. Jan leaned back provocatively, her legs straight out in front of her, her arms tucked behind her, resting on the back counter. She watched Brandon the way a hungry man watches a steak. Eventually, she straightened up. "Everything OK?" She asked.

Brandon nodded. "Really good. Thanks, Jan. I sure needed this meal, to keep me going for later."

Jan frowned. "Yeah? What's going on later?"

"I promised to look into some land for sale. There's a complex that might be built, out near here."

Jan sat up straight and glanced nervously over at Calista. "Yeah? Where?" She said quickly.

Brandon shrugged. "Oh, no, nothing, just forget it. It's not important."

He went back to eating. Jan nervously brushed her apron and straightened already straight plates on the rack behind her. She touched her hair, absentmindedly, and looked around for something to do. She was clearly worried about what Brandon had said. When she was at the far end of the counter, looking at something, Brandon leaned close to Calista and mumbled "You need the restroom."

Calista smirked and got up. She went around the corner of the counter to a side door, and into the restroom. Brandon watched her go, then waved Jan close.

"Listen," He whispered. "I have this friend who's coming to town. He looks like a biker, but he's really this eccentric guy, a multimillionaire my parents know. I want to take him by that property beside Miss Blake's. Do you know it?"

She nodded, stunned. "Sure, the Parsoner place. Why?"

"Right. That one. I saw the 'for sale' sign on the fence. Any idea what they want for it?"

Jan shook her head.

Brandon shrugged. "Anyway, he has a couple hundred thousand to play with this month, and if the complex does get built, he figures he'll triple his money."

Jan's eyes widened. Her mouth opened and closed silently, like a goldfish. "Yeah?" She said, softly.

Brandon nodded. "Yep. Anyhow, once he comes into town, I'll book him into the hotel here. Would it be all right if he spoke to Glen? I have no idea what prices are like here, so can Glen help him out?"

Jan nodded, slowly. Something clicked for her, and her eyes widened. "Complex?" She asked. "What kind of complex?"

He shrugged. "It's just a rumor I heard, but it's probably nothing. Forget that I even mentioned it."

Jan patted the sides of her head and looked off toward the street, thinking.

Calista came back and sat beside Brandon, and he sat up quickly, as though he was guilty of something.

"Anyway, Jan, as I was saying, Balboa Street has some really great vintage clothing places. You should check it out if you're in San Francisco."

Jan muttered something and went into the kitchen. Brandon smirked to himself, enjoying a private joke. They finished their meal, Brandon left a generous tip, winked at Jan, and ushered Calista back to the car. The engine roared to life, and he made a smooth U-turn, headed back toward the Ocean Dunes. Calista waited till they were out of Lincoln City, almost as though someone might overhear her, and turned to look at him.

"So, what was all that about?" She asked.

"I told Jan that a friend of mine has a lot of money to invest, and that POSSIBLY there is a building complex being planned near your neighbor's property."

"I don't get it. How would that benefit you?" She asked.

He smirked. "It wouldn't. But I'm going to have some fun, at Glen's expense."

The rain stopped, and the sun came out with a vengeance, scorching the highway dry in minutes, leaving only small pockets of fog here and there in the shadows, where the sun did not reach.

They drove past Calista's and turned in at the next driveway. It was a wooded property, with scraggly trees lining a grassy drive, leading to a small farmhouse off to one side. A pair of goats, held behind a wire fence, eyed Calista with curiosity, and a scattering of chickens ran across the road in front of the car, scurrying for safety.

Calista got out and waited for Brandon to join her. The door to the farmhouse opened, and a woman came out onto the porch. She was pale, about the same age as Maisie, but with a haggard look and disheveled hair. She wiped her hands dry on her apron, then brushed her hips casually as she walked down to meet Calista.

"Hello, Cali." The woman said. "I'm afraid I've never met you, though, sir?" She looked at Brandon.

Calista waved. "Freda Parsoner, Brandon Cooper. Brandon is helping us get the hotel ready for the summer."

Brandon reached forward and shook the woman's hand. "Hi, Freda. Lovely to meet you." He said.

The woman nodded behind her at the house. "Would you like to come in? I can make coffee, or tea?"

Brandon shook his head. "Sorry, I'd like to get back to working on the cottage. However, I have some information for you, in case you hear from your local real estate people."

The woman cocked her head to one side. "Go on." She said.

Brandon nodded at Calista. "Calista wants to offer you eighty thousand dollars for your property."

Calista's eyes widened at this. Brandon continued. "And I'm going to offer you eighty-five thousand. But you're not going to take either offer, right now."

The woman looked back and forth from Brandon to Calista and back. "Why aren't I?" She asked.

Brandon nodded. "You're still thinking about it. And you're going to get a visit from Glen, the tractor salesman. He's going to offer you a lower price for your land. When he does, tell him in all honesty that you've already received two offers, one of them for eighty-five thousand. When he asks who offered that, tell him that the offer was from a stranger, some man you've never met before. That's the truth, by the way, isn't it?"

Understanding spread across the woman's face. She grinned broadly. "What do I do if he offers me more?" She asked.
Brandon nodded. "Take it. But don't appear too anxious. Make him wait an hour or so, then get him to sign right away. Have him agree to pay you in cash then and there, as part of the deal."

The woman grinned again. "Do you do this for a living, mister Cooper?"

Brandon chuckled. "No, this is just for fun, but let us know how it goes, all right?"

She shook hands with him again and went inside. Brandon drove Calista home and handed her the car keys.

"There you go. I'm going to finish the painting." He said. He turned and walked back to the cottage.

Calista called to him. "Hey." She said. He turned to look at her.

"You can be really devious without half trying, you know?" She smirked.

He chuckled and went back to work.

That evening, he ate with Calista and Maisie, then sat with them after dinner and talked about his family. It occurred to Calista that he'd never really spoken about them before; he had brushed off any details when she had asked him about it, and he would only say that his family lived in San Francisco, and his mother worked in New York, for a charity.

This night, though, he told Maisie that the charity was one his mother had set up, that her family was even more prosperous than his father's, and that his parents had lived separate lives since he was a child. He had grown up with all the material things in life, but he had been lonely, too. He had learned that he could flatter, cajole and plead for what he wanted, but that life had been most fulfilling for him when he was in the army, part of a squad of soldiers, all equals.

Calista had never seen him so introspective. He seemed to be opening his heart to these two women, near strangers, really, telling them all his inner thoughts, his feelings of desperation and sadness.

Later, after coffee, he leaned back, rubbed his face, and smiled warmly at them.

"Thank you for a lovely meal and an enjoyable evening." He smiled. "I don't want to keep you up late. Good night, ladies."

He got up and walked casually back to his cottage. Calista got up and turned to Maisie. "I'm going to walk him over. He seems very sad." She said softly.

Brandon stopped on the lawn, halfway to the cottage, gazing up at the sky. There were a few cotton-white clouds in the west, their edges highlighted by the half moon, with bright stars peppering the sky around them. Brandon gazed up at them, his hands in his pockets. Calista walked up to him, and he glanced casually over at her then back up.

"Do you ever get tired of seeing this view?" He asked, softly.

"I don't often look up." She answered truthfully. "What is it about the sky here that fascinates you?"

He shrugged. "It's safe. It's comforting." He smiled at her. "Good night, Miss Blake." He walked to his cottage.

Calista helped her mother clean up, then Maisie climbed into her new bed and opened a book. She wiggled her shoulders to get comfortable, sighed at the luxurious bedding, and started to read. Ninety seconds later, she was fast asleep.

Calista was lying on top of her sheets, staring out at the night sky. Through the trees, barely visible between the branches, she saw the light from a tugboat, dragging a flat barge up the coast toward the Columbia River, a hundred miles north. The sound of the tugboat's engine, a steady 'putt-thump-putt-thump' as it struggled through the waves, echoed over the water and reverberated off the sand dunes.

Soon, Calista heard something else, a soft wailing that didn't seem to come from the tugboat. The sound got slightly louder, or she was listening harder, she couldn't tell. She soon recognized it as a harmonica.

Calista picked her way along the sandy path to the dunes, following the glow of a familiar campfire to where Brandon was sitting. He held a glass of wine in one hand, sipping it casually and playing a tune with the harmonica in his other hand. He glanced up at Calista as she came close.

"Hello, nice to see you." He whispered. "Will your mom be joining us?"

Calista glanced over her shoulder. "No. she's out cold. Those beds are *very* comfortable, by the way."

He grinned and put his wine down. "I thought you both might be coming. I brought out extra glasses." He reached behind him and picked up a glass, then held it out for Calista. He poured wine for her from a slim clear bottle and held his glass up high. "To life." He toasted.

Calista repeated it and took a sip. She wrinkled her brow. "Oh, gosh. This is amazing." She took another sip.

"Thank your friend for this wine, next time you see him. This is spectacular."

Brandon nodded. "Shall do. I'm glad you like it." He looked down at the sand, a distant, faraway look in his eyes.

She rolled the glass between her palms and leaned forward, watching him. "Is something wrong?" She asked.

He shook his head. "I just need to figure out where I'm going, that's all."

"You mean, after this summer?" Calista asked hopefully.

"Right. After the summer." He said. He looked sadly over at her. "What if the summer ended sooner than we thought it would?" He asked.

Calista felt a cold chill run down her spine. "What do you mean?"

"What if I wasn't able to be here till the end of August? I might have to leave sooner than I wanted to."

Calista shook her head. "That's not fair. You said you were going to be here all summer. You promised."

He nodded. "I know. Some things have happened, though. Look, it's not certain, and in any case I will be here until all the work is done. That much I can say with certainty."

Calista rubbed her fingers through her hair, trying to find a way to say what she was thinking. He had left, he had come back, and now he was leaving again. She felt angry, frustrated, and very much abandoned, and she didn't know how to tell him just how much this would hurt her.

"You said you were going to be here until the end of August." She pleaded. "What changed? Was it us? Was it me? Was it something I said, or something I did?"

He shook his head slowly, picked up a piece of shell and casually tossed it over the fire to the sand beyond. "No, no, it's nothing like that. Believe me, if it was up to just me, I wouldn't leave."

"Can you tell me why you're leaving, then? Why?" She sighed.

He shook his head. "No, sorry, I can't. Not yet, anyway. When I can tell you, I hope you'll understand, that's all."

Calista took a sip of the wine, feeling the rush of cool liquid fill her mouth and warm her throat. She put the glass down beside her and hung her hands between her knees.

"So, when you leave next time, will it be for good, or what? Will we ever see you again?"

He chuckled, took a large swig of wine and put his glass down beside Calista's. "Yeah, that's the thing. I won't have any say in whether or not I come back."

Calista smiled softly, trying to lighten the mood. "You're going to prison, or what?" She asked.

He laughed out loud and leaned back, then stretched his feet forward so far he had to point them to one side of the fire.

"Not quite, but not far off." He smiled. He looked at his watch. "Look, it's getting late, and I don't want to keep you. Would you like me to walk you back?"

Calista shook her head. "No, thank you. I'm just going to sit here for a bit, if you don't mind."

He nodded and stood up. He picked up the bottle and handed it to her. "Would you like me to leave this?" He asked.

She nodded, silently. He placed the bottle beside her log, picked up his glass, and nodded. "Good night, Miss Blake." He said softly.

She looked up at him. The glow from the fire, dying and fluttering in the light breeze, made her wet eyes twinkle.

"Good night, Mister Cooper." She took a sip of wine and listened to his footsteps, getting softer as he walked away.

Late the next morning, Calista was in bed. Still in that wonderful bed. The new sheets were like butter, the mattress was a cloud, and the pillows were like nothing she had ever experienced before. She didn't want to get up. She opened her eyes a crack to see the clock beside her. It took a minute for her eyes to open wide. The room was very bright, the air was warm, and the smell of coffee and chicken from downstairs meant that her mother was making lunch. She managed to get one eye to focus on the clock. Ten thirty. Ten THIRTY?

Calista sat up with a start. She threw on a pair of jeans and a sweater, then rushed downstairs. With every step she took, her head felt like something was hitting her skull. The staircase was narrower, more uneven, than she remembered. She gripped the banister for dear life, gingerly walking down to join Maisie in the kitchen.

Maisie glanced at her and smirked. "Good morning, sleepy head. What has you so tired this morning?" She asked.

Calista shook her head. "Hi, mom. I was talking with Brandon out at the fire pit last night, and we drank some wine. He went to bed, and I stayed out there to finish the bottle. I did finish it, didn't I?" Calista looked around, as though the empty bottle might magically show up.

Maisie chuckled. "I don't know, dear. I never saw a bottle. Did you enjoy your talk with him?"

Calista shook her head. "No. He thinks he might have to leave before the end of summer, he says. He won't say why, though. Just that he wishes he didn't have to go."

Maisie gave her a sad, worried look. "Oh, my dear. I'm so sorry for you." She said. "You must be feeling terrible."

Calista nodded. "Yeah, well, he hasn't left yet. Maybe the situation will change, he said, whatever it is. We'll have to see."

Brandon thumped up the steps to the house, looked back and forth at the women, and grinned a satisfied grin. "Morning, Calista. Hey, can I show you ladies something?"

He led the women out to the third cottage and opened the door. The paint was fresh, glossy, with crisp edges to the trim and a sheen to the floor. It looked and smelled new.

"Well, what do you think?" He asked proudly.

Maisie placed her hand gently on the floor, then rubbed it with her fingertips, the smooth wood silky to her touch.

"My word. This is wonderful." Maisie said. She walked around the main room, her footsteps echoing slightly off the walls. She poked her head into the bathroom, noticing the new paint on the walls above the tiles, and sniffed at the fresh paint smell in the air.

"This is better than it was thirty years ago. I'm beyond impressed." She beamed.

Calista sat on the edge of the bed, patted the mattress softly, then fell backwards with her arms out. "This is nice. Really, really nice." She sighed. She sat up again.

Brandon grinned, pleased. "I'm glad you both like it. You already have some tentative bookings for later in the summer. I wanted to make sure you have a couple of cabins ready in case you get some drop-ins."

Maisie looked around some more, thanked him profusely, and reminded him that lunch was at noon. She went back into the main house, skipping cheerily.

Calista was still sitting on the bed. She looked around at the room, then her eyes fell on Brandon. He was looking back at her, expectantly.

"So?" He asked.

"It's very nice." She repeated.

"No, about last night." He prompted.

She looked down. "Ah. Yes." She squirmed slightly. "I had an awful lot of wine last night. Mind you, it was very good wine, but I drank far too much."

"You're avoiding the subject." He said firmly.

She looked at him with a sad, sorry look. "Why do you have to leave?" She asked. "Why do you have to go so soon?"

He shook his head. "I can't talk about it. Sorry." He sat on the bed beside her. "Look, if this means you need to keep your distance from me, I will understand. I just hope we can still be friends, alright?"

She sighed, thought for a moment and nodded. "You've done some amazing things that have helped us. It would be selfish for me to be angry at you for leaving. I understand that. But it still hurts."

He put his arm around her and pulled her close. She leaned her head on his shoulder and sighed. "It's not fair. You come into my life and then you leave again, just like that. It's not fair." She sighed again.

He looked down at her and smiled. "Really? Thank you. That means more to me than you can imagine."

"What?" She asked.

He shook his head. "I've never had anyone say that they missed me like that- not ever."

Calista leaned back. "Really? With all the things you do for people, all the help you give them?"

He nodded. "You'd think so, but I'm often viewed as just a resource, not a person."

Calista reached up and kissed him, softly. "I think of you as a wonderful man."

Brandon ate lunch with Calista and Maisie, then went back out and cleared out the fourth cottage, getting ready to work on it.

He spent the rest of that week removing old paint and fixing the wood, working more carefully than he had on the first three. Calista told herself that it was his way of staying there longer, by working slower.

Maisie went into town for groceries on the Saturday, driving Jerry's Pontiac for the first time. She fishtailed as she started off, unused to the power of the car, but then she settled down, and roared off down the road toward Lincoln City.

The day was warm, even for early June. Brandon was busy in the cottage. Calista could hear him out there, hammering nails and thumping wood. Maisie called to say she would be at a friend's playing cards for the afternoon, but would be home in time for dinner, she thought.

Calista hung up the phone and looked out at the cottage. She had an idea; she went out across the lawn and waited at the cottage door, watching Brandon banging the door trim into place. He stepped back, checked his work, and saw Calista standing there.

"Hey, how's it going?" He asked, casually.

"Fine." She answered. "Listen, do you want to take a break and do something fun?"

He grinned broadly. "Sure. What do you have in mind?"

"Do you have a bathing suit with you?" She asked. "I thought we could go for a swim."

He shook his head. "I didn't plan on it. I could swim in the nude. If you don't mind, I don't mind."

Calista nodded. "Right. Just in case we're not alone, however, I'll lend you one."

Calista went to the main house and put on her swimsuit, a white one-piece that she hadn't worn in almost seven years. The last time she had worn it, she and Ed had gone to Pistol River Park for a long weekend, camping out in a tent. They swam in the ocean and walked along the beach. She had enjoyed that weekend more than almost any other time in her life. It was tantalizingly close to the California border, but back then she had no reason to think about California.

Today, she would give almost anything for Brandon to not go back, to stay here with her, whether he had work left to do or not. Just being around him lit a spark in her that she thought was long gone.

She came back out wearing a short robe, carrying a pair of Ed's old trunks and two large beach towels. She handed the trunks to Brandon. "Here you go. These were Ed's." She smiled.

He grinned like a schoolboy and went into the bathroom to put them on.

Calista was amused at this. "Really? Why are you changing in there? I've seen you naked before." She called to him.

He came back wearing the trunks, smirking. "I don't want you saying that I was trying to tease you. Besides, a guy sometimes needs his privacy." He said, haughtily.

He looked down at the trunks. They were wide, floppy, with brightly colored splotches printed on them. Brandon had to pull the drawstring tight, to keep them from falling off.

Calista snickered and covered her mouth.

"What?" Brandon asked, holding his arms out. "Do I look stupid in these, or what?"

Calista frowned and shook her head. "No, they're very fashionable." She said. She giggled and covered her mouth again.

Brandon sniffed. "I look like a 'Beach Boys' groupie." He joked. "What the heck, let's go."

They made their way along the path, past the fire pit, then fifty yards further to the beach. Brandon commented that he had never come this far before; he looked around, admiring the landscape as he walked. From here he could see the roof of the main house over his shoulder, poking up beyond the rise of dunes. Along the wide flat area heading to the beach, the low grass waved in the soft breeze, undulating in long, slow ripples.

Once they got beyond the grass the path opened out to sand, broad and smooth, with waist-high waves rolling onto the beach, leaving a line of dried seaweed and bleached shells. Calista laid out her towel just above the water line, and ran into the surf, kicking her feet high as she went. She squealed with glee as the chilly water splashed over her, then took a deep breath and dunked under. She popped back up a moment later and gasped for breath.

Brandon watched her bounce, fascinated at seeing her play, and rushed into the surf beside her. He dove in, hands over his head, and stayed under for almost a minute, surfacing a distance beyond Calista. She had her hands on the surface of the water, looking around for him, then grinned broadly when she saw him swimming back toward her.

"You swim very well." She said, over the roar of the surf. "Where did you learn to do that?"

"Escaping Alcatraz." He joked. He waded back to shallower water and shook his hair dry. "Seriously, I swam for our college team. I still have a medal or two from back then, I think."

They splashed for a few minutes, rolling over in the waves, diving and spraying each other, just having fun.

He curled up in a ball and plopped back under the waves, then stood up straight and shook his hair again. He glanced over at the goosebumps on Calista's skin. "I see you're getting cold." He smirked.

She glanced at her arms. "Yes, let's get some sun and warm up."

They plodded back to their towels, and Calista flopped face down onto hers. Brandon sat up on his, watching her.

"It's a shame you don't get a chance to have a swim every day, isn't it?" He said.

She folded her arms under her chin and nodded. "Yes, it is. The sun's very warm today, huh?"

He looked out at the water. In the distance, the same tugboat that had pulled a barge north was now headed back down the coast, towing a small freighter. Closer in, a sailboat bobbed over the waves, its sail flapping as it pitched in the wind.

He spread out his towel beside Calista and lay down next to her, then rolled onto his side to face her. She lifted her head slightly and turned to look at him.

"What are you thinking?" She asked.

"Has anyone ever told you that you have terrific legs?" He said.

She grinned and stuck her face down into her towel. "Yes. And they've described the rest of my anatomy in various ways, too. I got kind of tired of it in high school." She chuckled.

"What about in university? Was it any better there?"

She shook her head and put her face down into the towel. "I never went. I could never afford it." She became very still.

Brandon paused for a long minute. "I'm sorry. I didn't know." He said.

She sighed and propped herself up on her elbows. "Anyway, my dad taught me a lot more while he was alive than I would have gotten from any regular school. I'll always be grateful for that."

Brandon ran his hand casually down from her shoulder blade, along her back, over her backside and down the back of her leg. She turned to look at him and smiled. "That feels nice." She said.

He smiled back. "Glad to hear it." He leaned forward and kissed her shoulder, then lifted her hair and kissed the back of her neck. He leaned forward to kiss the side of her neck. She turned to look at him, her mouth open. He put his hand under her chin, tilted it up and kissed her softly, savoring the way she tasted, of sea salt and strawberry lipstick.

She watched him pull slowly away after the kiss, both of them tingling with the feel and the taste of the other.

She smiled slightly. "What now, Mister Cooper?" She asked.

"I think I love you, Miss Blake." He said it simply, without smiling.

Calista sat up and stared at him. "What did you say?" She asked it in a soft voice, almost a whisper.

"I said I love you." He repeated.

She got up and collected her towel. She stormed off toward the hotel, not looking back. Brandon was puzzled, completely confused. He grabbed his towel and ran after her, calling her name.

"Calista, Cali, wait, wait for me. Calista, please wait." He called.

Out on this beach, his voice didn't echo or carry- it just seemed to vanish in the breeze. Calista never looked back. She kept walking to the house, marched up the steps and in through the front door. He stopped at the base of the steps and waited, to see if she turned to look at him. She didn't- she just kept going into the house. He paused for a moment then followed her in. She was stomping up the stairs, so he quickened his step to catch up with her.

She was almost at her room when he caught her. He put his hand on her shoulder, and she spun around to face him. She slapped at him, hitting his hand, and glared at him.

"Don't you DARE." She spat. "Don't you even DARE say that to me. Do you hear? Never. Ever."

"Why? It's true." He said, softly.

She clenched her fists and pressed them against her temples. "Stop, stop. Don't talk to me. Why would you tell me something like that? Don't you realize what it would do for me to think that it was true, and then have you leave me?" She moaned.

She paced back and forth at the door to her room, not wanting to go in. Somehow, in her mind, going in with him there would have meant admitting that she loved him too.

She looked at the floor for a minute, thinking, then glared at him. "Look, you've done some very nice things for us, and for me, but god knows where you're going or what you're going to do after you leave. I can't control that. What I can do is to keep a distance from you, no matter what I feel about you. I need to have a part of me that isn't swallowed up by you, do you understand?"

He nodded. "Yes, I do understand. I'm sorry for what I said. Just for the record, though, I still mean it."

Calista stood there, dripping seawater on the floor, her towel over her shoulder. She glared at him. "You aren't just saying that out of pity for me? You aren't just telling me you love me to get me back into bed?"

He leaned back against the wall, his trunks soaking the floral wallpaper. "I said it because it's true. I have wanted to say it for a long time, but I didn't want to say it out loud; I wasn't sure how you'd take it. I'm sorry it came out the way it did." He said. He turned to leave.

Calista thought about that for a second. "So, why didn't you want to tell me? Because you didn't want to hurt my feelings? Or because you had no intention of being stuck with some country bumpkin for the rest of your life?"

He turned back and stood nose to nose with her. He spoke slowly, deliberately. "I had no wish to make you a widow again. I'll bring the trunks back at dinner." He walked out to his cottage.

Calista fell onto her bed and cried. She spread her arms out and hugged her pillow, the marvelous pillow that Brandon's friend had delivered. She didn't know what he meant by that statement, whether he was trying to spare her pain, or if he knew some terrible truth. Did it have to do with his heart operation? Calista sat up. She had overreacted, she decided. She would go out there and tell him she was sorry for saying what she said. At the very least, she told herself, she could convince him to not disappear in the night again. Maybe he would even stay until the end of the summer.

She changed out of the swimsuit, had a shower, then dressed. She took a pitcher of lemonade from the fridge and brought it, along with two glasses, out to the cottage where Brandon was working.

He was wearing his jeans again, and he was hunched over, scraping old paint off some blistered floorboards. Calista stood at the door and knocked. He glanced up and nodded, then went back to scraping paint.

"Hi. I thought you might like something cool to drink." She said.

"Sure. Thanks." He said, curtly.

"Do you want me to pour you a glass? Or just leave it here?" She asked.

"Leave it." He said.

"Do you want to talk?" Calista said. "I'm sorry, I realize I was kind of sharp with you there." She waited for his answer.

He stood up straight and dropped the spatula on the floor. He looked at her, thinking, and sighed. "My fault, entirely. I apologize for causing you distress." He said, formally.

Calista could see that he was locking himself away, shutting himself off, out of her reach. She shrugged, apologetically.

"So, do you want to talk, then?" She asked.

His eyes never left hers. "No."

"Do you want to explain what you said to me upstairs?" She continued.

He looked down for a moment, thinking. "No."

She smiled sadly. "Can you just stop for a moment and have lemonade with me?" She said it in a pleading tone.

He shook his head. "I'm not thirsty after all." He picked up the spatula and went back to scraping paint.

Calista felt devastated. In an hour, she had managed to destroy any feeling he had for her. He hated her now, she thought. And it was all her fault. She leaned back against the wall, slid down and hunched over her knees in a ball on the floor. She started to cry, slowly at first, then weeping, bawling, sobbing into her knees.

Brandon stopped what he was doing and groaned. He put down the spatula and stood over her.

"Snap out of it!" He barked. She had never heard him raise his voice before. She looked up, shocked.

He glared at her. "Get over it, Calista! You've just told me to get over you, then you get over me! Come on- do it!"

She wiped her nose with the back of her hand, looking out at the lawn. "Why are you being so mean to me?" She sniffed.

"Mean? I'm only being honest." He said. "You said you don't want me in your life, so I'm putting you out of mine. I'm just here to do work for you, that's all. I'm nothing more than that, remember? I'm just your paid handyman for the summer."

She looked up into his eyes. They were red, wet, rimmed with tears. The sadness in his face was painful to see. She stood up and wrapped her arms around his neck, but he pulled them away, slowly. "No, don't do that." He whispered.

She shook her head and reached her hands around his neck again. He put his hands over hers, as if to pull them away again, then pressed her hands tighter to his skin. She kissed him, gently, softly. She pulled back for a moment and kissed him again, longer this time, more passionately.

He gazed at her for a second, then wrapped his hands around her and pulled her close. They kissed, his hands running up and down her spine, feeling every bone, then he carried her across to the cottage where he was staying. She pulled him close, tugging at his shoulders, wrapping her hands around the muscles in his arms. They tore their clothes off and made love, forcefully, quickly, a carnal act, as though the world was about to end. She caressed his chest, his arms, his waist, as they made love, feeling him tingle with excitement at her touch. He moved like a large cat, smooth, driven, focused.

Afterward, he lay back on the bed, his arms on his forehead, catching his breath. Calista was draped over his chest, her fingers running through his hair, both of them covered in sweat.

"Wow." He said. "Maybe we should fight more often."

Calista smiled and looked down at him. "Maybe. What did you mean before?" She asked, serious.

"When?" He asked.

"You said something about making me a widow again. What did you mean?"

He looked up at the ceiling and sighed. "I felt we were getting very serious. I still do. I guess I was wondering where we were going, but I also have to keep in mind what the future holds, that's all."

"I don't understand." Calista said.

He sat up. "I went home to pick up some fresh clothes and check my mail. There was a letter waiting for me- I can't tell you what it said, but I can tell you that it said that I have to go away."

"Where?" She asked.

He wrinkled his nose. "A faraway land with an exotic name. Let's just say it's a country whose name ends in 'stan'."

He shrugged. "I told you I *was* in the army. Apparently, I'm *still* in the army. I thought I was out for good, but they called me back in."

Calista wrapped her arms around his waist. "They can't do that, can they? You can quit, or resign, or whatever, right?"

"They can, they did, I can't." He shrugged. "It's not so bad, really. Look, I'll be gone for eighteen months, but then I'll be retired, and out of the army permanently. Do you think you could wait that long for me?"

"What happens to us then?" Calista asked. "What happens to us in eighteen months?"

"I could move in here- I'm sure they'd hire me at that new casino at Porter Point. Or we could live in California- you'd like it there. It's just that there is an element of peril to what I'm doing and where I'm going, and I can't do it safely if I'm always thinking about you, living here, thinking about me. It would put me in even more danger to do that."

Calista brought her knees up to her chin and hugged her legs. "Are you a spy or something, then?" She asked, serious.

He laughed and shook his head. "Nothing so glamorous, no. But I still can't talk about it, in any case. I tell you what, after I get back, how would you like me to take you and your mom down to our place in Mexico for a break? What do you say- we'll sit by the pool, drink margaritas? It'll be fun."

Calista shook her head sadly. "Who'd watch the hotel? We don't have any staff, or helpers, or whatever. We only have each other." He stared at her for a moment then smirked. "I guess I'll have to stay here and rent a cottage from you, then."

Chapter Ten

Calista spent the afternoon sitting on the cottage porch, talking to him. She was in an old deck chair, stretched out at the doorway, while Brandon finished scraping paint from the walls and baseboards. Every so often, she'd catch him glancing over at her. Sometimes, he'd just go back to scraping paint. Other times, he'd grin at her, then he'd walk over and kiss her. By the time Maisie came back, the sun was low over the beach, and Calista had turned on the porch lights, bathing the main house in a yellow glow.

As the sun touched the horizon, Brandon said he'd change into clean clothes for dinner. Calista went out to his cottage and knocked on the door jamb. "Hi, mom's got food on the table." She called.

"In here." His voice said.

Calista went into the cottage, gingerly. "Everything OK?" She asked.

"It's fine. Come in here." He said again. Calista followed the voice to the bathroom. Brandon's hand grabbed her arm and pulled her around the corner, behind the door. She spun around, surprised by the action.

His arms were suddenly around her, pulling her close, and his face was right in front of hers. He kissed her, passionately.

She grinned and looked up at him. "What was that for?" She asked.

"That's for earlier. And for talking to me. It meant a lot. Thank you." He added.

They walked back to the house together, holding hands, smiling at each other. Maisie set out plates, then placed bowls of soup and trays of bread on the table. They started eating, passing food back and forth.

Brandon buttered some bread and took a bite, looking down as he ate. Calista thought she knew what he was thinking, what he wanted to say. He turned to Maisie and smiled.

"So, how was your day?" He asked.

"It was lovely, thanks. Your friend's car is certainly a handful. I can't imagine what he's doing to our old station wagon."

"Something similar, I suspect." Brandon smiled. He put his bread down, rested both wrists on the table and looked over at Calista. "Mrs. Blake, I need to say something." He said, firmly.

Maisie picked up the butter knife to butter a slice of bread. "Yes, dear?" She said casually.

Calista was staring at him, a look of apprehension and anticipation in her face. Brandon took a deep breath.

"Mrs. Blake, I am very much in love with your daughter." He said.

Maisie put down the knife and took a bite of bread. "Well, of course you are, dear. I knew that."

Brandon glanced at Calista and leaned toward Maisie. "You did?" He asked, puzzled.

Calista reached over, without thinking, and placed her hand on Brandon's. She kissed him softly on the cheek.

Maisie looked at him, a pleasant look, a warm look, but with a fierce determination behind it. "I'm old, but I'm not stupid. I could tell from the first day you showed up here that there was a spark between you two. I bet I noticed it before either of you did. Would you like more soup?"

Brandon grinned broadly. "Yes, thanks."

After dinner, Calista suggested sitting on the porch steps to have their coffee. Brandon sat beside her, no longer feeling the need to keep a distance, his hip pressing against hers. He talked more about his family; his mother's charity was funded by her family, and running it kept her on the East Coast most of the time. His father had long since found another wife, a younger woman who liked dinner parties and public events. Brandon said that his father had no illusions about why she had married him, and she had made no secret of the fact that she preferred the company of younger men.

Calista asked something which had been on her mind for a long time, but which she'd been reluctant to bring up. She took a deep breath. "Do you have any brothers and sisters?" She asked, tentatively.

He took a sip of coffee and hunched forward. "Not anymore." He said.

Calista digested this statement. "Oh, I'm sorry. Would you rather not talk about it?"

He shrugged. "My brother's passion was fast airplanes, to the point that he entered the Reno Air Races a few times. Some years ago, his plane crashed in a race. It was all over in a second, and he didn't feel anything, I don't think. Anyway, he died doing what he loved. What more can you ask from life?"

Calista leaned against his shoulder. "I'm sorry. Were you two close?"

Brandon smirked. "I was a fair bit younger than him, and sometimes I would steal his motorcycle. He pretended to get angry, but deep down I think he enjoyed knowing that I was a rebel, like him." He snickered. "Anyway, it's why I ride a bike now."

Maisie came out and sat beside Calista. She pulled her knees up and wrapped her arms around her legs, the way Calista did, then she looked up and took a deep breath. "It's a lovely evening out. Not too warm, not too windy, and the stars are very clear. Why don't you two go for a walk? The beach should be perfect for an evening stroll, don't you think?"

Brandon stood up. "That's a lovely idea, Maisie. Miss Calista, would you care to go for a walk?"

He held out his hand. Calista took it and let him pull her up. For a moment, she fell forward, almost crashing into him, just like she had at the fire pit. She turned to look at her mother. "Mom, do you want to come with us?" She asked.

Maisie shook her head. "No, you two go ahead. I promised to telephone a friend."

Calista led Brandon out along the path, past the fire pit and through the grass, out to where the low flat beach eased gently into the ocean. Down by the water, the air was cool; a soft mist of salt air hung low at the shore and muffled the sound of waves. The moon was only three-quarters full now, but it was big and clear, and the sea was almost glassy smooth. Moonlight reflected off the water, lighting up Calista's face. Brandon looked over at her, smiling.

Calista tugged his hand and smiled back. "What?" She asked.

He swung her arm playfully back and forth in his. "I can't tell you how nervous I was, telling your mother how I feel about you." He said.

"Do you really find her that intimidating?" Calista asked.

He chuckled. "Underneath that 'Dear Abby' exterior, I suspect she's very protective. She has certainly always done her best to help you, hasn't she?"

Calista bumped her shoulder against his. "Yes, she has."

They walked along the beach, talking about everything, about nothing, about life. They walked a long way before they turned around. Out to sea, a searchlight swung around, illuminating them for a moment, then swung away again. The boat attached to the light sounded its horn and turned north, churning water as it headed for Washington state.

Brandon stopped and looked straight up. Out here, the Milky Way was clear, bright, with innumerable stars filling the sky. Brandon pointed to a white dot, moving toward them from the east. "Another commuter flight?" He asked.

Calista looked up. "No, that one really is a shooting star." She smiled. "Make a wish."

He looked down at her. "Too late. I have everything I could wish for."

They took off their shoes and splashed in the shallows, then slowly, reluctantly, they headed back to the main house, still holding hands. Brandon walked Calista to the base of the steps and kissed her cheek. She wrapped her arms around his neck and pulled him close, then kissed him, firmly. She unwrapped her hands from his neck and stood back, smiling.

He grinned and backed away from her, toward his cottage, still looking at her. "Goodnight, Miss Blake." He said softly.

"Sleep well, Mister Cooper." She answered.

Calista went up to her room, slid under the luxurious sheets, and leaned over to see out the window. The light in his cottage went out; the yard was now illuminated by the soft yellow glow from the porch light, and a pale grey light from the moon reflecting off the driveway.

Calista leaned back, thinking. Brandon had told both Calista and her mother that he loved Calista, and he had been honest about why he couldn't stay after the summer. Calista's mind raced- what would she do while he was gone? Would he come back to her, after eighteen months? Was this trip real, or was it his way of leaving her as gently as possible, without hurting her feelings? If he did come back, what then? Would he be happy living in a small town in the middle of Oregon, after his glamorous life in San Francisco? Calista sighed. Too many questions, too few answers. She was too tired to think about that now; she fell asleep.

The morning was warm, bright, one of those glorious early summer days that drenched the yard in sunshine, with a soft puff of wind coming off the beach, gusting to a light breeze every so often, bringing in the faint aroma of sand and salt. Calista came down the stairs, fairly skipping, and looked around, expectantly. She couldn't see Brandon.

Her mother came in from outside and smiled. "Good morning, dear, sleep well?" Maisie asked.

"Very well, mom. Where's Brandon?" She looked over toward his cottage, feeling a slight panic at not seeing him.

"He had to run off to Lincoln for an errand. He asked me to bake up some muffins- apparently that friend of his will be here before lunch with our station wagon."

Calista was still anxious; Brandon had left once before, and a part of her still wondered if he would disappear again without telling her. She busied about, doing laundry, sweeping the porches on the two renovated cottages, listening with one ear for the sound of a motorcycle engine. By noon, she thought sadly, she realized he would not be coming back at all.

A little after one, the sound of crunching gravel made her come out of the house and look to see who was coming. Halfway down the driveway, their Pontiac wagon came toward her, silently. She went down to the base of the steps, held her hand over her eyes to shield the glare, and watched the car roll up to a stop beside her. Calista waved at the driver, the slim man with the tattoos, and turned to call out to her mother, in the house.

Maisie came down the steps and joined Calista, and they walked up to their old car. The man got out and smiled. "Hey, ladies, how's it going?" He said. He patted the roof. "She look OK to you?"

Maisie touched the front fender. "Hello, Jerry. The paint looks new. What did you do to it?" She asked, incredulous.

The man grinned. "We just touched it up. It didn't need much cosmetic work, so we concentrated on the mechanical stuff. Runs real good now, smooth and quiet. What do you think?"

Maisie opened the driver's door and peered in. "You replaced all the seats?" She asked, puzzled.

Jerry shrugged. "Yeah, the interior was kinda toast, so we reupholstered it. Hope it looks OK."

Maisie shook her head. "This is unbelievable. I can't thank you enough."

She sat in the driver's seat, caressing the steering wheel, and shook her head. "This is unbelievable." She repeated.

Jerry grinned. "So, does that earn me any more muffins, ma'am? The guys in the shop were just asking, you know."

Maisie muttered something, rushed up the steps and into the kitchen. She emerged a minute later with two huge baskets of muffins. The man's eyes lit up. "Hey, wow, thank you. I mean, we're all real fans of these, you know?"

Maisie waved her hands in front of her. "No, not at all. Listen, if you're ever driving by here, let me know and I'll bake you some more."

He grinned. "You got a deal. And I wanted to ask about renting one of your cabins later in the year. We plan to get away, me and my wife, and we wanted to go somewhere nice, you know?"

Maisie nodded. She was getting used to people actually wanting to stay at the hotel, now. "Certainly. I'll get you a card. We'll certainly let you have a cottage- for free." She went up into the house again.

Calista smiled at the man. "Do you have any idea where Brandon went?" She asked, hopefully.

Jerry snickered. "Yep. He's pranking some guy in Lincoln City. He told me he should be right…" at that, Calista heard the 'thump-thump-thump' of Brandon's motorcycle. Her heart raced, and she looked to the end of her driveway. Brandon was rolling toward her, but there was a woman in his sidecar. Calista felt a surge of anger and jealousy. As the motorcycle got closer, she recognized her neighbor, Freda Parsoner. Maisie came out of the house again, holding a business card.

Freda waited patiently for Brandon to help her out of the seat, then he pulled off his helmet and grinned at Calista.

"Hi, how is the car?" He asked, casually.

Maisie waved her arms. "It's remarkable. I can't thank you and Jerry enough. You're both wonderful." She gushed.

She handed the card to Jerry. "Whenever you want, I'll make sure we have room for you." She smiled.

The man shook her hand, playfully bumped his shoulder against Brandon's, then muttered something and drove away in his own car. Brandon and the three women silently watched him roll gently down the driveway, then as soon as he was on the highway the engine roared and he disappeared in a cloud of smoke.

"What was that about?" Calista asked.

"You mean the burning rubber?" Brandon said. "He's a hot-rodder, he likes to smoke the tires when he can."

"No, what he said to you." She said.

Brandon thought for a moment. "Ah. I said 'You go, Devil Dog', and he said 'Oo-rah'. Jerry is a Marine."

Maisie and Freda Parsoner were talking off to one side, whispering and laughing. "Where were you?" Calista asked.

Freda nodded at Brandon. "We just sold that land of ours. Two days ago, Glen offered me a measly forty thousand for it, like you said he would, so I told him that a man from California had offered us eighty-five. Today, Brandon and his friend Jerry went to meet Glen, asking about real estate in the area. Then after they left Glen drove to my place and offered me ninety thousand on the spot. I made him wait for fifteen minutes while I thought about it, just like you said I should, and then I agreed to sell it, but only for cash. We deposited the money this morning. I can't thank you enough, Brandon. This means the world to us." She giggled.

She skipped briskly down the driveway, cut through a low spot in the fence and crossed a field to her house. Brandon grinned at her, then he turned to look at Maisie. "So, how did he do on your Pontiac?" He asked.

Maisie looked down and realized she had the station wagon's keys in her hand. Brandon pointed to them. "Why don't you take it for a spin? I could use some lunch, by the way. What do we have in the house, Calista?"

Maisie covered her mouth with her hand. "We're out of most things. I should go get groceries. Do you want to come with me, Cali?"

Calista shook her head. "I want to stay here and talk with Brandon. I'll see you when you get back."

Maisie ran up the steps of the house, came back out with her purse and slid behind the wheel. She rolled down the window, started the engine, and glared at the dashboard; usually, the car shook side-to-side when she started it up, but now it ran smooth, quiet. She beamed and turned to Calista. "See you in an hour." She called.

She accelerated down the driveway, the car fishtailing before she realized it had far more power than before, then rolled onto the highway and headed for Lincoln City. Calista watched it go, then turned to look at Brandon.

She smacked his arm, hard. "Why didn't you tell me you were going away again? Why didn't you tell me last night, huh?" She snapped.

Brandon wrapped his arm around her waist. "Jerry called here early this morning, to tell me he was coming. You were still asleep when your mother answered the phone. Sorry, I thought she'd tell you when you woke up."

Calista pouted. "She did, but I still worried that you might not come back."

He grinned. "Do you really think I'd ever do that again, after I told your mother how I feel about you?"

Calista stared at him, puzzled. He was thinking something, she knew, she just wasn't sure exactly what. He pulled her close then he gave her a long, slow kiss.

"I'm very glad to see you." He said softly. "I missed you. Look, we've got some good weather for now. I should fix the leaky roof on this cottage, before it rains again."

Calista rubbed his arm, feeling a shiver as his hand caressed her hip. "Mind if I watch you work?" She asked.

She sat on the porch, watching as he pulled wood from under the roof overhang- fascia boards, he called them, and poked a flashlight up into the gap, looking for something. He squinted and contorted his face, bending his neck to look at corners and up high in the rafters. After a few minutes, Calista wandered up behind him, peering in with him.

"What do you see?" She asked.

He pointed up into the gap and said "Look in there."

Calista tilted her head to peek up where he was pointing. There was a square of light, shining down through the roof and onto the ceiling of the cottage. Where the light fell, a shallow puddle reflected the underside of the roof. Brandon leaned closer to Calista, pointed at a wooden rafter and explained that he needed to get rid of that pooled water, then stop rain from getting in again. His face was against hers, and her cheek brushed his as he spoke. Calista turned to face him, held his chin in her hands, and kissed him passionately.

He stood there, dumbfounded, then smiled broadly. "As I was saying, I need to fix this roof. I'm going to lift some shingles and patch this one, then I'll check the other cottages and see if they need fixing, too."

Calista had a thought. "Will that take very long to do?" She asked hopefully.

He knew exactly what she was asking. "It could add a week or so to the job, yes."

She grinned and sat back down. He continued working, peeling away wood from other areas, opening up the rafters to let the trapped water evaporate. He worked quickly, with an occasional grunt when he pulled away stuck pieces of wood, otherwise saying little. Calista walked into the cottage, admiring the work he had done on the walls and floors, breathing in the smell of paint and varnish, realizing that it meant that they might very well survive another year after all.

She heard the sound of gravel crunching, and went out to the yard to investigate. Her mother was back, and opened the passenger door of the station wagon to drag out some groceries. Calista went out to help her.

"So, how does our car drive now?" Calista asked.

"It's like new." Her mother smiled. "No, wait, it was never this smooth even when it was new. I don't know what that man did, but he can stay here for free, whenever he wants. He more than earned it."

Calista leaned into the car and grabbed a paper grocery bag. "Should I help you with lunch?" She asked.

"Yes, thanks, dear. What's Brandon doing?"

"He found some water damage in the ceiling of number three. He may take longer than he expected to finish the work."

Maisie grinned. "What a shame." She said.

A while later, Maisie went out to where Brandon was working. He was busily doing something on the roof, so she waited till he'd stopped scraping with a crowbar before she spoke. "Hello, Mister Cooper?" She called.

He looked down. "Hi there." He said.

"Lunch is ready. Would you like to stop and eat?" She asked.

He glanced at the roof. "Yeah, sure, I'll be right there."

Maisie and Calista set the table, laid out soup and sandwiches, and arranged the chairs around the table. By the time they were ready to eat, Brandon came in, wearing a clean shirt, his hair combed.

He thanked Maisie for lunch and sat down. The three ate, chatting about the work he was doing, what he'd found in the roof, what still needed to be done.

Maisie placed a hand on his. She gushed about how well her car was running, and how grateful she was for that. Brandon seemed slightly embarrassed by the attention, but smiled politely.

After Maisie had taken away the plates, she brought out dessert and coffee. Brandon took a large forkful of pie, mumbled appreciation, then looked at the two women and cleared his throat.

"Um, I wanted to ask you something." He began.

Maisie shrugged approval. He nodded.

"You might get more business if your sign was bigger, and out on the highway, not down in the yard. It's kind of hard to see there; the first time I came here I almost drove past the hotel."

Maisie looked out the window in the direction of the highway. She couldn't see their sign from here, but she looked in that direction. The sign he was talking about had been done by a local painter twenty years before. It was a white board about three feet square, a simple text that said 'Ocean Dunes Hotel', then the address and phone number. Brandon leaned forward. "I have a friend who's a graphic artist. I could make a call, and get you a really nice sign made. It would certainly help your business. What do you think?"

Maisie nodded. "Whatever you think. What would your fiend want to be paid for this work? We can't afford much, as you know."

Brandon grinned. "Let me ask."

He pulled his small black telephone book out of his back pocket and dialed a number. A few moments later, he said: "Hey, Tommy, it's Brandon." He waited and listened.

"Yeah, listen, what are you doing this week?" Another pause. "OK, how would you like to run an errand of mercy for me? It's a lovely pair of ladies, out here in central Oregon. They've got a hotel I'm fixing up, five cottages, really pretty, no exposure from the street. It needs a sign. What do you need?"

He picked up a pencil and paper and started writing. "Uh huh. OK, then. What would you want for it?"

He listened for another minute. "No, it's out in the boonies, on the beach, in the middle of nowhere. That's part of the charm, Tommy."

Another pause. "Let me check. Hold on." He put the phone to his chest. "Tommy will make you a sign for free, but in exchange for two nights in a cottage and meals. Is that agreeable?"

Maisie nodded. Brandon put the phone to his ear again. "You got it. So, you're bringing everything? Great. See you tomorrow. Bye."

He hung up. "Tommy will be here tomorrow to make you a sign. It's all set." He grinned.

Maisie nodded. "I'll have to make up cottage number one, I suppose. It's ready to go, isn't it, Brandon?"

"Yes, everything's all set there. I'm sure Tommy will enjoy her stay."

Calista sat up straight. "*Her* stay?"

Brandon laughed out loud. "Thomasina. Tommy's full name. Yes, she's a good friend of mine."

Calista raised her eyebrow. "How good a friend is she?"

He smirked at the question. "She's a very good friend."

Calista's shoulders stiffened. "She's *that* kind of friend, is she?"

Brandon's smile disappeared. "No, not that kind of friend. Her husband was like a brother to me."

Calista shrank back slightly. "Oh. I'm sorry. What do you mean, 'was'?"

Brandon frowned. "He was in my unit. He never made it back." He looked at his watch. "Thanks again for lunch. If you'll excuse me, I have to finish the roof."

He went back to work on the cottage, peeling away roof shingles and hammering tar paper underneath them. He was perched on a short ladder, peering into the underside of the porch, doing something. Calista waited for hours before she came out to talk to him; she felt she had hit a nerve, and upset at having implied he would do something to hurt her.

He worked until late in the afternoon; the sun sank behind the trees, headed for the ocean, and the mild breeze from earlier in the day was now stiffer, colder. Calista put a jacket over her shoulders and went out to the cottage. Brandon was hanging under the roof, nailing wood back into place.

Calista stood to one side for a minute, waiting for him to notice her. He hung the hammer on his belt and glanced over.

"How's it coming along?" She asked.

"Fine. This roof should be done by tomorrow." He said softly.

She took two tiny steps toward him. "Look, I'm sorry for suggesting, earlier, you know." She sighed. "I'm not very good at trusting men."

He stepped off the ladder and sat cross-legged on the porch. "Have I ever done anything that makes you doubt me?"

She shook her head, sadly. "No, you haven't. Again, I'm sorry that I said what I did." She turned to leave.

"Hey." He said. She turned back to look at him. "What's for dinner?" He asked.

She smiled. "What would you like?"

He thought for a moment. "Meat loaf?" He asked, hopefully.

She grinned. "You got it. Six thirty. Meat loaf." She ran back to the house.

Maisie had made roasted potatoes and apple pie to go with the meat loaf. She seemed to be trying to apologize for Calista's comment too, as well as to thank Brandon for the work on her car.

Brandon came in just after six thirty; he had washed and changed his shirt, and he had a bottle of wine with him. He placed the wine on the table and asked Calista to open it. Maisie went into the parlor to find their good glasses.

"I thought it would go well with meat loaf. It's a full-bodied red." He explained.

Calista pulled open a kitchen drawer and found a corkscrew, then struggled to unfold it. She stared at it, frustrated. Brandon watched her, amused. "Do you want me to do that?" He asked.

"Certainly not." Calista said, firmly. She held the corkscrew in her lap and leaned forward, prying it open. Her hand slipped, and she jumped, startled, then she looked down at her thumb; it was bleeding.

"Damn." She mumbled. She stuck her thumb into her mouth and rummaged through the same drawer, looking for a bandage. She wrapped a paper napkin around her finger and kept looking, without much success. Maisie came back in, holding three ornate crystal glasses, and put them on the table. She looked at Calista's thumb.

"Oh, dear. That old thing will be the death of me yet." She muttered. She went to a cabinet by the phone and pulled out a small tin box, got a bandage from it and calmly wrapped it around Calista's thumb.

"When you were a little girl," She said, "You were such a tomboy. You used to climb trees and jump over rocks and chase rabbits. All the boys treated you like just another boy."

"Then I turned thirteen." Calista said.

"Ah. Yes, then they 'discovered' that you were a girl." Maisie smiled. "You bought makeup and did your hair, you wore skirts and heels, and all of a sudden the boys started noticing you.”

Calista shrugged. “It was a mixed blessing. Anyway, you don’t want to hear all those old stories, do you, Brandon?”

Brandon shrugged. “Absolutely. I don’t have any stories like that. Yours are great. Keep going.”

Maisie shook her head. “But, you have all these interesting friends, all these people who have done fascinating things. You must have stories to tell, about places you’ve been, things and people that we could never imagine.”

Brandon leaned back. “Let me open the wine, then I’ll tell you some stories.”

Calista handed him the corkscrew, reluctantly, and tucked her bandaged thumb into her fist. Brandon whipped out the corkscrew and twisted it into the cork, pulling it out with a satisfying ‘pop’. A tiny cloud of swirling vapor followed the cork, then he placed the opener on the table and poured wine for the three of them. He raised his glass.

“To old friends, new friends, and may they all be true friends.” He said.

“Cheers.” Maisie said, and took a sip of wine. She opened her eyes wide and glared at the glass. “Dear lord, this is potent.” She muttered. She took another sip. “But very, very good.” She drank some more.

Calista took a long, soothing drink, feeling a rush of warmth as the wine went down her throat. The wine reminded her of being out at the fire pit with Brandon, of making love in the sand, of soaking in the casino tub. She wouldn't tell her mother that, though. She nodded. "I agree. It's exceptional."

Maisie served coffee and pie after the main meal, and told Brandon some more stories about Calista and their life here at the hotel.

Calista's father had been in the army; he had seen action in the far east, then came back to get a degree and teach. Maisie was aware for some time that he was sick; he went from being robust, cheery and always happy to being quiet, then after he went to the doctor he would sometimes find a quiet place on the beach to sit, by himself. More than once, Maisie had found him sitting in the tall grass, crying. He never cried for himself, she said, but for Maisie and Calista, and that he wouldn't live to see his grandchildren.

Calista spoke about her husband. Ed had been a teacher, like her father, and he was a cheery, even-tempered man who loved her dearly. He sometimes told her that he was surprised that a girl like her would marry a man like him.

Calista said that he did everything he could for the hotel. He did most repairs himself, as best he could, even though he wasn't very handy. He didn't spend money for anything he didn't have to; he would wear the same jacket to school for weeks at a time, he would have Maisie make his lunches to save the cost of cafeteria meals, anything he could do to help keep the hotel going. And, Calista said, he did it cheerfully, with love, because he knew the hotel meant so much to her.

"So," Brandon said, "When I said that you should tear down the hotel and sell it off, that's why you were so angry at me?"

Calista shrugged and raised her glass. "Yep." She said, and took another sip. Her glass was empty, and she held it out for a refill. Brandon smiled and obligingly poured her more wine.

Calista pointed a finger at him, keeping the other four wrapped around the glass. She slurred her words slightly, now.

"And what about you, Mister Brandon Cooper, what about telling us some of your stories, huh?" She asked.

He swirled his wine slightly in the glass and looked at it, thinking. "My father took me with him once to Buenos Aires, when he was working on a project there. I was twelve, and I remember thinking that this would be a great trip- exotic places, exciting things to see, tropical beaches- so many expectations. Anyway, he was there for four days, and I spent most of the time in the hotel, watching the Argentine game shows on TV. I found out later that he had to bring me along because my mom was off on some junket, and she didn't want me in the way. I was an inconvenience to her."

He looked up at Maisie, a solemn, serious look. "See, now you've gone and made me talk about myself." He said. He smiled slightly. "A very boring subject, I have to say. It looks a lot flashier on the outside than it is to actually be me, you know."

Maisie reached forward and put her hand on top of his. "Don't ever think that, Brandon. Don't ever tell yourself that you're just a 'thing' we want to use. Without your money, you are still a good man, and there is nothing in the world that can buy that. Remember that."

Brandon looked at her, wide-eyed. He seemed surprised at Maisie being so philosophical, so blunt. He took her hand and kissed it, gently. "Thank you for that, Mrs. Blake. Thank you very much." He looked at his watch. "If you will excuse me, it was a lovely meal, but I should get some sleep. Tomorrow will be a busy day. Good night." He stood up and turned toward the door. "Good night again. Please, keep the wine." He walked down the steps toward his cottage.

Calista put down her glass and ran after him. She caught him near the door to his cottage, and touched his arm. He looked down at her hand, casually, and looked back up at her. "Hey, Calista. Sorry about getting all gloomy back there. I just don't like to talk about myself, you know?"

Calista pulled his arm close, reached up and brought her face up to his. She kissed him, softly. "I'm so sorry for you. You didn't have an easy childhood, did you?"

He shrugged. "You don't get it, do you? I envy you, I envy you so much. I envy that nobody wanted you for just your money, or your name, or your contacts. They may have been attracted to you for your looks, but they liked you, not what was behind you."

Calista glanced over at the path to the beach. "Are you going to the fire pit tonight?"

He shook his head sadly. "Sorry, no, I'm really tired. I'm going straight to bed. Good night."

She kissed him again. "Good night. Breakfast at seven?"

He smiled, for the first time that night a genuine, happy smile. "Sure. You're going to have a guest tomorrow, remember. Tommy should be here before noon."

Calista nodded. "We look forward to it. Good night, again."

She walked slowly back to the house, and Brandon stood in the yard, watching her go. When she got to the top of the steps, he called out to her.

"Hey, Calista?" He said. She turned to look at him.

"Thank your mom again for dinner. Very good meat loaf. Sleep well." She smiled and went inside.

At six thirty the next morning, Calista was awake. She made coffee, mixed up pancake batter, and let it sit, so the cakes would be tall and fluffy. Fifteen minutes later, she heard the door open, and Brandon came in, wiping his hands on his pants and shuffling his feet, as though nothing had happened the night before.

He leaned against the sink and picked up a mug to pour himself some coffee. "Morning. Where's your mom?" He asked.

"She had to go into town. Listen, last night, I realize I said something that really hurt you. I'm sorry for that, it's just that I'm not used to someone saying what you said." She almost whispered the last words.

"That I love you?"

"Yes."

"Do you feel the same way toward me?" He asked.

She nodded.

"Then you say it, too." He ordered.

She pursed her lips. "You're going away. You won't even be here the whole summer." She protested.

"Does that change how you feel about me? Come on, say it." He dared her.

"All right, I love you." She blurted out.

She took a step back and covered her mouth. She whispered it again. "I love you. I do, you know."

He smiled. "Good. It's not one-sided, then." He wrapped his arms around her, lifted her off the ground, kissed her softly, then gently let her back down again. Calista looked up at him and beamed. She threw her arms around him, hugging him tight.

"Tell you what." She said. She sighed, thinking. "Let's not focus on the future. Let's just enjoy the present- the summer, today, this morning, the next five minutes. All right?"

He nodded, digesting the statement. "Well said. Sure, that works for me." He kissed her again, softly.

"Is breakfast ready?" He asked.

Calista pointed at a chair and Brandon sat, smirking, his hands squeezed between his knees. She made pancakes and eggs, slid them onto a large plate and placed it in front of him. He looked down at them, waited patiently for her to join him, then he began to eat.

They ate quietly, the clatter of silverware on plates the only sound in the room, and occasionally grinned at each other.

Brandon slid his empty plate away and leaned back. "Man, way too much food- now I need a nap." He said.

Calista took the plates and refilled their coffees. She sat across from Brandon, stretched her arm out and touched his hand, playfully, then she leaned down and rested her head on her elbow.

"This was fun. I like having breakfast like this, with you." She said.

He placed his other hand over hers, protectively. "A year and a half. I'll be back in just a year and a half. Can you wait for me that long?" He asked, softly.

Calista was silent for a long time. Brandon almost took his hand away. He thought he'd said something wrong. Finally, she nodded, very slowly. "I can wait." She whispered.

Brandon was in the third cottage, finishing up the final trim work before he put the furniture back into it. Calista came out with some lemonade for him, an excuse to see what he was doing. He put down his hammer, gave her a kiss and gratefully accepted the lemonade. They talked about the way the cottage looked; Calista commented on the fresh smell of the floors and ceiling, and Brandon showed her all the things that were once broken, but were now fixed.

They both smiled a lot. Out on the drive, they heard gravel crunching, and Calista went out to greet her mother's car. Instead, there was a dark blue van rolling to a stop on the grass in front of the house; Calista went out to meet this stranger.

The driver's door opened and a woman jumped out. She looked a bit like Calista, only shorter, wearing dungarees over a denim shirt, her long dark hair pulled tight in a ponytail, a brightly colored handkerchief holding it back. She puffed on a stubby cigarette, then dropped it and stepped on the butt. She saw Calista, waved and bounced cheerily over.

"Hi!" She squealed, a shrill, schoolgirl voice. "Where's Brandon?"

Brandon walked slowly out of the cottage, wiped his hands on his jeans, then held his arms out wide for the woman.

"Hey, Tommy, it's really good to see you." He said warmly.

She rushed up to him, threw her arms around him, and hugged him tight. Calista felt a rush of jealousy. This woman was hugging HER boyfriend. The woman squeezed him tight then took a step back.

"Hi, Bran flake, how are you?" She asked.

Brandon rubbed the top of her head, playfully, and put an arm around her shoulders. "Tommy, meet Calista."

Tommy reached a hand out and Calista took it. "Hi, Calista, is it? Nice to meet you." She said. "We all wondered what Brandon was doing out here in the wilds."

Calista nodded. "Hello. Yes, he's offered to fix up our cottages. He's been terrific- we can't thank him enough."

Tommy shrugged. "Yeah, that's the Bran flake for you. So, anyway, I drove past this place three times before I finally noticed your puny little sign. You guys need my help, seriously."

She looked over her shoulder at the main house. "Anyway, do you want to put me in the big house, or what?"

Calista waved at the first cottage. "Sure, or if you'd prefer some privacy, you could have a cottage to yourself. It's up to you, whichever you like."

Tommy looked back and forth, deciding. "Yeah, all right, I'll take a cottage, then. Thanks, let me get my stuff."

She walked back to her van, opened the passenger door and hauled out a large tote bag. She swung it along as she walked, took it into the cottage and dropped it on the bed. She looked around, admiring the curtains, the bathroom, the view out the back window towards the beach. She slid the window open and took a deep breath.

"Wow, this place is terrific. I can see why Brandon wants to spend the summer here." She said.

Calista had a brief memory of herself and Brandon, making love in the sand. "Yes, he enjoys the peace and quiet out here." She said.

Tommy pulled balls of fabric out of the tote; shirts and socks, underwear, pants, all rolled up like wash rags.

She stuffed them into the dresser drawers, then scattered a toothbrush, toothpaste and her toiletries on the bathroom counter. She bounced on the bed, patting the blanket. "Hey, nice. This is classy." She commented.

Calista chuckled. "This is the first time I have EVER heard anyone refer to the cottage as 'classy'."

Tommy finished stuffing her things into the dresser and slammed the drawers closed with force. "So, what's there to do for fun in this burg?" She asked.

Calista shook her head. "Sorry, this is Oregon, not Las Vegas. We're pretty low-key here. There is a dance next Saturday in Lincoln City, at the fire hall. Maybe we could all go there together?"

Tommy grinned and smacked Calista's arm, playfully. "Yeah, sounds like fun. Let's work up an appetite, stir up the locals."

The sound of more crunching gravel brought Calista out again. She left Tommy to organize her toiletries and went to see who it was this time. Maisie's station wagon rolled slowly around the van and stopped by the main house.

Maisie got out, struggled to drag some groceries out behind her, and looked toward Tommy's cottage. Calista walked over to join her.

"Hi, mom. We have a guest. Brandon's friend just showed up."

Maisie looked at the van, then the cottage, then back at the van. "She's already here? Wonderful. I should say hello."

She handed the groceries to Calista and shooed her into the main house. Maisie went up to the cottage and knocked on the door frame. "Hello? Hi, I'm Calista's mom, Maisie."

Tommy came out to meet her. "Hey, Maisie. I'm Tommy. Brandon told you I was coming?"

Maisie nodded. "Yes. He said you paint signs?"

Tommy shrugged. "Yeah, among other things. Once an artist, always an artist, I guess. This is a lovely place you have here, by the way."

Maisie chuckled. "You wouldn't have said that a month ago. Brandon has done wonders here."

On cue, Brandon walked through the door. "Ladies, has everyone met, then?"

Maisie waved her hand. "Yes, I was just saying how much you've done for us here. Tommy, I'm very glad to meet you. Would you like some lunch?"

Tommy looked at Brandon for guidance. He nodded. She turned to Maisie. "That sounds great. I'd love some lunch, thanks."

Maisie hurried back to the main house and started cooking. Calista helped her, but kept peeking out the window to see what Brandon and Tommy were doing.

Maisie glanced at her. "Leave it, Cali; I'm sure there's nothing going on with them. I'm sure she's just a friend."

An hour later, everyone was eating, seated around the dining table. Tommy finished her food, patted her mouth dry with a napkin and nodded approval.

"Very nice, very nice indeed." She said. "Bran was telling me that you can get to the beach from here?"

Calista waved in the direction of the path. "Yes. There's an opening in the fence, and it leads down to the shore. Would you like me to show you later?"

Tommy nodded enthusiastically. "Sure. I always like to paint unusual scenery, different places. Would you mind sitting for a portrait while we're out there?"

Calista looked at Brandon, puzzled. "Tommy is a talented portrait artist, as well as a sign painter." He explained. "She did a large oil painting of my father a few years ago."

Calista looked over at Tommy. "I see. Why would you want to do my portrait?"

Tommy leaned forward. "You have an interesting face. It says a lot about you."

"Like what?" Calista asked.

"For one, the fact that you've had a lot of pain in your life, but you stay positive. You try to see the best in people, but you won't let yourself be taken advantage of. How am I doing?"

Calista smiled. "You've been talking to Brandon, I see."

"Nope. He never said anything about you. I got all that from looking at your face."

Calista leaned back and glanced over at her mother. "All right, I'm impressed. What else can you tell me?"

Tommy reached her hand out. "Give me your palm." She said.

Calista held out her hand. "You're a palm reader, too?" She smirked.

Tommy shook her head. "I'm an observer of people." She stared at Calista's hand. "You do some manual labor; not much, but enough to keep you in shape. You're quite well-educated, and you read a lot, but you don't read stuffy books. You take care of your appearance, but you don't obsess- you're not a princess. How am I doing so far?"

Calista pulled her hand back. "How did you get all that? Not from my face that time."

Tommy pointed at Calista's hands. "You have some calluses, but not dark or thick, like a farmer's. so you do some work, but not heavy labor. You have a smudge of ink on your middle finger, where you licked it to turn a page. You don't do that with newspapers, only books. So far, you haven't quoted Freud, or Chomsky, or any of the pop-psych gurus. You don't suffer fools gladly, as the saying goes. Next item, your nails are neat, lightly painted, but not extravagantly so. Your hair is clean and well-styled, but without a ridiculous hairdo. So, am I right so far?"

Calista chuckled. "Bang on. Well done, I'm impressed."

They talked for a long while over coffee. Tommy lived in Sacramento, a ten-hour drive away, and she didn't see the ocean nearly often enough, she said.

Calista was surprised by this; Tommy pointed out that very few people were as lucky as Calista and Maisie, that this was a pearl of a place, and they should feel very lucky to live here. Tommy said her apartment was her studio, and it was big enough to work in, but she missed green grass and fresh air.

Brandon thanked Maisie for lunch and went back to working on the cottage. Maisie collected the dishes to wash, and Tommy turned to look at Calista.

"So, when can I sketch you?" Tommy asked.

Calista shrugged. "I don't know. I've never had my portrait done before. When do you want to do it?"

Tommy looked out the door. "Now. The beach is over there, right? Let's see if there's a spot out there that feels right."

Calista waited patiently as Tommy gathered together an easel, some large sheets of paper and a clutch of colored pencils, then the two women trudged down the path, toward the beach.

Tommy stopped at the fire pit. "Hey, this is perfect." She said.

Calista felt distinctly uncomfortable. "Are you sure?" She asked. "There's a long flat beach down the way."

Tommy shook her head. "Nope. This is the place. You sit over there." She pointed a pencil at the far log, and Calista sat down.

Tommy set up her easel, then she placed Calista's hands on the log, just so, and had her turn her head to one side slightly, tilting her chin up. "Good. Stay like that, please." Tommy ordered. Calista sat still.

"Can I talk?" Calista asked.

"Sure. Just don't move around much. I like you right there- good subject, good setting." She muttered.

They were both silent for a few minutes. Tommy sketched feverishly, looked up every few seconds and added strokes to the paper. Calista sat still, waiting for instructions or comments.

"Ok, turn your head a little left." Tommy said. "More. No, back a bit. Perfect." She scraped her pencil along the paper with short, precise swipes, focusing on the tips of her fingers, clutching the pencil just above the lead.

"You come out here very often?" Tommy asked, still sketching.

"As often as I can." Calista said. The image of her and Brandon, naked in the sand, went through her mind.

"Lots of good memories, huh?" Tommy asked.

Calista blushed slightly. "Sorry?"

Tommy stuck the pencil in the sand and leaned back, checking her work. "I guess you would come out here with your husband, right? Romantic nights on the beach?" she looked up and smiled. Calista was now blushing a deep red.

Tommy's face dropped. "Oh, god. No, it wasn't... it was. It was Brandon, wasn't it?"

Calista covered her face, embarrassed, and bent forward. Tommy started to laugh. "It IS Bran, it IS." She cackled. "Well, what do you know?"

Calista shook her head. "Look, he's different from any man I've ever met before. He's handsome, he's charming, and he likes me. What can I say?"

Tommy shrugged. "Hey, it's good for him to get out there again. After his marriage broke up, he was completely miserable. That's why he finally went off on this walkabout, I guess, to get his head straight."

Tommy changed pencils, clutching a stubby yellow one. "So, what brought him out here?"

Calista pointed back at the house. "We advertised for a handyman, and Brandon offered to work for room and board. He has done more good in a few weeks than we could have in years. He has saved our hotel. Whatever else happens, I'll always be grateful to him for that."

Tommy shrugged. "It's just nice to see him happy again. He really is a great guy, you know, through and through." Tommy gathered up her pencils and folded up the easel, the sheet of paper still clipped to it. "Shall we go?" She asked.

"That's it?" Calista said. "You're done?"

"Almost. Some clean-up and final coloring to do, but it should be ready by dinnertime."

"Can I see it?" Calista asked, curious.

"Certainly not."

"Why not?"

"Do you eat raw steak? Same reason." Tommy laughed. "But, I do need your help with the road sign, all right?"

Calista grinned. "Glad to help. What do you want me to do?"

"Ever handle a power auger?"

"What's that?"

Tommy nodded. "I'll take that as a no. We'll start tomorrow. I'm going to rest up for a bit first, OK? It was a long drive."

Calista watched her wave a brief hello to Brandon then go into her cottage and close the door. Calista wandered over to the cottage where Brandon was working, nailing wooden trim around the main window. He stood back to check that it was straight, saw her and smiled. "Hello, come to check on my work?" He joked.

Calista stood beside him and admired the window, then she playfully stuck her hand into his jeans' back pocket.

"Your friend was sketching me earlier," She said. "Out at the fire pit. She knows." She smirked.

Brandon looked at her, reading her face. "Ah. I swear, that girl's psychic. She must have some gypsy blood, I tell you."

He grinned. "What the heck. How does the window look?"

"Terrific. I'm going to help mom make dinner. See you at six."

Calista went to Tommy's cottage and knocked at the door. Tommy opened it quickly, a thin paintbrush in her teeth, another stuck in her hair, above the ponytail. "Yuh?" She mumbled.

"I just wanted to tell you that dinner is at six, all right?" Calista said.

"OK." Tommy said, distractedly, and closed the door.

Calista went back to the main house; her mother was chopping vegetables and pushing them into a roasting pan. Calista picked up a small chunk of carrot and nibbled on it.

"Hey, mom, can I help?" She asked.

"No, I've got it, dear. How did you get along with Tommy?"

Calista sighed. "Well, she was asking about me and Brandon."

Maisie kept chopping vegetables, not looking up, not missing a beat. "I see."

"She said it's nice to see him dating again. She thinks he's a very nice guy."

Maisie looked up at her. "I would agree. He's also very cute." She giggled.

At six o clock exactly, Calista sat on the front porch of the main house. From there, she could see the sun just touching the tip of the tallest pine tree in the yard. Brandon had washed up and pulled on a clean shirt, his hair combed back to expose a line of untanned skin on his forehead. He sauntered over to the house and hopped up the steps. Calista stood up and gave him a hug and a long kiss.

"Hello there." She purred. "Good amount of work today?"

He smiled. "Absolutely. The third cottage should be done by Monday. It's coming along really well, despite the rotten wood."

The door of the first cottage opened, and they both looked over, still embracing. Tommy came out, wearing jeans and a bright orange hoodie that read

'Florida Grapefruit', and stepped off the porch. She strolled to the middle of the path, looked up at the darkening sky, put her hands on her hips and leaned back, stretching. Brandon turned to face her, his hand around Calista's waist, and waved.

Tommy reached into her hoodie's pocket, pulled out a pack of cigarettes, lit one and took a long drag. She blew a thick, blue column of smoke into the air, walked around in slow circles and smoked the cigarette down to half way, then stubbed it out on the sole of her shoe and crumpled it.

She jogged up the steps to join Calista and Brandon. "Evening, kids. Everyone's feeling the love, I see?" She smiled.

Brandon took her arm with his other hand and led both women through into the house. Brandon and Tommy sat, as Maisie instructed, and Calista helped serve.

Tommy looked over at Maisie. "What's for dinner, then?" She asked.

"Well, we have a couple of things...." Maisie started.

"As long as it isn't pot roast." Tommy interrupted.

Maisie's mouth dropped open.

Tommy laughed. "Just kidding. I love pot roast."

Maisie chuckled at the joke and loaded pot roast onto plates, passing them to Calista for the side vegetables.

Everyone was soon eating, chatting back and forth, handing plates to each other. Brandon snuck a piece of beef from Calista's plate, and Maisie pretended not to notice. Calista leaned forward and caressed his leg, and Tommy pretended not to notice.

Maisie watched the others, talked cheerily, passed plates, asked how the food was. Tommy thanked her for the meal, apologized for joking about the pot roast, and offered to help clean up. Maisie flatly refused.

Calista suggested coffee in the living room; everyone nodded agreement.

Tommy turned toward Calista and grinned. "I have something for you." She said, with a Cheshire cat grin. She looked at Brandon. "You too. Both of you, wait here."

She marched out to her cottage. Maisie and Calista looked at each other, puzzled. Tommy came back a minute later with a large sheet of cardboard under one arm and a wooden box under the other. She rested the cardboard by the door.

She dropped the box in Brandon's lap, making him go 'oof' involuntarily. "It's from our mutual friend. Don't worry, I got one too." She said.

Brandon opened the box and pulled out a clear glass bottle. He read the label. "Hm. Good for after dinner, do you think?" He asked. "Yeah, I think it's good with coffee. Calista, would you mind getting some glasses?"

Calista pulled four wine glasses out of the cupboard. These were the glasses they had only used on very special occasions; when she got married, then for the reception after her father's funeral, and for the reception after Ed's funeral. Once or twice they had been pulled out for New Year's or Christmas, but after Ed died they had always been left in the cupboard. She placed them gingerly on the table and slid them toward everyone.

Tommy pulled a pair of reading glasses from her hoodie pocket, grabbed the bottle out of Brandon's hand, and read the label, slowly. "Any idea what he charges for this stuff?" She muttered.

"He drives a Porsche. Do the math." Brandon shrugged.

"And that Benz, remember?" She added.

For a brief second, Calista had a glimpse of the life Tommy and Brandon had, far away from her little hotel. Those simple statements, the casual way they said it, told her just how different their world and hers really were. It scared her- how would he feel about her when he came back- if he did come back? Was she fooling herself about how he felt? She didn't want to think about it now- she decided to think about that later.

There was a 'pop' as he pulled the cork out of the bottle, and a near-silent 'glug-glug-glug' as he poured the wine. It was clear, pale, with bubbles that wandered lazily up the sides of the glass and danced on the surface before dissolving. He handed a glass to Maisie, then to Calista, then Tommy, before pouring one for himself. He turned to Tommy. "Care to give a toast, then?" He asked her.

She glanced around the table and thought for a moment, then raised her glass with an impish grin. The others raised theirs too. "May we always be close to the ones we love." She said.

Everyone repeated it, and took a drink. Maisie stared down at the liquid, rolling the stem of the glass in her hands. "All right, now I'm truly impressed. What is this, exactly?"

Brandon sniffed his glass. "It's called 'prosecco'. Think of it as poor man's champagne."

Tommy snickered. "Just pity the poor man, driving his Porsche."

Calista drank all of her wine, in large sips. "This is like liquid dessert." She said. "It's divine."

Brandon grimaced. "It really sneaks up on you, you know. Be careful."

Calista held out her glass for a refill. "More, please." She said.

Brandon smirked, poured a second glass for Calista, and watched her drink half of it, quickly. "See? No effect." She said.

Tommy rolled her eyes and shook her head. "Ah. Something for you." She remembered. She went back to the front door and brought back the sheet of cardboard. It was actually two sheets of cardboard taped together, Calista saw, and Tommy took one of the dinner knives to slit the tape.

She flipped up one sheet and carefully tucked it behind the other, then presented the cardboard to Calista. Taped to the cardboard was the portrait Tommy had done earlier, now finished in charcoal and colored pencil.

It was as lifelike as a photograph; it captured Calista's smile, the way her hair wisped away from her face in the soft breeze on the beach, with the long stretch of scrub grass behind her, leading off to the ocean. She could almost feel the warm sun, sketched onto the page, from the subtle golden shading on the sunward side of her face.

Calista moved her hand over the painting, her fingers hovering just above the paper, afraid to smudge the work. She handed the paper to Maisie. "What do you think, mom?"

Maisie took the painting and examined it, tilting her head as though to look around the picture, behind Calista to the shore beyond her. "This is remarkable, Tommy, you have exceptional talent. You should be very proud of that."

Tommy grinned. "Thanks. Portrait work helps pay the bills between sign commissions. It's something I enjoy very much, something I'd do for free, but don't tell anybody that." She smirked.

Tommy took another sip of her wine. "So, when's this dance?" She asked.

Calista nodded. "Two nights from now, on Saturday. Would you like to go?"

"Sure. I assume the dress code is casual? I didn't bring my evening dress, you realize."

Brandon grinned. "You'd be overdressed in jeans. You look fine, Tommy. Let's go, we'll enjoy ourselves."

Tommy put her glass carefully on the table. "Sold. Now, if you'll excuse me, I'm going to get my beauty sleep, out here in the wilds of Oregon. Good night all, thanks for the lovely dinner." She stood up to go.

Maisie touched her arm. "What would you like for breakfast?"

Tommy thought for a moment. "Surprise me. Good night again."

She went out to her cottage. Through the kitchen window, Calista could see the cottage porch light come on, then the main room lit up, then the door closed, the porch light went off, and the yard was dark again.

Brandon offered more wine to Maisie, who refused, and Calista, who took a small glass. He waited politely until she had finished her drink, then he said good night and went out to his cottage.

Chapter Eleven

Calista helped clean up, then went up to bed. She leaned out her window and looked out at the cottages; she saw a shadow cross the window where Tommy was, then that cottage went dark as Tommy went to sleep. Calista felt a vague sense of jealousy, a part of her wondering if Tommy and Brandon had ever been more than friends. She shook her head. Let it go, she thought. She went to bed, slid under the lovely, luxurious sheets and tried to sleep. The night was warm; a hint of a breeze from the ocean barely cooled her, and the bright moon shone in through her window, so bright that she threw an arm over her eyes to get away from the light. She still couldn't sleep. There was a sound in the distance, soft and melodic, that caught her attention. It was Brandon's harmonica.

Calista slipped on a pair of shorts and a sweatshirt and crept past a snoring Maisie, down the stairs, and out the front door, without thinking. She stopped on the porch and sighed. 'What am I doing here?' she asked herself. 'I don't even know why I'm going out there. He might not even be alone. Tommy might be there too.'

That thought made her even more decided. She picked her way through the grass to the fire pit. This evening, the fire was small, the warm night making a larger fire unnecessary. Brandon sipped wine from a glass and smiled at her.

Calista sat beside Brandon and bumped him, playfully. "Hi there, come here often?" She joked.

He smiled and kissed her, softly. "Long time no see." He quipped. "Care for some wine?"

He lifted up a thin, dark green bottle, and a second stemmed glass. Calista took the glass and held it out. Brandon poured a half glass for her and some for himself, then held his glass up. "To infinite possibilities."

Calista drank her wine in a long gulp and smacked her lips. She held out her glass. "More, please, a full drink this time."

He raised one eyebrow. "Are you sure? This is a different prosecco- and pretty potent stuff, you know."

She shook her head. "More." She repeated. He shrugged and poured, nearly to the rim of the glass. Calista gingerly moved the glass to her lips and drank half of it. "Wow, that is good." She purred. She started to wobble slightly on the log, spread her feet far apart to steady herself, then put a hand on Brandon's shoulder.

Brandon shook his head. "I think that, as your bartender, I should cut you off, miss." He said.

Calista sighed and sipped the rest of her wine. She handed him the empty glass and leaned back, looking up at the sky. She pointed into the air and smiled. "Look. A shooting star; make a wish." She slurred.

He looked up, following her finger. "Sorry, that's the commuter plane to Seattle, again." He said.

"You don't think you should make a wish on an airplane?"

He nodded. "All right. Let's see." He closed his eyes for a few seconds.

"Well? Did you get your wish?" Calista asked.

He opened his eyes. "You're still here, and so yes, I did." He smiled.

Calista leaned against him. "So, do you want to take cruel advantage of me out here on the beach?"

He shook his head. "There are rules about that. I wouldn't feel right, with you like in this condition."

"I'm offering you a very good time. Don't you want to?" She asked, trying hard to focus.

He stood up, hooked his hand under her arm and lifted her upright. "Come on, Calista. Let's get you to bed."

She threw her arm around his neck and tried to walk, shakily. "You're a true gentleman, you know that, Mister Bran flake Cooper?"

"Yes, I know. Now, get some sleep and we'll have a nice breakfast and lots of coffee in the morning, OK?"

He half-walked, half-carried her back to the house, opened the door and maneuvered her to the stairs.

She lifted a foot to climb up, but missed the step and slipped. Brandon caught her, his hand reaching automatically around her waist and planting itself on her breast. She turned to face him and grinned.

"Having a change of mind, are we?" She joked.

He sighed, bent down and lifted her up, effortlessly. "Come on, let's go." He whispered. "Quiet, your mom's sleeping."

He crept up the stairs, the wood creaking softly under their weight, and used his knee to push her bedroom door open. He sat her on the bed, peeled off her top, pulled the sheets down, slid her under them, then covered her up.

He leaned down to straighten the covers and Calista wrapped her hand behind his head. He looked at her, nose to nose, her eyes examining him, it seemed. She lifted her head slightly and kissed him. "Thank you. Good night." She whispered.

"Sleep well, Miss Blake." He whispered back.

He went back down the stairs, stopped the middle of the yard, and looked up at Calista's room. She had stirred something in him, something that he thought was gone, a part of him that was warm, kind; happy. He went to bed.

At seven thirty in the morning, Calista woke up. The sunlight in her room was blinding; the sound in the yard deafening. It was the sound of two people talking, she eventually realized. There were smells from downstairs that made her gradually open her eyes a slit, despite the light burning through her eyelids. Bacon, coffee, and toast. She squinted at the clock and took a minute to focus, finally reading the time. She groaned, threw on her sweatshirt and shorts, and went downstairs.

Maisie was in the kitchen; Tommy said something, then laughed loudly. Painfully so. Calista squinted at the noise. Brandon was leaning against the door frame, sipping coffee from a thick mug, chatting with Tommy. He saw Calista walking slowly toward him and smiled.

"Hey there. Good morning." He boomed. Calista winced at the sound.

"Hi. Morning." She whispered. She looked around. "Fresh coffee?"

Maisie nodded. "Right here. Too much wine last night, dear?" She asked.

Calista squinted a 'yes', and Maisie snickered. Calista scowled at Brandon.

He shook his head. "Don't look at me- I didn't say anything bad, just that you came out to the fire pit and shared another glass or two with me. That's all."

Calista shrugged. "God, that's powerful stuff. Where do they get that wine?"

Tommy nodded. "California- Napa Valley. Good, huh? But it does pack a sneaky kick, doesn't it?"

Calista poured herself a coffee. "Like a mule." She agreed.

Maisie ordered everyone to sit and eat, and two coffees later Calista's mind was clear enough that she could carry on a conversation without a pounding pain in her head.

Everyone talked, Brandon glanced over at Calista, keeping a straight face, not gloating about her being drunk the night before, and everyone ate. Maisie cleared dishes and shooed everyone out of the house.

Tommy touched Calista's arm. "So, I need your help doing the signs today, all right?"

Calista grinned. "Sure. What can I do?"

"Be my gopher. Let's go."

They dragged two large sheets of plywood out of Tommy's van and placed them on the grass. Tommy took out a thick carpenter's pencil and drew, freehand, an image of the main house and two of the cottages. Then she pulled that sheet of wood aside and did the same for the second sheet of wood. Calista helped her move the plywood onto a large piece of canvas, and Tommy went back to her van to retrieve buckets of paint and brushes.

She painted the plywood in broad, sweeping strokes, random-looking swaths of tan and green, then a panel of blue above. She switched to a finer brush and changed to a pale yellow paint, putting two cottages and the main house on what Calista realized was an image of the yard. Another brush change, and Tommy drew clouds, tufts of grass, and a few seagulls. Calista stood back and examined her work. It had taken about an hour to do all this, and it looked terrific.

"Dear lord, you're good." Calista said, shaking her head. "I wish I was a quarter this talented."

Tommy grinned and wiped a brush clean. "It's a mixed blessing, actually. Everyone expects perfection the first time out. That's a lot of pressure, though." She looked at her watch. "It should be completely dry in an hour. For now, let's do the other panel."

She repeated the same procedure with the second sheet of plywood, painted it exactly the same way, and placed it beside the first panel, comparing them. She grunted, satisfied, and packed up her brushes.

"Good, nothing to do now but wait." She said. "Let's dig some post holes."

Tommy went to her van and dragged out something that looked like a monstrous dental drill- an auger, then a pair of thick wooden posts. She placed the posts flat on the ground about three feet apart, spray painted an 'x' beside the base of each, and brought the auger over, standing it up on top of one 'x'.

"I've seen these before- road crews putting in signs." Calista grinned. The auger had a pair of long handles, one on each side, and Calista held it steady as Tommy started up the small gas motor on top of the auger, and the corkscrew drill wormed its way into the soil.

They drilled two deep holes in the ground, sank the posts into them, and stomped in rocks to set them straight. Tommy stood back, eyed the posts, then nodded, satisfied. "Good enough. Time for a cigarette before lunch."

They sat on the fence, Tommy inhaling on a long, thin cigarette, looking over at her artwork, chatting openly. Tommy was much more casual, more forthcoming about herself, it seemed, now that she and Calista had worked together. Tommy's husband was in the army, along with Brandon. They had been ambushed, and their vehicle caught fire. Brandon had risked his own life getting her husband out, but he died of his wounds nonetheless. She felt she owed Brandon a debt of gratitude for just trying to save him, and not leaving her husband in there to die, she said.

Maisie called them from the house, waving her arm in the universal signal to come and eat. Tommy stubbed out the cigarette on the sole of her shoe, crushed it in her hand and tossed it onto the grass. She dusted off her jeans and walked with Calista up the steps to the main house.

They ate lunch, making small talk about the signs and progress on the cottages. At one point Calista started to say something about Tommy's husband, but Tommy gave her a look that spoke volumes, and Calista changed the subject.

After coffee, they all thanked Maisie for the meal and went back out. Brandon went back to working on the cottage; he gave Calista a subtle wink and smile which nobody else saw.

Tommy spoke little until they got out to the two posts in the ground. She shook them firmly, checking that they were set into the ground properly, then she stood back, looking up and down at them, and spoke softly to Calista.

"Listen, let's not say anything about what I said before, OK?"

Calista understood. "All right. I'm sorry. I didn't realize how sensitive you are about it still."

Tommy was still looking over the posts. "It's a year tomorrow. Yeah, it's a sore point. After all, I'm not going to say anything about that wink he gave you just there."

Calista blushed. "You saw that, huh?"

"Yep. Point made?"

They carried one of the plywood sheets to the posts and Tommy carefully placed it where she wanted it then bolted it in place. They put the second sheet of plywood on the other side of the posts, made sure it lined up with the first, and bolted it into the post too. Tommy dabbed some paint on the bolt heads, and from five feet away they blended in to the background.

Calista stood back, admiring the work. In a few hours, Tommy had made their little hotel truly visible from the road. Anyone driving by would certainly see this sign, she thought.

Calista and Tommy wandered over to see what Brandon was doing. He had redone the main room in the cottage, and was dismantling the vanity in the bathroom. He was on his back, unscrewing something under the sink.

Tommy crouched down to look under the sink too. Calista stood back, amused, as Tommy poked Brandon's stomach. "Hey, mister, whatcha doin'?" Tommy joked.

He stuck his head out. "There's a wobbly sink in this vanity. I'm going to replace the seal." He said.

Tommy stood up. "Well, you have fun. I'm going into town to get some gas and stuff. Want to come, Calista?"

"Sure."

They climbed into her van and headed up the road to Lincoln City. Calista gave directions; up the Oregon Coast Highway, over the Stiletz River, through the wildlife refuge, telling Tommy the history of the area and pointing out landmarks as they went. Tommy was talkative; she mentioned that her husband had always wanted to take a long road trip. He had always wanted to drive through New Mexico, to see the great big sky of the desert at night, to smell the dust and feel the heat. Then he was deployed overseas, she said. He never got to New Mexico.

She got quiet after that, but after a few minutes she perked up again and started waving at people on the side of the road.

They drove to the second gas station in town. Calista said that the first one had higher prices, because all the tourists stopped there first. A scruffy young man filled up her tank, nodded recognition at Calista and ogled Tommy. He watched the pump numbers roll up to match the cash Tommy had given him, hung up the nozzle, then wished them a nice afternoon, watched them get into the van and went back to reading his newspaper.

Tommy announced she wanted to buy some cigarettes and candy bars; Calista pointed out the grocery store a few blocks down the street, so they parked in the store's lot and walked in. Calista nodded to the clerk by the front register, pointed Tommy in the direction of the candy counter, and chatted with the clerk. Tommy came back with a handful of candy bars and pointed to the cigarettes behind the clerk, indicating the brand she wanted.

A few seconds later, Calista was aware of a large shadow coming closer. Glen, the real estate salesman, hovered over her, flashing a crocodile smile, an expression that said he had gotten the better of someone, but was trying to be modest about it.

"Hi, Calista, how are you doing?" He cooed, in a reassuring voice.

"Fine, Glen, how are you?"

He ogled Tommy. "Great, just great. Who is your friend here?"

"Glen, Tommy. Tommy, this is Glen."

He grunted and scanned her up and down, then he turned back to Calista.

He took Calista's hand in both of his. "I just wanted to tell you, I didn't know you were after the Parsoner land too. I mean, if I'd known you wanted to buy it, I wouldn't have bought it myself. You do realize that, don't you, Calista?"

Calista stifled the urge to smirk, to laugh out loud, to tell him that he'd been had. "Yeah, well, we had wanted to expand the area around the hotel, but there was just no way we could do it, you know? It was a stretch any way you look at it."

He shook his head reassuringly and closed his eyes. "I know, believe me, I know. I understand your friend, the investor from California, was also interested in that property?"

Calista had to force herself to not giggle. "Yeah, well, he wants to invest a bunch of money in some land here, I'm told, but I don't know the details."

Glen's eyes widened. "Yeah? Do you know where he is now?"

Calista had a flash of inspiration. "He's back in California, I hear. He may be back later in the summer, I think."

Glen fumbled through his pockets, desperately looking for something. "If you see him, would you give him my card?"

He thrust a card at Calista. She read it.

"John Deere tractors?" She asked.

"No, no, the other one. Right. Damn." He muttered.

He took the card back and held out a different card. She took it and nodded.

"'Real estate sales professional'. Sure. I'll pass it on."

Glen shook her hand again, glanced at Tommy's cleavage as discreetly as he could and said goodbye. He almost ran toward a pickup truck in the parking lot.

Tommy watched him go, amused. "What was all that about?" She muttered.

Calista saw the cashier watching them, out of the corner of her eye. She didn't trust the cashier. "Tell you on the way home." She said.

They walked out, looking up into a bold blue sky, a warm, early-summer kind of afternoon, with streaks of cirrus clouds off in the distance, over the open ocean, and only the barest tufts of puffy white cumulus clouds to the east, where the mountains blocked the wind.

They took a long, winding route back to the hotel, meandering along back roads and following the ocean wherever they could. They had the windows open; the warm salty air blew through the van, and Tommy played Willie Nelson on the stereo, her speakers blasting 'On the Road Again' at passing cars as they sang along with the music.

Tommy asked Calista about Ed and her father. She wanted to know about them, she said. She followed Calista's directions and ended up at the cemetery where Calista had taken Brandon. They stood there for a minute or two, talked about Calista's father, talked about how he had lingered, but how Ed had gone so suddenly. Tommy's soft smile was still there, a gentle feature that made Calista feel like talking to her. As they walked back to the van, Calista decided to ask the question she had been avoiding.

"What about your husband? What happened to him?"

Tommy shrugged casually. "There was a roadside bomb. Ollie was closest to the blast, and it blew off his legs. He died before the medics could get to him. Still, all the other men said that Bran spent the last moments of Oliver's life holding him, talking to him. Brandon was hurt, too, but his only thought was letting Ollie know that he would not die alone."

Calista was silent for a long period. "I'm so sorry. It must have been terrible for you."

"Yeah. It wasn't easy, what can I say. Ollie once wrote me a letter, and said I should only open it if he didn't come home. I read it after his funeral. It said that he wanted me to live my own life, to be happy. So I will be happy, if only for him."

Calista put an arm over Tommy's shoulder and hugged her tight. "If you ever need somewhere to stay, or someone to talk to, you know you have a friend here." She said.

"Thanks, Calista. I really appreciate that. Thanks a lot."

They got back to the hotel, skirted a minivan parked beside the main house, and parked Tommy's van out back by the fence. Calista went up the stairs to the house. A tired looking man in shorts and a polo shirt was talking to Maisie. A woman, around Calista's age, held two small children close to her while listening to the man, looking over when Maisie spoke, nodding approval every few words.

"So, two nights in the cottage, and that includes breakfast for all four of us, right?" He said.

Maisie smiled calmly. "Yes, that's right. Would you like eggs or pancakes for breakfast?"

The man glanced at the woman, an unspoken question. "Could we get both?"

Maisie nodded. "Certainly. What time tomorrow do you want breakfast?"

"Eight o clock?"

"Sure. We'll have the breakfasts ready for you then."

"And it's one-fifty a night, for the four of us? With breakfast?" He asked, cautiously.

"Yes, that's right. Enjoy your stay."

The man grinned, grabbed one child and the woman took the other. They headed out to the minivan, pulled some luggage out of the back and disappeared into cottage number two.

Maisie watched them go, then she gasped. "Oh, heavens, Cali. They saw the sign! They were driving through from Canada and they said they saw the sign! They stopped because they saw the sign. Can you believe it?"

Tommy chuckled. "You're welcome."

Brandon wandered into the house and studied the women's expressions. "Something wrong?" He asked.

"We just got a drive-by. We haven't had drive-by guests in years! And for two nights! Can you believe it?" Maisie said.

Brandon smiled. "Good, well, that means I won't be doing any noisy work on cottage number three while they're around, then. Do you have anything for me to do in the main house?"

Maisie waved her hand in front of her, dismissively. "Never mind that. Cali, we need to get groceries. Come with me."

Calista shrugged and followed her mother out to their station wagon, then they rolled out onto the highway and accelerated as they headed up to Lincoln City. Tommy watched them leave, amused, and turned to look at Brandon. He was still looking down the driveway, watching the dust settle in the afternoon sunlight.

"So, you're really stuck on this girl, huh, Bran?" Tommy asked.

He turned slowly to look at her. "Why do you say that?"

Tommy shrugged. "You got the look. Every time she moves, you follow her. Every time she comes into the room, you light up. What is it about her? The face, the hips, the boobs? All of the above? What?"

Brandon grinned sheepishly and looked down at his feet. "You've still got a bit of the gypsy psychic, you know, Tom?"

Tommy tilted her head back and laughed loudly. "So, are you going to tell me why you really came here? Cause I don't believe the 'taking the summer off' story, you know."

Brandon shook his head. "I was supposed to be discharged this year. I planned to ride up to Alaska, and visit one of my buddies from the unit. Trouble is, he's in Indonesia now. I ran into Calista at this greasy spoon in Lincoln City, and I just couldn't get her out of my head. So I figured I would come here, do some work for her, clear my mind. The Army had said I was done, but now they've pulled me back in for one last tour. I found the induction letter when I went home to get some clothes. So, I'm going to enjoy the summer here, help out Calista and her mom, and then see what life gives me."

Tommy stopped smiling. "Will you be… there?" She sighed. "Where Ollie was…?"

"Yes."

"Does she know?"

"Who?" He asked.

"Calista. Did you tell Calista where you're going? I don't think your ex really cares about anyone except herself. And her cosmetician. "

"That's not fair. We have a beautiful daughter, and I'm very proud of her. The rest of what happened is only between us."

Tommy grunted and pulled a rumpled pack of cigarettes out of her back pocket. She lit one and took a long, slow, puff. She stuck her other hand in her back pocket, scratched her nose with her ring finger, and looked around. The sun had moved southwest, just touching the trees between the cottages and the scrub grass that led to the beach.

The couple from the minivan came out of their cottage, tentatively, like bears coming out of hibernation, and led their children along the path to the ocean. As they crested the low rise, the father saw waves in the distance and walked faster. His wife saw them a moment later, and soon all four were racing along the path and out of sight. Tommy watched them, amused, then turned back to Brandon.

"Look, she's a good kid- Calista, I mean. She doesn't need the grief, that's all, you know?"

"I know, Tommy. She knows I'm deploying. I've been very honest with her."

From over the crest of the sand dunes, they could hear soft squeals of delight, of children splashing in the water, their parents laughing, calling them by name. Tommy smiled at the sound then looked down sadly.

"Well, at least you have a daughter. Ollie and I never got that chance." She said.

They sat on the lower step of the main house, watched the sun set lower into the pines, talked about things they both knew, reminisced about the old days. The family came back from the beach, dripping wet, smiling broadly, and ran into their cottage. They came back out twenty minutes later, washed and dressed, and asked Tommy for a good place to eat dinner. Brandon directed them to Lincoln City, and suggested the hotel or the diner, depending on their taste. The father thanked him and the mother pulled the children behind her to the minivan, skipping as they went, and they drove off.

"Another happy family." Tommy said, sadly.

Brandon watched the minivan roll down the drive and turn onto the highway. "Ollie always said he wanted you two to have kids, you know?"

"Yeah, well, it never happened." Tommy sighed.

"Maybe you'll still find someone- someone nice, like Oliver. Never say never."

"Maybe, Brandon."

Calista and her mother came back a few minutes later. Maisie hurried to get the groceries out of the car, then disappeared into the kitchen and started dinner. Calista set the table, carefully placing herself between Brandon and Tommy, and helped her mother serve. Tommy went out to her cottage and returned with a different bottle of wine. She uncorked it and poured a small glass for everyone, then waited for glasses to be raised in a toast.

"To the end of a perfect day." She said. Everyone repeated it.

Maisie took a sip of the wine. "This is rather tart, isn't it?" She said, rolling the glass in her hand.

"It's a dry Reisling." Tommy explained. "It's supposed to taste like this."

Maisie took another sip. "My, but it does rather grow on you, doesn't it?"

After dinner, Tommy told everyone that she would be leaving on Sunday. She needed to get back to a project she was working on, she said, as they needed her help. She quickly added that she wanted to come back soon, though, and stay for a week or so. Maisie informed her, in no uncertain terms, that she could only come as a friend, not a paying guest.

They retired to the living room for coffee and ice cream. Brandon was most of the way through a story about growing up in San Francisco when the family with the minivan pulled up to their cottage. They piled out, holding hands in a line and singing, then filed into the cottage. The mother rubbed her forehead, tired from the day's drive, and the father squinted and yawned. Ten minutes later, the lights went out in the cottage and the yard went quiet.

Tommy thanked Maisie for dinner and strolled out to the yard. Calista's eyes followed her as Tommy lit a cigarette and leaned back, blowing a cloud of smoke into the sky; it hung around her face then disappeared into vapor. She scratched her leg and wandered into her own cottage, casually.

Brandon was watching Calista, amused. Maisie had gone downstairs to load the washing machine. Calista looked back and saw Brandon grinning at her.

"What?" She asked.

"Are you jealous?" He asked.

Calista raised one eyebrow, melodramatically. "Why? Should I be?"

He chuckled. "She's a friend, just that. No- much more than that. The bond we share is through her husband, however, not through her. But in the way you mean, she's just a friend."

He leaned forward and gave her a soft kiss. "I should let you get some sleep. Good night, Miss Blake."

She finished the routine. "Sleep well, Mister Cooper."

He wrapped an arm around her and gave her a hug, then went out. Almost as if it was choreographed, Maisie came up the stairs at the same moment. She watched him hop down the steps and pause in the yard, just where Tommy had. He stuck his hands in his pockets, leaned back and took a deep breath. Then he turned back to the house, waved at Calista and Maisie, and sauntered to his cottage.

Maisie let out a long sigh. "Well, wasn't that exciting?" She said. "Between the sign and the drop-ins, and everything, I can't recall the last time it was this busy here. Are you all right, Cali? You look tired."

Calista nodded. "Just a bit. Let's get an early night. I want to be fresh for our guests' breakfast tomorrow morning."

They closed up the house and turned out the lights. Maisie went to her room, read a book for a few minutes, and fell asleep with her light on. Calista brushed her teeth and put on a loose T shirt, then gingerly took the book from her mother's hands and turned out the light. Calista slid under her sheets; it was a warm night, with a soft wind heading up from California, up from where Brandon would go back to, after the summer was over. She could almost smell the salt from the beach, carried all the way from Mexico to her room here in Oregon, bringing with it a hint of something exotic, something mysterious. That was not real, she thought. All she could really smell was the clover in Freda Parsoner's field.

She looked out at Brandon's cottage. His light was on, and his door was open. Was this an invitation? Then she saw that Tommy's door was open, too, and the light was on in her bathroom. Calista felt a rush of jealousy at that. Without thinking, she pulled on a pair of sweat pants, crept down the stairs and went across to Brandon's cottage. She knocked softly at the door- no answer. She pushed it open an inch, afraid that she was intruding or interrupting something, then a few inches more. There was nobody there. Brandon wasn't there. Neither was Tommy. She went out to Tommy's cottage and knocked at that door, again softly. Again, there was no answer. she poked her head around the corner and looked in, but again there was nobody there. Tommy's easel and luggage were stacked in two neat piles at the foot of the bed, but she was not there.

Calista went out into the yard, wondering where they were, then she heard it. It sounded like laughing, a low, quiet sort of laughing, coming from the fire pit. She walked toward the sound, picking her way through the gap in the grass, so familiar to her she could do it with her eyes closed, and started to crest the rise before the short walk downhill to the fire. Then she heard another sound, a grunting, moaning sound. Calista stopped. Tommy and Brandon were making love! No, they were having sex! On the beach, her beach, by her fire pit, the one where she had made love to him.

She was filled with fury. She briefly debated storming over and yelling at him, and at Tommy, for betraying her. Then she decided instead to walk away, to say nothing until Tommy left, then later she could tell Brandon that she knew how he had betrayed her. She knew that the love she had for him was gone, and she was angry that he had treated her the way all the men in town treated her. She would talk to him in the morning, after Tommy left. She turned to leave, then she heard another moan, another sigh. This one was different. She stopped. It was Brandon's voice:

"But why? I was the squad C.O. It should have been me, not him. It's not fair. I mean, why him, Tommy, why him?"

Then she heard Tommy's voice. "I know. Listen, I blamed you for so long, Bran, but it wasn't your fault, it was never your fault. I know that now. He was just not meant to be with us for very long. That's all there is to it."

Calista found herself walking toward the fire pit, automatically, not aware of what she was doing. She sat on the log beside Tommy, across from Brandon, and looked into his eyes. There were tears on his face, his eyes were a deep red, and he sniffled, wiping his nose with a large handkerchief. He looked embarrassed, insecure, as though this was a part of him he didn't want her to see.

He coughed, straightened up and smiled slightly. "Good evening. Would you like some wine?" He asked.

"Yes, please."

He reached behind him and picked up a glass. He poured some wine into it and handed it to Calista. Tommy held out her glass and he poured her some too.

He looked back at the main house. "Will your mom be coming out to join us?" He asked.

Calista shook her head. "She's asleep." She took a sip of wine. "Anything you want to talk about?"

He shrugged. "Just catching up on old times, you know. Good times, bad times, old times."

Tommy leaned forward. "Bran still feels guilty about Ollie. Tell her, Brandon. Go on."

Brandon sighed and leaned back, stretching his legs forward, ankles crossed, and looked up, thinking.

He mentally decided something and sat up. "All right. So, a year ago this week, we were ambushed. Where it happened is unimportant. We went there to do good, and we still got shot at every day. Monday will be the anniversary of the incident. That's why the bad memories came back, that's why all the demons were let loose."

Tommy turned to face Calista. "That's why he came here. He wants to get as far from the memories, the people that remind him of the battle, as he can. Right, Brandon?"

Brandon nodded sadly. "Sorry, Calista. I only meant to stop by for the summer to get away from it all. I never expected to meet anyone like you. I never expected to fall…" He stopped himself there.

Tommy stretched her leg out and kicked the bottom of his shoe, playfully. "You old romantic, you." She grinned. "Well, kids, I'm going to get some sleep. Don't do anything I wouldn't do. Good night."

She downed her wine in one quick slurp and left the glass by the log. She leaned over Brandon, gave him a kiss on the cheek and rubbed his hair, playfully. Then she picked her way back to her cottage, slowly, gingerly, following the path in the darkness until she crested the rise and disappeared.

Brandon rubbed his face and sighed again. "So, Calista, why are you out here on this fine night?" He asked.

"I saw your door open. I wondered if you wanted company."

"Company?" He grinned.

She shook her head. "I miss you. I miss being with you, even just spending time alone with you. Is that so strange?"

"That's a very nice thing to say, Cali."

"It's true. Is that why you're going back into the army? Because of Tommy's husband?"

"No, I'm going because they recalled me. That's the only reason."

"Can't you refuse to go, or resign, or something?"

He laughed out loud. "That's not how it works. I'm back in for eighteen months, then I'm out for good. Period."

She looked down into her glass, thinking. "Then what? What will you do after that?"

"I have no idea. What would you like to do? Do you want to sail the South Pacific, or live in a cabin in Switzerland? Whatever you want to do, just tell me, and we'll do it."

"What about running a little hotel in Oregon?" She asked, tentatively.

"Sure, if I can be your one and only handyman."

She looked down at her wine again and watched the inch of pale liquid slosh along the inside of the glass.

"I liked the bubbly one better." She said. "Presto? Prosco?"

He smiled. "Prosecco. It means 'very dry', I think."

"Right. It was very good. This is not bad, but that stuff was really good."

She shrugged. "How do you do it, Brandon? How do you go from being someone with no money worries, to camping out here in the middle of nowhere, with two women who don't have a spare dollar between them?"

He shook his head. "Money won't buy you love, or security, or anything. All it does is give you another ball to juggle. Some people can juggle it better than others, that's all. I've been juggling our business, my work, the army, and the future, as long as I can remember. I guess I'm tired of juggling."

"So, what does that mean, exactly?"

He squinted his eyes. "When I get back, do you want to make it permanent between us?"

Calista studied her wine glass for a long moment. "Maybe. Ask me when you get back. You might change your mind."

"Or you might get a better offer." He said, seriously.

"Could be." She grinned.

She sat on his lap and stared into his eyes, studying them, trying to see into his mind, looking for some insight. She leaned forward and kissed him, gently. He wrapped his arms around her, his hands caressing her spine, rubbing her vertebra, giving her a tingle as his hands touched each one, then he kissed her, too.

She pulled back slowly and stood up. "Good night, Mister Cooper." She whispered.

"Sleep well, Miss Blake."

They walked back hand in hand, saying nothing. They had said everything that needed saying. She went up the steps of the house, turned at the porch and saw him, leaning at the front door of his cottage. He waved, smiled and went in. The light went out, and she went into the main house. She crept upstairs, past her sleeping mother's room, and went to bed.

She closed her eyes, but she could still see Brandon, the fire illuminating his face, his sad smile. She would be awake all night, she thought. She immediately fell asleep.

Chapter Twelve

The next morning was very warm; it started off with big, puffy cumulus clouds drifting north towards Portland. They got darker and thicker up the coast, and dispersed, giving way to a deep blue sky, further south. At a quarter to eight, Maisie had set out plates for the guests, laying the chinaware and cutlery around the big oval table in the front room.

Calista prepared the pancake batter, flipped stacks of thick buckwheat circles and placed them on a warming dish by the stove. Maisie grilled sausages and scrambled eggs, checking every so often that the coffee was percolating.

Brandon wandered in and sat at the small table in the kitchen, keeping out of the way. Calista set a place and placed a plate of pancakes and eggs in front of him. He smiled warmly at her, and she sheepishly smiled back.

Tommy sauntered out of her cottage, stretched her arms high, and swung them in a big circle. She hopped up the steps and gave Maisie a warm hug.

"Gosh, I slept well." Tommy said. "It's too bad I have to go back so soon. I could get used to this."

Ten minutes later, the family came out of their cottage and filled the dining room, full of comments about the beach, questions about Oregon and hungrily sniffing the air for breakfast. They sat at the oval table, and quietly waited while Maisie brought out their food. They ate quickly at first, devouring the food, then they slowed down, talking and stretching between mouthfuls. Tommy and Brandon ate with them, chatting

Maisie appeared with a pitcher and a hot carafe. "More coffee? Anyone want milk?" She asked.

The woman nodded. "Yes, please. You have a lovely hotel here. I'm so glad we stopped on our way south."

"Where are you going?" Maisie asked.

The man wiped his mouth on a napkin and pointed out the door. "We're going down to Eureka, California. My cousin lives there, and he always bugs us to come and visit him, so we finally decided we'd go see him."

Maisie poured coffee into his cup, and he grunted approval. "I see. Where do you live?" She asked.

"Calgary, Alberta. We left Calgary on Wednesday, made it all the way to Yakima, Washington, and stayed there overnight. We wanted to drive straight through to Eureka, but the kids were getting restless, so we stopped here."

"Well, we're glad you did. I hope you enjoy your stay." Maisie said. She turned to leave.

The man touched her arm. "When do you get your first snowfall, down here? How bad is the drive over here in winter?"

"Snow?" Maisie shook her head. "I think we got a dusting about eight or ten years ago. We don't get snow, usually."

His eyes widened. "So, would you have any vacancies around Canadian Thanksgiving? In October?"

Maisie reached behind her and took a business card from the sideboard. "Possibly. Call us with your preferred dates, and we'll let you know what we have." She handed him the card.

He took the card, read it slowly, and tapped it against his other hand. "If I wanted to rent one or two cottages besides ours, with some friends, could we get them in some kind of package deal?"

Maisie's expression didn't change. "What did you have in mind?"

He pointed the card at the door. "I figure next time we'll all fly down to Portland and rent a couple of vans. Let's say we wanted three cottages for three nights."

Maisie glanced into the kitchen. Brandon had heard everything, of course, from behind the wall, where the others couldn't see him. He held up a hand with one outstretched finger, and the other hand with two fingers. Maisie blinked gently. "Certainly. We could offer you the cottages at one twenty per night per cottage. Would that be acceptable?"

"How much would it be with this breakfast thrown in?" He asked.

Maisie didn't bother looking at Brandon. "Oh, we could add that on for just ten dollars a cottage." She smiled.

The man grinned approval, pocketed the card, and went back to eating. Twenty minutes later, the family slowly pushed away from the table, thanked Maisie profusely and sauntered out for a walk on the beach.

Maisie watched them leave and turned to look at Brandon. "My goodness! Three cottages, for three nights! And for over a hundred dollars a night, too! What people are willing to pay for a room these days!"

Brandon shook his head and put down his coffee. "I told you, people don't just want a bed for the night, they want to enjoy a new experience. This hotel gives them that experience. That's worth something, Maisie. Never forget that."

The family said they were driving down to Newport for the day, and that they would probably be back late. The husband pulled a wad of money out of his pocket and gave it to Maisie, for the two nights' stay. He told her he wanted to be sure he paid her, and besides, he wanted her to know he was serious when he called her later in the year.

Brandon spent the day scraping paint off the outside of the fourth cottage. After the family left, he said he'd get going on the noisy stuff, sanding the floors and so on. Calista made up the bed in their cottage, cleaned the bathroom and swept the floor. She couldn't remember the last time they'd had someone stay over for two nights, so she wanted to leave a very good impression. Tommy announced that she had a friend out near Coos Bay she'd promised to visit, but she'd be back in time for dinner. She roared down the drive and onto the highway again, Willie Nelson still blasting from her stereo.

Maisie served lunch on the porch, just sandwiches and coffee, and the hungry gulls circled overhead, hoping for scraps. Brandon peeled a crust off his sandwich and tossed it into the air; a passing seagull caught it before it hit the ground. He finished his meal and leaned back in the wicker chair, sighing along with the creaking wicker, and closed his eyes.

Calista went in to do the dishes, and Maisie announced that she had to go into Lincoln City; she wanted to pay some bills and deposit the cash in the bank. She giggled at the wad of bills, stuffed it into her purse and said she'd be back within a couple of hours. She fired up the station wagon, kicking up gravel as she momentarily forgot about the new power it had, and sped down the driveway.

Brandon was now almost asleep. He felt good, calm, more at peace than he had felt in a very long time. Calista came back out of the house and placed her arm on his shoulder.

"How are you feeling?" She asked.

He wriggled in the chair, his eyes still closed. "Wonderful. If I could bottle this feeling, I'd be a very rich man." He said.

"So, um, we're all alone for a few hours." Calista said. "Anything you'd like to do?"

He opened one eye, slowly. "Like what?"

Calista leaned forward and kissed him. He glanced down her top and saw that she was no longer wearing a bra.

"Oh." He smiled. "I see."

They walked hand-in-hand to Brandon's cottage, closed the door and made love. Even after having lived here all her life, being in the cottage with him, alone, with nobody else at home, felt like the night they had made love in the casino hotel; it felt exotic, hedonistic, sinful, in a 'good sinful' sort of way.

Afterward, she lay on the bed on top of him, her hair cascading over his shoulder, her cheek against his neck. He rubbed her spine with two fingers, pausing at every vertebra, moving slowly down to the curve of her backside and back up again. He leaned back slightly to look into her eyes.

"Why did you suggest we make love this afternoon?" He asked. "Not that I'm complaining, you understand."

"Carpe diem." Calista said. "Why pass up the chance?"

She lifted her head and looked toward the door. "After all, I'm not sure if I'll see you again, after the summer."

He looked at the door too and sighed. "Believe me, Calista, you'll see me. That's for sure."

She slumped down again and rubbed his arm. "You promise?" She repeated.

"I promise."

An hour later, Brandon was back at work on the fourth cottage, humming to himself. Calista prepared dinner, swept the porch and waited patiently for Maisie to come back. They occasionally looked over, catching each other's eye and grinning like mischievous school children. Brandon sanded the cottage's floors, cleaned up the mess and packed away the equipment before the visiting family came back. Maisie showed up a while later, bubbly and pleased with herself at having paid some bills, and helped set the table for four. Right on time, Tommy's van crept down the drive and parked out back, away from the road.

They ate dinner, talking and laughing. Tommy told stories about Brandon, how he had done silly things in the past, how he had used his charm to get out of embarrassing situations, and Brandon smiled good-naturedly as she spoke.

They had coffee on the porch, at Tommy's suggestion, and watched as the sun went down to the horizon. The sky went from deep blue to a golden orange color, painting the western wall of the house and cottages with a soft glow. Just as the last light of day left, the distant streetlights out on the highway came on, and two beams of yellow light turned down the driveway. The family in the cottage, returning from their day out. They got out of their van, laughing at something, and stopped to say hello at the bottom of the steps.

"We saw whales today." One of the children giggled. "They were jumping this high." He leapt up and twirled around, giddy with delight. His mother took his arm, faced him toward the cottage and wished everyone a good night.

The father took his other child's hand and squatted down, pointing at the crescent moon, and said something to her. She nodded, smiled, and they headed for the cottage. The child turned a few steps later and waved at Calista. Calista waved back, automatically. The father was almost at the cottage steps when he turned back to look at Maisie.

"So, if we were to come back this way, would you have vacancies later this month?" He called.

Maisie nodded. "Call us. I'll let you know."

He waved goodnight and went into the cottage. Maisie watched the door close, then she leaned over and kissed Brandon on the cheek. He blushed a deep red. Calista didn't think she'd ever see him blush like that.

"What was that for?" He laughed.

"Happy guests. Thank you from the bottom of my heart. I don't know how we can ever repay you." She said.

Brandon shot a quick guilty glance at Calista; she smirked and turned away. Maisie never saw either look.

The next morning, the family in the cottage ate breakfast, took a last walk out on the beach and thanked Maisie for a lovely stay. They loaded up their minivan and drove off. It was suddenly very quiet.

Brandon finished a second coffee and announced that he wanted to finish work on the fourth cottage. Tommy asked Maisie if she'd mind her doing a portrait of the main house.

By noon, Tommy was lost in thought, her easel set up on the far side of the driveway, a tub of water beside her to soak her paint brushes, and a canvas in front of her, holding all of her attention. She had two thin brushes in her hair, sticking out comically like feathers on a hat. Brandon finished the cottage floor, and got ready to paint the outside walls. Maisie called them in for lunch, and both Tommy and Brandon straggled in, reluctant to leave their activities. Calista was in the kitchen, setting out portions of shepherd's pie.

Tommy went upstairs to wash up, and Maisie followed to show her where the clean towels were. Brandon leaned over and stroked Calista's hip.

He leaned close to her ear. "Hey there, sexy." He whispered.

Calista glanced over to see that Maisie was still upstairs. She kissed him, quickly. "Hello to you, too." She said.

They giggled like children for a moment, then Brandon looked down, serious.

"Listen, I've already told your mom how I feel about you. Do we really have to sneak around like high school kids? Why can't we be more open in front of her?"

Calista shook her head. "It's not just for my mother, Brandon. It's for me, too. I've been hurt before. I don't think you'd want to hurt me, but in all honesty. I don't know where you'll be in a year, and you can't guarantee that life will bring you back here. I need some space, some emotional distance for myself. Please understand that."

He shrugged. "Fair enough. So, there's a dance in town tonight, as I remember?"

She grinned. "Yes, at the fire hall. Are you asking me to the dance, Mister Cooper?"

"I am. Miss Blake, would you do me the honor of accompanying me to the dance?"

"I would be delighted. What about Tommy? Can she come too?"

"Yeah, she's a party animal. I think we'll have to bring her along." Brandon said.

They spent the afternoon doing normal things; Brandon papered, taped and sanded the fourth cottage then painted it. He waited a couple of hours for the paint to dry then pulled the paper and tape off. It looked like unwrapping a Christmas gift; the cottage was a crisp off-yellow color, with vivid white trim and shiny wood deck. It looked new. He loaded the furniture from one of the other cottages and set it up, ready to rent.

By six that night Maisie had dinner ready; Brandon had washed and changed to good clothes for the dance. Tommy and Calista chatted and laughed like old friends, finishing each other's sentences and speaking in short phrases. Everyone ate quickly, Maisie rushing in and out of the kitchen, swapping plates and filling glasses, then Tommy announced that they were heading into Lincoln City, and Maisie said she was going to telephone some friends.

Tommy roared down the drive. Brandon sat in the back seat, hanging on for dear life, and Calista sat beside Tommy, laughing at something Tommy had said. They pulled up to the fire hall as the dance was just starting. Groups of people, in twos and fours, sauntered up to the front door. A young woman sitting behind a folding table had a metal box in front of her; she took people's money then stamped their hands, and pointed at the entrance door. Brandon climbed out of the van's side door and opened the passenger door for Calista. He held her hand as she stepped out, their eyes meeting in an unspoken conversation, and he wrapped his arm around her waist to lead her to the other side of the van.

Tommy jumped down and brushed herself off, casually. Both she and Calista were in jeans and blouses, with sensible shoes for dancing. Brandon wore khaki slacks and a polo shirt, with an army crest on the shirt. As they hurried across the street, Brandon saw a familiar figure leaning over the young woman at the front door. She seemed uneasy, nervous.

Brandon recognized Glen, wearing an ill-fitting suit and too-shiny shoes. He was smiling, leering, persistent, and the young woman seemed relieved when she saw Brandon and Calista. She sat up and looked at them.

"Hi." Brandon said. "Three, please." He handed her some money and she stamped his hand, pausing as she held it, then quickly stamped Tommy's and Calista's hands.

Brandon turned to Glen. "Hello again. Are you here by yourself, or will your lovely wife be here too?" He asked.

Glen seemed uneasy at the comment. He glanced at the young woman and mumbled "Yeah, she's here."

"Good to hear." Brandon effused. "I'd like to say hi to her again." He nodded at the young woman then steered Tommy and Calista in front of him, toward the door.

Tommy leaned close to him and whispered "Who's the butt hole?"

Calista snickered at the comment. Brandon tilted his head back. "He's a real estate guy. He bought the place next to Calista's."

Tommy grunted. "I smell a weasel. Am I wrong about him?"

Brandon chuckled. "No, you're not, Tommy."

They went into the fire hall and Brandon looked around. A long table was set up by one wall, selling coffee and cookies, while another table beside it sold soft drinks. A pair of lanky firefighters stood behind the tables, fidgeting as they waited for the dance to start.

A third firefighter was on a raised platform, working controls on a panel in front of him, turning dials as he looked intently at a pair of speakers just in front of him. There was a soft hiss, then a loud guitar twang, and the firefighter grinned with satisfaction. The music started, and the small group swelled in size as if by magic, covering the floor.

Brandon grabbed Calista and dragged her out to the floor. They spun and bopped to the music; old rockabilly songs, pounding rock & roll, and country tunes that Brandon didn't recognize. He danced to them anyway. He glanced over to see Tommy out across the floor, laughing and spinning around with a slender young man in a cowboy shirt.

Five songs into the dance, Brandon asked Calista if she wanted a break. Reluctantly, she nodded and they picked their way through the crowd to one of the side tables. He bought drinks for them and handed her a cola.

He leaned close to her ear, and spoke loudly through the music. "Having fun?" He asked.

She looked into his eyes, smiled, then nodded. She leaned close to his ear. "And you?"

He stroked her arm and let his hand brush over her thigh. "With you, always."

Tommy came up beside them, dragging the young man with her. "Hey, Bran. This is Warren. Warren, Brandon. Warren is in the army, too." She said it proudly.

Brandon nodded. "Glad to meet you, Warren. Enjoying the dance?"

The young man nodded. "Yeah, I am. You're regular army? I'm in the Army National Guard, out of Newport."

Brandon smiled, but seemed uncomfortable. "That's great. You guys do good work. Nice to see you here."

The young man continued. "So, I'm a Sergeant, in the infantry. Can I ask your rank, Brandon?"

Brandon shuffled his feet. Calista had never seen him so ill at ease. "You know, we're all just here for a good time. How about we leave it at first names?"

The young man frowned, obviously unhappy with the answer. "Sure. Enjoy your evening, mister."

He walked away, and Tommy went after him. Calista watched as she tugged on the man's sleeve, then said something to him, poking him in the chest. Tommy pointed at Brandon then wagged her finger at the man. She said something else, and the man's mouth dropped open. He looked over at Brandon, surprised. He walked back, quickly.

"I'm so sorry, sir." He stammered. "I didn't know, like, I never realized, you know..."

Brandon held his hand up and grinned. "That's ok. But if you salute me, I'll have you court-martialed."

The man laughed nervously and went back to rejoin Tommy. The music started and he took her in his arms, dancing to the tune. Within a minute, he was talking to her casually, the conversation with Brandon gone from his mind.

Brandon turned to Calista. "Want to dance some more?" He yelled over the music.

She shook her head and pointed at the door. "I need some fresh air." She said.

They went out into the cool of the evening, breathing in the clear air, refreshing after being in the heat of the fire hall.

Calista took his hand and pulled him across the street to a small park, then sat on the bench under a sprawling oak tree. "When I was a little girl, I remember climbing this tree." She said. "My mother used to get so upset at me for doing that, but I think my father was just happy that I was active, even for a girl."

Brandon looked up at the thick branches. "Why does it not surprise me, that you'd do that?"

"Are you saying that I'm reckless?" She asked.

"I'm saying you have an adventurous soul." He answered.

He looked over Calista's shoulder at a figure walking toward them. It was Glen, the real estate salesman, and his wife, the waitress. Glen came over to the back of the bench and leaned over it, hovering over Calista.

"Hi there, Cali." He slurred. "Enjoying the dance?"

Calista scowled at him. "Have you been drinking, Glen? You sound a little sloshed."

He shook his head. "Not much. I just need to talk to your friend here about the Parsoner land. You do know I bought it, right?"

"Yes, Glen. Freda Parsoner told me you did."

He walked around the bench and poked a finger at Calista, almost into her face. "You think I'm an idiot, don't you?"

Brandon gritted his teeth, his face turning slightly red. "Glen, you may want to take a step back right now."

Glen pivoted and shook the finger at Brandon. "You stay out of this. It's your fault that I ended up buying that worthless piece of dirt. You stay out of this."

His wife looked around, trying to avoid staring at her husband, shifting her weight from foot to foot. She sighed. "Come on, Glen, let's just go home. Leave it alone, all right?"

Glen glared at her and turned back to Brandon. "You think you put one over on me, don't you?"

Brandon shook his head. "Glen, you're drunk. Why don't we talk about this in the morning?"

He went to stand up but Glen pushed him back down. "No, we'll talk about it now."

Brandon went bright red and his expression changed to solemn, determined. He raised one foot and kicked Glen in the inside of his knee. Not hard, just forcefully enough that Glen's leg buckled. Glen fell backwards onto the grass and grabbed his sore leg. Brandon stood up, slowly, and casually stood on Glen's calf. Glen grimaced in pain.

"I have tried to be civil to you, despite everything you've done to me." Brandon said, his voice a staccato, chopped speech. "And you still keep trying to annoy me. How stupid can you be, Glen?"

Brandon squatted down to stare at the big man, his foot still firmly on Glen's leg. "I should tear you apart-brick by lousy brick. But you know what? If you think I've cheated you, I will buy the Parsoner land from you. How about that?"

Glen winced with pain, but looked up at Brandon, surprised. "Huh?" He said.

Brandon took his foot away and let Glen get up. Glen brushed off his jacket and stared at Brandon, incredulous.

"Why would you do that?" He asked.

"How much did you pay for the Parsoner land?" Brandon asked.

Glen thought for a moment. "A hundred thousand dollars." He said.

"That's a lie. I know you paid ninety." Brandon said. "However, I'll write you a check tomorrow for a hundred and ten thousand dollars for that land. Do we have a deal?"

Calista stared at Brandon. He had said the price casually, as if he was buying a toaster, she thought.

Brandon repeated it. "A hundred and ten thousand dollars. Do you want to sell the land?"

Glen thought for a moment. "Why? What do you want to buy it for?"

"My business. My money, my business. A hundred and ten thousand dollars. Yes or no?"

Glen snickered. "I think I'll pass. Thanks, but that land is mine. Good night."

Glen stumbled off into the dark night. His wife muttered something apologetic to Calista and shuffled after him.

Brandon watched them go then turned to Calista. "All right, want to dance some more?" He smiled.

She stared at him. "Why would you do that? Why would you offer to buy Freda's land from Glen?"

"I was sure he wouldn't sell it if I offered to buy it. For the next year or two, he'll convince himself that I was trying to cheat him out of a valuable property. That's exactly what I was betting he'd do."

"Why did you think that?" She asked.

"He tried to cheat you, and he tried to cheat Mrs. Parsoner. That's what he is- a cheat. He can't conceive of someone trying to do right by him, so he turned me down."

Calista shook her head. "And if he'd accepted your offer?"

"Then I'd have yet another reason to come back this way."

Calista looked over at the fire hall. "That man in there, the one in the National Guard, what did he mean?"

"About what?" Brandon asked.

"He said he didn't know. What didn't he know?"

Brandon shook his head. "That I outrank him, that's all. Want to dance some more?"

Calista grinned and took his hand. They danced long into the evening, the altercation with Glen now a distant memory, then around midnight Tommy gave Brandon a quick nod, and Brandon casually guided Calista out the back door toward Tommy's van. They piled in, Tommy looked around quickly, started the engine and raced out onto the highway.

Brandon was thrown to the floor. He struggled to sit up and found his seat, eventually. He leaned forward, resting his wrists on the front seats.

"So, Tommy, are we outrunning the cops, or what?" He asked.

She laughed. "No, but I think soldier boy back there was about to propose or something. Sorry, no more of that commitment stuff for me, thanks. I need my space."

Brandon glanced at Calista. She smirked and rolled down her window, then leaned out and took a deep breath. She hung her arms out the window, letting the cool air rush over her. Brandon reached around the seat and caressed her waist; Tommy didn't see it.

Calista looked at his hand on her hip and smiled at him.

They turned off the highway and onto the long gravel drive to the hotel; only the porch light was on in the main house, but two cars were parked in the yard, and there were lights on inside two cottages. Calista turned to Brandon.

"It seems we have guests." She mumbled.

Tommy thanked Brandon for a fun evening and went into her cottage. The light went out a minute later and the yard was dead quiet. Brandon looked up at the sky and took a deep breath. He closed his eyes, savoring the fresh air, the quiet, the evening.

Calista wrapped her arms around him and kissed him, gently.

"Thank you for a wonderful evening, Mister Cooper." She said.

He smiled warmly. "The pleasure was all mine, Miss Blake. Good night."

She kissed him again. "Good night, Mister Cooper."

Calista crept up the steps to the main house and turned on a small table lamp in the living room. A soft yellow light filled the room, dim enough that it did not feel annoying, but bright enough that Calista could see her way to the top of the stairs. She walked through the dining room, towards the kitchen, and noticed a note on the table. It said, simply, 'two cottages, six guests, breakfast at eight.' Calista read the note, silently thanked tommy's large sign, and went to bed.

Seven thirty the next morning, and the sun beat in through the open window, warming Calista's left foot, which was sticking out from under the crisp white sheets. She half-opened one eye, pulled the foot back under the sheet, and tried to sleep some more. It was no good- her foot was too warm, and there was laughing and the sound of slamming car doors in the yard. She got up, threw on a sweater and skirt, and went downstairs.

Maisie was racing back and forth, making breakfast. She glanced at Calista and sighed.

"Hello, dear. Have a good time at the dance? Sorry, I'm rushing here." Maisie said.

"Yes, it was wonderful, thanks. Can I help?" Calista answered.

"Yes. Set the table for six, if you would. Four adults, two children. Everyone wants eggs. Everyone wants waffles."

Calista pulled napkins, place mats, cutlery and glasses out of the cupboard, almost mechanically. She was halfway to the dining room when it occurred to her to ask the obvious question.

"When did these people show up?" She asked.

"Late last night. They're friends of our other guests- the ones from Canada. Those people talked about our place here, and this group is staying just for the one night, but with breakfast too. I tell you, Cali, if this keeps up, I'm going to have to hire some help." She grinned at the statement.

At eight o clock exactly, two groups of people came in, a couple in their thirties who looked like bankers in casual clothes, and a family with two teenage boys, both of whom kept looking at Calista. Everyone talked with everyone, it seemed. Conversations were going back and forth across the room. Brandon and Tommy appeared and introduced themselves as family friends. Maisie came through with breakfast, and the room went suddenly quiet. The sound of voices was replaced by the sound of clattering dishes and cutlery. A half hour later, Calista was leaning against the sideboard, sipping coffee. One of the teenage boys was still watching her very move, while the other wanted to ask about the ocean.

"There is a sandy beach through there." Calista explained. "If you have time, you can go for a walk this morning."

One boy sat up straight. "Do you ever go swimming there?" He asked.

"Sometimes, when the water's not too cold." She answered.

His eyes glazed over slightly, as he imagined seeing her in a wet swimsuit. Calista knew the look. She turned to look at the woman who was not the 'banker type'. "Where are you headed?" She asked.

The woman patted her lips and nodded at the door. "We're driving through to San Diego. I promised my nephews we'd all go see Disneyland this summer. Right, guys?"

The two boys nodded. She took a sip of coffee. "I'm glad we stopped in. This is a real little gem you have here."

Calista smiled and nodded. "Thank you. We like it."

Two hours later, the six guests had walked down to the beach and back, collected seashells from the sand and business cards from Maisie, and packed up their vehicles. They gratefully accepted a dozen muffins in a box and drove in tandem down the highway, headed for California.

Maisie watched them leave, then gave a deep sigh. "My word, Cali, that was unexpected. They just showed up here last night, right after you left, and booked a cottage each. Can you believe it? They asked what our rates were, and I told them it would be a hundred and fifty dollars a night, and one fellow said 'is that each person?' and I said 'no, for each cottage'. And they just said 'sure' and gave me the cash. Can you believe it?"

Brandon smiled. "See. There you go. I told you, this is a special place. I should get going on the last two cottages, before you have to start turning people away."

Calista helped Maisie clean up the breakfast dishes, then Tommy walked into the main house, a forlorn look on her face.

"Well, I should be going. This has been a wonderful time, ladies. I hope I can come back again." She said, hopefully.

Maisie put down her tea towel and put her arms around Tommy's shoulders. "Oh, dear, listen, any time you want to come by, please feel free to just drop in. We'd love to have you stay with us, wouldn't we, Calista?"

Calista nodded. "You will always be welcome to stay here, you know that, right?" She said.

Tommy nodded. "Thanks. Thanks to both of you, for everything. I'm just going to pack up my stuff."

She turned and went out to her cottage. Maisie watched her go and sighed. "She's a good person, isn't she, Cali?"

"Yeah, she is, mom. Do we have any muffins left to send off with her?"

"Of course we do."

Twenty minutes later, Tommy had thrown her bag into her van and lit the last cigarette in her pack. She stretched backwards, arched her spine, and swung her arms in a circle. Maisie handed her a basket of muffins and gave her a hug. Calista gave her a hug too, wished her all the best and made sure Tommy had their business card, to keep in touch.

Tommy got in her van, blew a kiss to Brandon and pointed at the highway. She stuck her head out the window and grinned at Calista.

"Hey! I didn't accidentally leave anything behind. It's for you!" She called, and sped off.

Calista and Maisie went to Tommy's cottage, filled with curiosity. Propped up on the bed was the painting Tommy had been working on, a painting of the main house, almost as realistic as a photograph. There were three people in the painting; Maisie was standing on the porch, wiping her hands on her apron, and Brandon was in the yard in front of the house, kissing Calista.

Calista froze for a minute, wondering what to say. "Ah." She finally said.

Maisie looked at it for a long moment, not saying anything. She sighed and tilted her head. "Well, she certainly captured the feeling of the place, didn't she?"

Calista smiled and tilted her head slightly as well. "I think I'm a little taller than that, though."

Maisie nodded. "Well, if you don't mind, this is going up in my room."

She carried the painting to the main house, and Calista walked out to the fourth cottage. Brandon was touching up the paint on the outside windows, waiting for the lacquer to dry on the floor inside before he put the furniture back in the cottage. He put down his paint brush. "Hey, how are you feeling? Are you sorry to see Tommy go?" He asked.

Calista shrugged. "Yeah, it was nice to have another woman around, for a change."

"I suppose." He said. "I want to finish this cottage, then I'm going to take the afternoon off, if that's all right."

"Sure." Calista said. "Is there anything you want to do?"

"Yeah. I'd like to have a picnic up at Porter Point, out where they're building that casino. Want to come with me?"

"I'll make lunch." She grinned.

They rode up past Lincoln City, along Highway 101, the sun at their backs, with Calista stretched out in the sidecar, a wicker basket in her lap. The motorcycle slowed with a 'whump-whump' sound as they turned down Wi Ne Ma Road, and chugged as they followed it to a parking lot at the end of the street.

Brandon turned off the engine and took Calista's basket. She stretched out one leg to hurdle out of the sidecar, fell forward and landed against Brandon's chest. She grinned, embarrassed.

"This feels like déjà vu." He joked.

They walked, hand in hand, down the path to the beach. Brandon looked for dead crabs, like the one that had them both falling into the water before, but found none. Calista scowled at him about that, then they turned the corner and saw the large rock in the water by Porter Point.

It was as big as a house, sitting alone a few feet out from the beach, like a large grey egg on a sandbar. Calista set up a blanket and opened out her basket, placing dishes and napkins around the basket, then sandwiches and a thermos of coffee on one corner of the blanket, to keep the breeze from lifting it.

Brandon sat with her, nibbled on a sandwich and potato chips, then looked out to sea, a faraway look in his eyes.

"Something wrong?" Calista asked.

He shook his head. "I'm just enjoying this moment, that's all. I'm having lunch with a beautiful woman, sitting on a beautiful beach, on a beautiful day, and enjoying a beautiful sandwich. What more could a man want?"

Calista lay down on the blanket and closed her eyes. The warm sun and the soft breeze soothed her. Brandon leaned over her, momentarily blocking the sun, and kissed her. "Penny for your thoughts?" He asked.

She shielded her eyes with her hand and looked up at him, the sun behind him forming a halo around his head.

"I was just remembering the times we came here when I was a little girl." She said.

She sat up and pointed at the rock in the water. "I used to climb up there, and once I found a big spike or nail or something, and carved my initials on the top of the rock. My mother was furious at me for climbing up there, but my father said 'let her climb'. He was always a lot more forgiving than mom about my behavior."

"Do you think the initials are still there?" Brandon asked.

"Maybe. It's been a few years, after all."

He stood up and unlaced his shoes, then peeled off his socks. "I'm going to check." He announced.

He ran out into the water, barely ankle-deep in the low tide, and got to the rock. He surveyed it, carefully deciding how he should scale it, and leapt up unto a narrow ledge on the side. He teetered, then pushed away and landed on the sand again, stumbled backwards and sat down. He laughed at the misstep and stood up, brushing sand off.

He took another run at the rock, got most of the way to the top, and slowed, deciding on his next step. He wobbled slightly, stepped on the slippery seaweed covering part of the stone, and suddenly his foot slid to one side. He slammed sideways into the rock, bounced like a rag doll and landed on his feet on the sand. Calista started to laugh, then she saw the pained expression on his face. He grimaced, grabbed his left leg and hobbled back to her.

"Well, that was stupid." He muttered.

He looked down at his leg, and Calista's eyes followed his. There was a gash on his calf, with blood streaming out of it.

He slipped his belt off and wrapped it tightly around his upper calf like a tourniquet. He had a scrape on his knee as well, and a purple mark on the side of his foot.

"That looks bad." Calista said. "We should get you to the doctor's. Doctor Maddox is our family GP, in Lincoln city. He should be in today. Come on, let's go."

She quickly packed up the picnic basket and waited for Brandon to walk beside her. He hobbled a few feet, then his knee bent under him and he fell over. "Damn." He grunted.

He stood again, hopped on his good leg and tried to walk some more. This time he got about twenty feet before he stumbled. Calista looked around and found a long, fairly straight piece of driftwood, and he held this up like a staff and leaned against it for support.

With Calista tucked under his good arm, he managed to hobble back to the motorcycle. They put the picnic basket down in the sidecar, and Brandon tried to throw a leg over the motorcycle's seat. He grimaced in pain and leaned back.

"Can you ride a motorcycle?" He asked her.

She laughed. "No, I've never been on one before yours."

"Ah, right. You told me that. Look, here's what you do."

He explained the throttle, the brakes, the gear shift, then told Calista to start the motor and lifted himself into the sidecar. Calista put on her helmet and gingerly let out the clutch. The motorcycle sputtered and stalled. She looked over at Brandon, embarrassed.

"It's OK." He said. "I did that a lot when I first started riding it. Try again."

She started the motor, gave it gas, then let the clutch out, more carefully this time, and the motorcycle started to roll.

Calista squealed with glee, looked over at Brandon, then remembered to steer and pointed the wheel toward the road, and back to the highway.

Within five minutes, she was feeling confident, steering, shifting and braking smoothly, and she bounced up and down in the seat, laughing at the sensation of speeding along.

Brandon watched her, amused, and had to remind her as they entered Lincoln City that he needed to see the doctor. Calista had almost forgotten, in the thrill of driving the motorcycle, that they were going there.

They rolled to a stop in front of the doctor's office, and Calista helped Brandon out of the sidecar. They hobbled up the steps to the doctor's front door and went in. there was only one other person in the waiting room, a sad-faced old man who stared at Brandon as though he had landed in a flying saucer.

The doctor's nurse came out from the back and recognized Calista. "Hi, how are you, hon?" She said.

She looked down at Brandon's leg, blood still oozing despite the belt around his calf, and grabbed his arm. "Ooh. Looks bad. Come with me." She said.

She guided Brandon into the doctor's office and they disappeared into a back room. Calista heard voices from behind the door. The nurse was walking back and forth, Calista could see from the shadows on the frosted glass doors, and Doctor Maddox was talking in his low, careful way of speaking. Then Brandon's voice, clear and confident, every so often.

"No, I'm just helping out the two ladies who own it." She heard him say, through the door.

Then an older man's voice, doctor Maddox, said something, and his nurse said 'Triple O silk, right."

Brandon's voice again; "That's fine. My insurance will cover it."

Calista waited for what seemed an eternity, then the frosted glass door opened and Brandon walked out, still limping, with a wide bandage on his leg. He grinned at Calista and turned back to face the nurse.

"Thank the doctor again for me, would you? He does good work." He said.

He turned back to Calista. "There, all done. Can we go home now?"

"What happened in there?" Calista asked.

"Ten stitches in my leg, and a tensor bandage to stop the bleeding." He said.

Calista helped him down the few steps to the street and toward the motorcycle. "Can you drive home?" She asked.

He shook his head. "Working the controls might tear the stitches. Can you drive us home?"

Calista's heart raced. She had half-hoped he would say that; driving the motorcycle was more thrilling than anything she had ever done. Brandon wedged himself in, his bad leg up in the air, hanging comically over the front of the sidecar, and put his helmet on. Calista put her helmet on, looked over to see he was settled comfortably, and started the engine. She wriggled in the seat, grinned broadly and rolled out onto the road.

Brandon watched her, amused, as she bit her lip and concentrated on shifting gears, then pointed the machine straight and roared toward home.

She hunched over the gas tank, leaning into the handlebars, and glanced over at Brandon every so often, smiling at him as she did. She turned the final corner to the hotel, slowed as she saw Tommy's large plywood sign, and rolled smoothly down toward the main house. There were cars scattered over the yard, with people milling around, talking and laughing. Maisie was in the yard, talking to the people, pointing and waving at the cottages. She casually noticed the motorcycle headed toward her, but did a quick double-take when she saw Calista driving, with Brandon in the sidecar, his leg sticking out.

She walked over to join them. "My goodness, what happened?" She gasped.

"I was clumsy. I slipped off a rock." Brandon said meekly.

"Does it hurt?"

"Some. Actually, it kind of tired me out more than anything."

Maisie frowned. "Oh, my. Well, Cali, we have four cottages rented for tonight. It seems that word has spread about the hotel. Brandon, I had to move your things out of your cottage. Is it alright if you sleep in the main house for now?"

"I could stay in the fifth cottage." He offered.

"Nonsense, it's chaotic in there. Would you mind being in the main house?" Maisie said.

He glanced over at Calista. "Not at all. Do you need any help getting me set up?"

Maisie shook her head. "No. You go inside and lie down. We'll manage just fine. Come, Cali, let's go."

Maisie went back to the yard; she greeted everyone, directed them to their cottages, explained where the beach was, and waved at the main house, describing the procedure for breakfast. In their groups, the people piled into the cottages to unpack. Brandon sat in a chair on the porch, amused at the sudden swarm of activity.

He leaned back, closed his eyes, and relaxed, letting the heat of the afternoon sun warm him, while the overhang of the porch kept most of the light out of his eyes. His body slumped, went limp, and he fell asleep.

A while later, a hand on his shoulder made him jump. He woke up and opened his eyes. Calista was looking down at him, smiling. "Hey there. Sorry to disturb you." She whispered.

"No, it's all right. How long was I asleep?" He asked.

"Three hours. You must have really been tired. Anyway, I've set up the spare room for you, in the house."

He followed Calista to a door behind the dining room. He opened the door, to what must have been the servants' quarters when the hotel was built. It had one of the beds that he'd brought them, a tall dresser, and a sink, but nothing else. A square window looked out over the dunes, toward the beach. It was clean, and it smelled fresh, but it was small and simple.

"This is fine." He said.

"I'm sorry that it's rather plain, but it's the only room we have. We didn't plan on being fully booked." Calista apologized.

"Get used to it. I have a feeling you won't be running empty for much longer." He said.

Calista stared at him for a moment and hugged him tight. He grinned, amused. "What was that for?" He asked.

"Thank you. You saved our home." She said. "You do realize that, don't you? I can't thank you enough for that."

"So, do you forgive me for leaving so suddenly before?"

"Yes. Dinner will be in a half hour. Are you hungry?"

He sighed. "Yeah. I really am. It must be the shock of the stitches and all, I guess. What's for dinner?"

"Shepherd's pie."

"Sounds perfect." He said.

Chapter Thirteen

Maisie prepared dinner, with Calista's help, while Brandon sat at the table, feeling vaguely useless. A few times, they were interrupted by people from the cottages, coming to ask whether it was a public beach, how to get to Lincoln City, and if there was a good restaurant there. Maisie cheerfully answered their questions, and then all the people eventually went off in two cars, headed out to dinner. The hotel seemed very quiet again. Maisie served the shepherd's pie while Calista set out salad.

Brandon went to the spare room, rummaged through his things and came back to the table with a bottle of wine. Wordlessly, Calista brought out three glasses, and he poured wine for everyone. They made a simple toast and took a sip.

Maisie rolled the stem of the glass between her thumb and forefinger, examining the deep red liquid.

"Well, this is certainly...full-bodied." She said.

"It's a Merlot. It goes well with the shepherd's pie." Brandon explained.

"Goes with pretty well everything." Calista mumbled. She drained her glass and held out the empty for Brandon to refill.

He grinned and poured her more wine. "Be careful, you know how this stuff hits you." He said.

Maisie drank hers more slowly, sipping between mouthfuls of food, but Brandon still had to refill her glass two more times. Calista finished her third glass and squinted, rubbing her eyes in fatigue. Groggily, she helped Maisie clear up and prepare for the morning's breakfast rush. Brandon sat on the sofa, out of the way, and watched the choreography of these two women, moving plates, pots, eggs and milk in a dance through the kitchen, setting up for the morning, doing what they best knew how to do for their guests.

Brandon suddenly sensed just how desperate Calista must have been when she placed the ad that brought him to the hotel. He realized just how little they had to cling to, and how close they had come to losing even that little they had.

He felt glad at having been here to help them, but he now felt an obligation to keep them going. He also owed it to Calista. Whatever his feelings were for her- whether it was pure love, physical attraction, or both, mixed with admiration, he wasn't sure- but he wanted to make certain she would be all right. And his leg hurt now; the stitches had started to bother him and the wine didn't help, so he just sat back.

A knock at the door made him sit up straight. Maisie answered it, smiling. She expected that one of the guests had a question, or request. She opened the door to see Glen, the real estate man, rocking from foot to foot on the porch. He had his back to her, and he turned to face her when the door opened.

"Hi Cali... ah, Maisie, I mean. How are you?" He said.

He had a pasted-on smile, the kind of smile a cat gives just before attacking a mouse.

Maisie stood square in the doorway, leaning against the frame, blocking him. "Hello, Glen, can I help you?" She asked.

He looked nervously over her shoulder at Brandon. "Well, yes, you can. Do you mind if I come in for a minute? This shouldn't take long."

Maisie took a cautious step back and Glen strutted in. Brandon watched him carefully, trying his best to act casual, but sensing there was something in this visit that he didn't like. Glen sat at the dining table without being invited to and looked around, surveying the room.

"Do I smell coffee?" He asked, expectantly.

"Yes, we had coffee- with dinner." Maisie said curtly. "Now, what can I do for you?"

Glen leaned forward and knitted his fingers together on the table. Brandon knew that body language; his father used it when he was negotiating with a competitor. It made the hairs on Brandon's neck bristle.

"Maisie, you know I've always had the greatest respect for your family." Glen said.

Brandon's mind raced. He could think of about five different directions this conversation was going, so he kept a poker face, waiting to see which one it was.

Glen continued. "We've had our differences, I know, but you and Calista have always been seen as good people here, and Lincoln City is proud to have you as its citizens."

Brandon narrowed the conversation's possible directions to three, but stayed quiet.

"As you know, there may be a development going in at Porter Point. They're buying up land all around it, and they're trying to push out people who've lived here for years, just to make a quick profit."

"I see." Maisie said. "How does this affect us?"

Glen nodded, solemnly, like a preacher giving a sermon. His sales skills had improved, it seemed. "Well, you know, there is a problem with the Ocean Dunes Hotel. I had hoped that if you'd sold it to me, I could have kept it as a going concern, you know, but then I was made aware of something."

Maisie's back stiffened. "A problem? Go on."

Glen pulled a slip of paper out of his jacket and handed it to her. "You had mortgaged this place a while back to try and keep ahead of your expenses." He said. "But it's a demand mortgage, and the bank says that they want the note retired right away. Maisie, they're foreclosing on your hotel."

Maisie looked at the paper. "I've been paying my bills. I've been paying this off." She whispered.

Glen shook his head sadly. "I'm sorry, Maisie, I'm so, so sorry, but this was just given to me, and I told them that I wanted to let you know about it. I didn't just want the sheriff to show up at your door next week."

Calista shook her head. "Mother, what's he talking about? We've been making regular payments on that loan, haven't we?"

Maisie sighed. "Yes, we have. Glen, Calista is good with figures. She arranged the loan, and I've been paying it off little by little, sometimes making up the payment from my widow's pension. I thought we'd surely make it, that we'd survive. Heaven knows, if Brandon had come to the hotel sooner, we'd be fine now."

Brandon had guessed what was going to happen next. "So, Glen, what happens now?" He asked.

Glen looked over at him, sympathetically. "Yup. I hear you injured your leg, huh? Does it hurt bad?"

Brandon suspected he really hoped it did hurt. "No, it's not painful at all. The bank just gave you a copy of this foreclosure notice, you said?"

"Yeah."

"Just like that? The banks don't usually do that, Glen. You'd need to have a good reason to get a copy of it."

Glen's eyes darted over at Maisie and back at Brandon. "In any case, it's out of my hands. You got a notice of foreclosure three months ago, Maisie, you should have dealt with it sooner."

Calista glared at her mother. "You never said anything, mom. You got a warning from our bank, that could lose us our home, and you never said a word to me. That's irresponsible. Now what do we do?"

Glen leaned in, clearly going for the kill. "Look, I can still help you out, if you let me. I will buy the hotel, at a fair price, and you can pay off the loan, plus you'll have a good few dollars left. Beyond that, I'll let you stay on and run the hotel until you get a new place to live. What could be more fair, I ask you?"

Brandon snickered. "How much does the bank want?"

Glen looked at him warily. "A very large sum. A lot of money."

"What you call 'a lot' and what I call a lot are two different things, Glen. How much?"

Glen looked at the paper in Maisie's hand. "Almost a quarter of a million dollars."

"When exactly did you get the first notice of foreclosure, Maisie?" Brandon asked.

Maisie looked up, thinking. "About three months ago. Yes, it was the end of March, just before Easter, as I remember."

Brandon nodded. "Right. Oregon has a one hundred and twenty-day grace period after notice of foreclosure, and you have seven days before due date to pay the amount owed. You're safe, for now."

Glen's mouth fell open. "How could you possibly know that?"

"So, you knew it too, but you still came here to try and cheat these two women?" Brandon sneered.

Calista said nothing. She had never seen Brandon act like this hard, cold, like a businessman.

Maisie stood up quickly. "Well, Glen, thank you for the visit. Please give my regards to Jan. Good night."

Glen stood automatically and stared at her, dumbfounded. He grabbed the notice out of Maisie's hands, turned around and stormed out. He slammed the door as he left.

Brandon watched him go and waited for a minute. Nobody said a word- it was dead quiet.

"Well, that was interesting." He muttered.

Maisie looked down at her feet then up at him. "Brandon, thank you for stepping in. This gives us a month, at least, a whole month to find some way to save the hotel."

"How? How exactly do you plan to save the hotel?" He asked sharply.

Calista shrugged. "Do you have something in mind, Brandon?"

"Yes. I'd like to buy a one-third share in your hotel, ladies. Is that agreeable?"

Calista shot a look at her mother. "In exchange for what?"

"In exchange for the knowledge that my good work here won't be bulldozed to make a strip mall."

Maisie nodded. "Go on."

"I will own a third of the hotel. In exchange, I get to stay here whenever I want, for free. You pay off the loan. You carry on running the place, like you do now. Period. Do we have an agreement?"

Maisie stretched her hand out. "It's a deal." She grinned.

Chapter Fourteen

Brandon opened his eyes slowly. The light was wrong- the sun, which usually streamed in through his window about now, was missing. He looked toward his bathroom- it wasn't there. Of course not- he was in that spare room in the main house.

He heard voices, noises coming through the door, sounds of people talking, Calista laughing. He sat up, pulled on jeans and a tee shirt, and went out into the dining room.

A dozen adults and four children were in the room; Maisie had pulled out the center leaves of the dining table for the adults, and set up a small table to one side for the children. Calista was rushing back and forth, serving eggs and coffee, while Maisie cooked bacon and buttered toast. All the adults were smiling and laughing, and they nodded at him as he walked in, but kept talking amongst themselves. Brandon picked his way past everyone and sat in one corner of the kitchen. He looked around, found an empty cup, and filled it with coffee.

Maisie charged into the dining room with a large plate of pancakes, to a collective gasp from the adults, and Calista rushed into the kitchen to refill the coffee pot. She glanced over at him furtively, checked that nobody could see him from the dining room, and quickly kissed him.

"Good morning. Sleep well?" She asked.

He rubbed his hair and yawned. "Yeah. I guess whatever they gave me for the pain yesterday really knocked me down. I'm good now, though."

"Maybe it was the stress of dealing with Glen?" Calista asked.

He shook his head. "He's a low-grade pest. I've dealt with Glens every day in San Francisco."

He looked around, looking for food somewhere nearby. Calista read his mind.

"Stay right there. Do you want eggs, toast, pancakes, what?" She asked.

"Yes, to everything. Please." He mumbled.

Calista slid two eggs onto a plate, lifted pancakes from a warming tray and scooped hash browns onto the plate, then set it in front of him. He muttered thanks and started eating.

An hour later, the guests had packed up their belongings, loaded their cars, accepted the obligatory muffins from Maisie, and left in a convoy, headed down toward Utah, they told her. Maisie waved at the departing cars, watching until the last one had turned down the highway, then put her hands on her hips, pleased with herself.

"Well, that certainly went well, didn't it, Cali?"

"Yes, mom. A few weeks like that every year and we'll be all set, thanks to Brandon and his friends."

Brandon stepped out onto the porch. "You called?" He asked.

Maisie put her arm around his waist. "That one group paid us enough to live on for more than a month, Brandon. Do you know how exciting that was?"

"I can imagine. Now, you realize you're going to have to call me 'partner' from now on, right?"

Maisie nodded. "It's going to be very strange, you know, not owning the place outright. I hope you realize just how much trust we're putting in you, Brandon."

He grinned. "I know. I won't let you down."

After breakfast, Brandon asked Maisie to show him the bank notice she had received. He called someone, introduced himself on the phone, and casually asked them to transfer two hundred and fifty thousand dollars to Maisie's account. He said it like he was ordering pizza. Later the next afternoon, Maisie went into the bank. The bank manager welcomed her into his office, had her sign some papers, and asked if she wanted to set up another loan? She politely declined. The hotel was now clear of debt, and Maisie drove her station wagon back to the hotel, faster than she usually drove, excited at the reversal of fortune. Brandon seemed mildly amused as she described paying off the loan, nodded politely at her detailed explanation about clearing the loan, and laughed at Maisie's description of the shock on the bank manager's face, when she told him she had the money to pay it.

He spent the next five days fixing up the final cottage. He sanded, painted, patched and repaired it, as though it was his own home. He hobbled slightly for a day or two, until his leg was better. Once he'd finished the work, he called Maisie and Calista over to see how it looked.

Like the other four cottages, this one smelled clean, fresh, and new. The walls were a crisp cream color, the outside walls were a pleasant putty shade, and the floors were silky smooth, gleaming under their new coat of varnish. This cottage had been the first one built, back when the main house was built, and it was somewhat larger than the rest. Brandon suggested that this one could rent for a little more, since it had room for a fold-out sofa and a sitting area, and it was closer to the beach path. Maisie was not so sure, but he pointed out that, as a shareholder in the enterprise, he had a right to protect his interests. Maisie conceded that he was probably right.

He moved into the fifth cottage, then spent a week fixing up things in the main house. It was in better repair, and most of what he fixed- door hinges, sticky windows, the like- were quick jobs.

The following week, a truck came and took away all the rented equipment. Suddenly, the yard looked very clean and spacious.

Almost every day, they had guests in two or three of the cottages. Maisie quickly got used to asking for a room rate she would have thought impossible just a few weeks before. They were taking in enough money to pay their bills, with enough left over to live comfortably during the slow days of winter, and then the cottages would be ready to open up again in the spring, as the next year's group of visitors came through.

Tommy's sign drew in most of the business; word-of-mouth brought the rest. Maisie was sure to always give her guests a basket of muffins to take with them. That seemed to have been part of the word-of-mouth, apparently.

Some nights, Brandon went out and sat at the fire. When he did, Calista would see the glow of rising embers, or hear his harmonica, or somehow just know that he'd be out there, and she'd join him. They drank wine and talked, or they went to his cottage and made love, or both. By the end of June, he was almost out of wine. He would have to go back for more very soon, he said.

The hotel was in better shape than it had ever been, the cottages were renting steadily, and for the first time since she was a little girl, Calista was truly proud of the place where she lived.

Brandon's friend Jerry had come out for a couple of days with his wife, in a sleek old pre-war Pontiac, with purple-black paint and nearly invisible flames pinstriped on the fenders. It rumbled down the gravel drive, smooth and throaty, and stopped in front of the main house. Jerry's wife looked like a 1950's girl, with a poodle skirt and polka dot blouse, but with bright pink hair and a leopard tattoo on her arm.

They were very nice, and they enjoyed their stay, but they seemed slightly embarrassed when Maisie refused to let them pay for the cottage. His wife bashfully asked for a large batch of muffins to bring back with them; apparently they'd made a real splash at Jerry's auto shop.

A couple of the men from the gravel trucks also came by and booked a series of dates later in the year, after the busy season in their jobs, they'd said. Maisie wrote down their names, dates, and preferred cottages in a ledger book, keeping track of available space for the first time in recent memory.

One evening in July, Calista was in her room. It wasn't late, only nine thirty or so, but her mother had been up early with a group of guests who wanted to be on the road by seven, and she had already gone to bed. The light was on in Brandon's cottage. Although the other cottages were empty tonight, three groups had booked for the following night. She leaned out her window, hoping she would hear his music. She did.

She picked her way out to the fire pit, following the sound of a harmonica, and sat beside Brandon as he played a tune. She bumped her shoulder against his, rubbed her head against his arm, and looked up at him, waiting for him to kiss her. He wrapped his hand carefully behind her head, reached down and kissed her, passionately. . His lips tasted of wine and smoke, of salt air and sweat.

Calista opened her eyes as she pulled back and looked into his face. He was smiling, but it looked like he was in pain. "What is it?" She asked.

"I have to go, to California." He said softly.

"I know." She said. "You told me. When will you be back?"

He shook his head. "No. I have to go." He whispered it.

Calista still didn't quite understand what he was telling her. "What do you mean?"

He picked up a small piece of shell and tossed it into the fire. "Yesterday, I got a phone call from my commanding officer. They've moved my deployment date up a month, so I have to leave. Tomorrow."

Calista's mind raced. Life had been going well- she was secure, safe, happy for the first time in a long while, she had a man who treated her with warmth and love, and now he was going away for a long time, maybe forever. It suddenly felt like her chest was about to explode.

She covered her face with her hands, trying to think of how to say what she was thinking. "You can't! You can't just go away and leave me- leave us! Can't you just tell them you're not going, that we need you here, that you love me, that I love you? Tell them I need you. Can't you just tell them that?"

He shook his head. "It doesn't work that way, Calista. I have to go. I'm sorry."

Calista ran her fingers through her hair, desperately trying to make sense of what he was saying. Nothing made sense. He was leaving, but he didn't want to. She wanted him to stay, but she knew he couldn't. He might never come back to her now, even after leaving the army. None of it made any sense.

She took a deep breath and stood up. She would be alright, she told herself. She had been abandoned before, and survived, and she would be alright this time, too. She would hurt, she knew. She had known hurt before and she knew it now. It would pass.

"Well, then, you should get some sleep. You have a busy day tomorrow." She said, coldly.

He turned to face her. "Look, Calista, I don't like this any more than you do, but it's something I have to do, something I can't get away from. I made a commitment, and I have to keep it."

She slapped his arm. "You made a commitment to fix up the hotel, too. You said you'd be here all summer, but you won't be back. I know it. *You won't be back.*" She hissed.

"No, you're wrong, Calista. I've done all the work that needed to be done, all the work I promised I'd do, and you'll be fine until I get back. And I *will* be back. I promise."

Calista scowled. "Well, you need to pack up your things. You should get some sleep. Good night." She stormed off and marched along the path, back to the house. By the time she got to the house, she was almost running. She raced up the stairs to her room and threw herself on her bed.

She felt completely abandoned, betrayed by this man she had come to love, a man who said he loved her, but who said he was going to leave her. She buried her head in her pillow, trying to think of what she could have done to make him stay.

Was it her fault he was leaving? She couldn't think. She was filled with pain and rage, angry at Brandon, at herself, at Glen, at the world. She covered her head with her lovely pillow, the pillow Brandon had gotten for her, and tried not to think about it.

She woke up with a start. There was a commotion downstairs, people talking loudly, car doors closing. She scrambled out of bed, pulled on a pair of jeans and a sweater, and combed her hair. Maybe he'd changed his mind. Maybe.

She vaulted down the stairs, looking around the base of the steps to see where Brandon was. She would apologize to him for being so angry the night before, she decided. That would help, she thought.

There were two families in the hallway, four adults and a handful of children, with luggage and road maps, all talking. Maisie directed them to two of the cottages, and they piled out, slamming car doors and laughing as they went.

Calista looked around. "Where's Brandon?" She asked.

Maisie looked into her eyes. "He left already." She said simply.

"Left?"

Maisie reached behind the kitchen counter and pulled out a brown paper package, larger than a license plate. She handed it to Calista.

"He left this." She pulled an envelope from her apron. "And a note."

Calista tore open the envelope and unfolded the letter inside.

'Dear Calista;' It started. 'I can't begin to tell you how much it hurts me to leave, but if I had waited to say goodbye to you in person, it would have been impossible to go. I will be back for a very brief visit in a while. I don't know exactly when, but when I come, I will give you something to prove that I'm coming back. You'll understand when I get there.

In the meantime, the package is a gift from Tommy, for your mother. She said you'd understand and appreciate it. I have no idea what it is, by the way.

See you soon. Love, Brandon.'

Calista handed the package to Maisie. "This is for you." She said.

Maisie tore off the brown paper. Inside were two signs, in black lettering with a white background, that read 'Sorry- No Vacancy". Despite herself, Calista laughed.

Chapter Fifteen

Calista went through the following days on autopilot. People came and went, they rented all the cottages, and occasionally they had to hang out the 'Sorry- No Vacancy' sign. Maisie hired Freda Parsoner for a couple of days a week to help her out. Every waking moment, Calista thought of Brandon. His voice, his smell, the touch of his hands, all filled her mind. Every time she passed what had been his cottage, she almost thought she saw him, lounging in the doorway, smiling at her.

The couple that had rushed away just two months before, that had lied and said they were heading back to San Diego, came back. They wanted to rent a cottage for a couple of nights, they said, and they were willing to pay whatever the rate was. Calista smiled and pointed out that they were full, but later in the year there might be room. The man scowled at her and they drove off in a hurry.

Days later, Calista was sweeping the front steps, as she did every morning. She finally felt able to breathe, to smile, to believe that life could get back to normal. The clouds in the sky this day were puffballs, rolling over the beach like sailboats in the sky, darkening the grass with round shadows as they passed. The summer promised to be warm and long, and Calista eventually settled into a routine.

A car rolled down the drive and stopped outside the main house, and Calista put her hand above her eyes to look up at it.

It was a black sedan, very shiny, very new. The man who drove it got out. He was in a crisp green uniform, and he looked about eighteen years old.

He marched over to Calista and gave her a sharp nod.

"Morning, ma'am; are you Miss Blake?" He asked.

Calista nodded. She felt a cold wave come over her; something terrible was wrong with Brandon- she could feel it. This man was here to give her the bad news. He had come to let her know the worst had happened.

"I was sent here from the army base, ma'am. I was told to ask for you. I'm supposed to talk to you about the officer, ma'am. About Colonel Cooper, ma'am." He said, looking around.

"Colonel Cooper?" Calista repeated. She began to tremble.

"Yes, ma'am. Colonel Cooper. I was sent here, by the army." He said again.

Calista's knees went weak. "What about him?" She whispered.

The young man looked sadly down and opened his mouth to speak.

A familiar sound, a thump-thump-thump noise, came from the end of the road. A motorcycle with a sidecar, rolling toward them. Calista's heart pounded so hard she thought she might faint.

The man in the uniform looked over at the motorcycle and smiled. "I was sent to pick him up. Here he is now." He said.

The motorcycle's rider stood on his foot pegs and pulled up behind the sedan. Brandon swung a leg over the bike and pulled off his helmet.

"Hi, Calista. I'm so very glad to see you. Did you miss me?" He asked.

The young man got into the sedan and closed the door, waiting patiently.

Brandon pulled a folded suit bag from the sidecar and slung it over his shoulder. He reached out to Calista with his free arm and wrapped it around her.

"See, I told you I'd be back." He said softly.

She glanced at the young man and back at Brandon. "What's going on? Why is he here?" She asked.

Brandon looked over his shoulder at the sedan and back at Calista. "Look, I only have five minutes. There's so much I want to say, so much I want to tell you, but I just don't have the time right now. Is there a cottage I can use?"

Calista shook her head. "We're full. The spare room in the house is empty, though."

He kissed her quickly. "I'll be right back."

He sprinted up the steps into the house. Calista heard her mother's voice say 'what?' then scream in delight. Maisie came rushing out a moment later, wide-eyed.

"Cali? He's back. Why is he back?" She asked.

Calista shrugged. "I don't know, mom. I just don't know."

Three minutes later, Brandon came out. He was now in the same uniform as the young man, a dark green dress uniform, with two rows of colored ribbons over the left breast pocket, and gold eagles on the shoulders. His shoes were a mirror black, and he had an army cap tucked under his left arm.

He walked stiffly down the steps to join Calista and Maisie. "Look, I told you I'd be gone eighteen months," He started.

"But the general owes me a favor. I told him about your situation here, and he has agreed to let me leave the army earlier."

Calista tilted her head. "How much earlier?"

He glanced at the sedan. "How does this Christmas sound?"

Calista beamed. "How do I know you'll really come back?" She teased.

He pointed to the motorcycle. "I've left my bike here for you. Ride it whenever you like, but please take care of it."

"Couldn't you just buy yourself another one?" Calista said.

He shook his head, serious. "Not like that one. It was willed to me by Ollie."

Calista looked over at the motorcycle. She realized just why he was so attached to it, and what it meant for him to leave it with her. Her heart felt warm again.

Brandon hugged her mother. "Keep well, Maisie, I'll be back before you know it."

Maisie wiped her eyes with a handkerchief and started to cry. She ran up the stairs and back into the house. Calista was now alone in the yard with Brandon, wondering what to say to him, how she could explain that the last few days had felt like torture, how to tell him that every day he was gone would be more torture till the day he came back.

She took a deep breath. "Christmas, you said?"

"Christmas. Look, I really, really have to go. I love you." He whispered the last three words.

She smiled. "I love you, too."

He kissed her, slowly, gently, as though she might break, then he took his cap and put it squarely on his head. He stood up straight and spun around, then walked briskly to the sedan.

The young man jumped out and saluted. "Colonel, sir." He said.

Brandon returned the salute then got in the back. "Sergeant." He answered. "Let's go."

The young man closed the door, the car turned silently in the yard and rolled down the smooth gravel driveway.

Calista stood there for a very long time, watching the car go, watching as the small cloud of dust that it left swirled and blew away in the breeze, watching the man in her life go away, knowing that this time he would come back.

This time, she would not be left alone. This time, she would still feel loved. She smiled and looked up at the sky.

It could turn out to be a lovely morning, thought Calista.

The End.